Ships and Silhouettes:

Setting Sail

For Alyssa

Ships and Silhouettes:
Setting Sail

Allyson Faith

Critiqued by Lena Debb's Critique Group.
This is a work of fiction. While I've taken from elements of life, none of these characters, places, cultures, or events are meant to represent any real life people, events, and places.

This book is dedicated to the one true God, who gave me the gift to write, my family, who push me to be better, Paulie Ayala, my coach and one of the humblest men I know, and all the adventurous, reckless, and stubborn people that make this world better.

Table of Contents:

Dictionary

Titles:

Deb: A nobleman of Iecula, meaning someone with status. Usually someone who has proved themselves in combat.

Debna: A noble woman, usually receives her status because she is a member of a deb's household.

Chief Deb: The head of the council of debs which handles all governmental issues of Nileal, and, by extension, the island since Iecula follows Nileal's lead.

Iecula Praeti (Pray-tee): The civil protectors organized and funded by the deb council.

Places:

Iecula (EE-coo-ay): The biggest island in the Speckled Region.

Nileal (Nih-lee-ool): The capital of Iecula and fight capital of the Eastern Realm.

Valsquel (Val-skwell): A nation which sprawls the plains across the sea. Known for their large universities and knowledge hungry culture.

Asium (Ah-sea-um): The outdoor pavilion which houses rows upon rows of punching bags for training. It also holds practice rings, training equipment, and wooden boxes for storage. It is situated behind Deb Rez's castle and part of his grounds. Named "Asium" because this means red in Ikuela, and the wood which holds the boxing bags has red grains. When the sun shines, these grains cast red sunbeams on the ground.

Zafiere (Zaf-fee-air-uh): The monstrous, tiered outdoor stadium built some four hundred years previously for Banli Boxers. Its name means *Fire of the Sea* in Ikuela. It was named this because of the red blood spilt there in the middle of the sea, as, originally, all fights were to the death.

People (The two ages represent the time jump in the book):
Ishel (Ish-el): Family last name.
Reznaldo (Rez-nal-do) Ishel and Le (Lay) Ishel: Father and Mother.
Silohski (Sih-low-ski) "Ski" Ishel, 19 then 22.
Adnesier (Add-neese-ee-er) "Adnesi" Ishel, 18 then 21.
Obedium (O-beh-dee-um) "Dium" Ishel, 16 then 19.
Rosquevalarian (Roska-val-ar-ee-an) "Rosca" Ishel, 15 then 18.
Jack Ishel, 9 then 12.
Mar-Iecula "Mar" Ishel, 6 then 9.
Hela (Hell-lah) Ishal: Rez and Adnesier's sister.
Adnesier Ishel: Rosca and Ski's father and Rez's brother.
Arienvalarian Ishel: Rosca and Ski's mother.
Fuerzalin "Lin": Dium's friend and newcomer to the island.

Chapter One
Victory

The fear was the worst part. And the best.

Rosca ducked under the gold-dyed ropes and faced her corner. Adrenaline pounded a rhythm in her ears. "It's just another fight." Sweat coated her brow while her stomach curved into knots. *Maschiach, please speed this up,* she prayed as her courage threatened to mutiny.

"You'll be fine once it starts. Instinct takes over." Adnesi's compassionate gaze cut like glass. He could see her nerves. She wasn't putting on a good enough show.

"I'm just excited." She smiled and met her older brother's narrow eyes.

He pursed his lips, looking unconvinced.

Pushing off her back foot, she trotted around the ring and swung her arms. As she warmed up, she sneaked a glance at the tiered stadium stands. Strangers' silhouettes fleeted by like smoke. Their expectations hung over her, making the cool evening air as muggy as a humid high noon. Terror gripped her heart. Short, frantic breaths escaped her. Like a bug about to get swallowed, she shrank. The outdoor ring would better be called the pit of terror than Zafiere – *fire of the sea.*

Soar out or get swallowed. She forced steady inhales through her nose. "If I can't face this," she hissed to herself, "I don't deserve an adventure. I don't deserve to be called a fighter."

Determination set her jaw. She wanted this. No one told her to fight. She chose this, and she would see it to the end.

"To your corner." The wizened, bald watchman, who'd manned the fights at Zafiere for as long as she could remember, pointed to Rez, her adopted father and blood uncle, and three brothers.

She shuffled to her corner. All except her older brother Dium, who could have had a cannonball aimed for his head and still would have laughed, wore masks of taut attention.

The deb, as the Nileal islanders called their chief noblemen, slammed his hands into her padded gloves and drove his determined stare into hers. "You ready?"

"Am I supposed to feel ready?" Nerves shot adrenaline like a volley of arrow-fire. She could have rambled on, but her father's raised brows froze the words in her throat.

The one thing she feared more than a flying fist was his disapproval.

"Those punches are coming whether you're ready or not." He softened his curt, militant tone and put a hand on her shoulder. "What do we say?"

A burst of confidence inflated her chest. "I'm an Ishel. I'm a fighter."

A smile split his weathered features. "Not bad for a Valsquelian."

She held down a glare. Did he have to mention that right now? Even if they did share the unfortunate bloodline, she didn't want to think about her intellectual, shriveled ancestry pre-fight. While the Valsquelians' national intelligence probably equaled every other country's put together, they had no grit or courage. Or so the islanders said. And she trusted the islanders.

Of course, Deb Rez confounded that stereotype. But he had broken every whip people laid on his back. Born and raised in

Valsquel, he'd come to the island as a young man then built a name for himself through acts of heroism in the island militia and victory in the boxing ring. Nilealians all but synonymized his name with strength and stoicism. Though, they didn't see him during a morning hangover, where he could barely creak his old bones to the breakfast table. Hanging her head, she stamped her feet. "Focus, focus."

Catching her muttering, her father squeezed her shoulder in wordless encouragement. "Kill her." He stoned his features until they could have sliced ice.

"Kill? Tall order for a fifteen-year-old in a boxing match." The knot in her belly tightened. For once, snarky comebacks didn't help.

Deb Rez nodded as though this was non-negotiable.

His confidence washed over her. He wouldn't put her in that ring to fall flat. And his Valsquelian heritage had never held him back, so neither would hers. No matter what the island natives claimed.

She exhaled a puff of air through her nose. With every second, her body tensed tighter. Between waiting or actually fighting, she'd pick the second any day.

Finally, her opponent's team made their way across the bare, dusty floor to the elevated ring. In front, the fighter Lilith's stoic expression revealed nothing. Her thick chestnut hair had been carefully plaited with golden string, like a pampered carriage horse. The girl had a broad chest, corded calves, and a square face.

Rosca pushed her own braids over her shoulder, each tiny one gathered into a ponytail by the white strip from her brother's shirt. He'd ripped it off just before the fight, as she'd forgotten to bring her hair ribbons.

She bounced on her toes. She'd only seen Lilith spar once since her competitor trained at a different deb's gym. Yet, the girl's power-house reputation preceded her. According to many of the fighters, the long-armed girl had crumpled some of the toughest female competitors.

Rosca swallowed. Hard.

Use it. Use the nerves. She shadowed a few punches, throwing them into the air.

Lilith ascended into the ring, and Rosca assessed her quickly. Tall. Much taller, and longer limbed. Fighting from the outside would end in a mauling but close the distance and uppercuts should serve. Still would be a war. High volume punching. And for sea's sake, she had to slip! If she kept forgetting to dodge, Father would have her hide put on the next trophy, and then the crowd would ship her back to Valsquel.

The watchman shouted, "Fight!" and moved out of the middle of the ring.

Lilith's upper lip curved in contempt as they circled. Her first jab whipped in and out, measuring the distance between them.

"Be first." Her father's advice echoed in Rosca's mind. She stepped in with a one-two combo, throwing first the left jab then straight right.

Lilith slipped one and ate one, letting her close the distance.

Too close. Rosca tried to circle away but Lilith's long arms shot out like arrows from a bow.

Rosca fell back, and Lilith followed. The big girl's hammering straights whipped Rosca's neck back like a snake in its death throws. They came faster and faster. Lilith had found her rhythm.

Rosca's vision blurred.

"Get out!" Her brothers yelled.

Frozen, Rosca shelled her head with her hands. The blows rained down, but her guard held. Tucked behind it, she used the half-seconds to reset her mind. Gym gossip hadn't exaggerated.

Lilith hit like a charging boar, but Rosca stayed up. Finding her feet, she shuffled left.

Her father's disembodied voice cut in, demanding she, "Slip, shel it!"

Pain is a part of it. She locked eyes with Lilith.

The girl's smirk set a fire in her.

She forced her anger into a box, and refocused on Lilith's chest, where she could best spot each incoming punch.

Lilith shot forward, stepping with a jab then following with a power right, uppercut, hook.

Rosca slipped the first two, blocked the upper, and rolled under the hook. As she popped up to Lilith's right, she sunk her glove into the girl's solar plexus twice, then slammed a straight right into her body.

Lilith grunted. She tried to return with body shots, but Rosca used her elbows to cover her middle. Lilith slowed, and Rosca threw six punches starting at the body then moving to the head. Her target fell back into the ropes.

Rhythm gripped Rosca. Her mind blanked. Her hands knew what to do. One, two, double uppercut, right hook, left hook. Roll to the side. Repeat. The combos blurred into just throwing whatever looked open.

Lilith moved to shuffle out, and Rosca stepped to block her escape.

The gong announced the end of round one.

Rosca caught herself almost skipping back to her corner. She hadn't won yet.

Her brother Ski gestured to the stool, and she shook her head. She'd sparred five-minute rounds in training. In comparison, the fast-paced one-minute round felt like seconds.

"Rosca!"

At the snap of her father's voice, the satisfaction of her success burst. He'd find something she could have improved. As a good coach should, but that didn't make it any less frustrating.

Her second-to-oldest brother held out his hand for her to spit out the hardened clay protecting her teeth. She did so, and he poured water into her mouth using a leather-hide bottle. "That was a great finish. You're wearing her down. Just keep doing what you're doing."

She nodded at him then directed her attention to her coach for the coming advice. Adnesi tended to paint a rosy picture of reality. She needed the black-and-white to win.

Her father took the mouthpiece from his son and replaced it in her mouth. "Stop letting her have free hits. Do the basics and do them well. Throw your one, two combos. Slip. Block. It's that simple. Quit freezing. That's how you get head injuries."

Rosca winced. "Yes, sir."

"Don't tell me 'yes, sir,' if you aren't going to do it. Slip the punches! Duck right, left." He mimed dropping low right to left, his body shifting weight as he dodged imaginary blows. "Use your defense."

Nodding with extra vigor, she met his gaze. "Yes, sir."

He patted her helmet. "Good girl." His broad cheek bones jutted out with stoic strength. He exuded an imperturbable calm, but he always did.

At a sign from the watchman, she rose.

"Fight!"

Advancing, she picked a combo to open.

Lilith walked into range.

Rosca jabbed forward, then followed with a right, hook, right, hook.

Lilith ducked under the last hook, throwing Rosca off-balance. She landed a punch on Rosca's temple and followed it with a barrage of blows to the body.

Rosca's head rang from the clean hit. She forced clear thoughts to stamp out the gathering panic and shuffled out of range. She had to win this. Had to.

Once she got away, the pain of the body shots registered. Exhaustion settled in her tight limbs. She looked to her father, then focused in on her opponent. He couldn't save her. She'd asked for this. She'd trained for this. Only she could take her victory.

The gong sounded. Round two ended.

When they returned, Lilith sprang like a hare. The same downpour of punches rained on Rosca, forcing her into the ropes. She tucked herself behind her guard.

Her opponent did not get winded, alternating head and body shots like Rosca was a practice bag.

A vicious growl erupted from Rosca's throat. She pushed forward, blocking the pain behind a mental wall. But Lilith hit harder. Faster. When Rosca shuffled left, her opponent hammered her side with a hook. Slipping right earned her an uppercut. She couldn't find an escape.

A sense of failure deadened Rosca. What business did a Valsquelian female— really any outsider have in a Banli ring. They were the fight island natives. Victory was their birthright.

Her right hand dropped, and a shattering hook crashed into her skull. Her vision blurred, then blacked. That was it. She couldn't see. The watchman would stop the fight now. She'd lost.

The hailstorm of blows continued to batter her body. Minskhead! She had to get out. She wasn't fighting. Get out! She used her footwork to circle away.

A primitive instinct for space, sound, and light arrested her as she moved. For the moment, she had cleared the bully. As though her body took the safety for all its worth, light crashed into her senses, sending ripples of hazy rays over a tall girl's merciless snarl. Lilith approached, triumph in her expression.

Rosca's small frame quaked with rage. The raschuka had almost taken her sight. She ground her teeth, quoting to herself. *Lose your temper, lose the fight. Lose your temper, lose the—* Baring her teeth, she tucked her chin and sprung in. A sweet and simple one, two combo. Her straight right-hand connected.

Lilith's head jerked back, but she stayed firm on her feet.

Rosca didn't stop. Right to the body. Right to the body. Hook to the body. Pivot. Right, hook, right. Double left uppercut. Angles employed on every punch kept a moving target for Lilith. Two of her competitor's punches grazed the top of her head as she sunk low and alternated right and left hooks to the body.

Lilith retreated.

Rosca chased her. She looked for a drop in the hands, a moment of distress, or a loose chin. But the girl had too much experience to give her these. By switching between head and body punches, Rosca spread out the girl's defense enough to touch her with three true power shots, ending with a blow to the liver. Lilith doubled.

Another hit from the gong ended the last round. They went to each other's corners to shake hands with their opponent's coach.

Returning to the center of the ring, Rosca let the watchmen grab her wrist and waited for the announcement.

He lifted both hers and Lilith's arms in acknowledgement. The cheering crowd filled Rosca's senses. Her chest swelled. *Maschiach,* she prayed, *please, I need this win! I'm a fighter. Let them see it.*

At a sign from the judges who sat on a platform level with the ring, the watchman raised Rosca's hand.

The cheering turned into roars of joy. Like crashing waves, they flipped her heart with speechless gratitude. She hadn't expected so much attention as a new, juvenile fighter, but she should have known better. Afterall, she had Deb Rez, island Chief and four-time Banli Boxing Champion, in her corner. With such notoriety on her side, nobody cared that she'd only done small tournaments, or that she was a juvenile competitor.

Her brothers lifted her on their shoulders. Adnesi shouted the loudest. "You won! You did it! My sister is a Banli Boxer!"

Her cheeks ached with a wide smile. She'd done it. Valsquelian or no, she'd earned the island title. She'd earned her place. "I'm a Banli Boxer!"

Her oldest brother Ski grabbed her shoulder, pulling her toward the ground. "One more fight and you qualify for the final fifteen. The championship tournament."

A weight mounted on her chest. She huffed and rolled her eyes. "Can't I enjoy my win for five minutes without you talkin' 'bout the next fight? Is being Banli Boxer not enough for now?"

Ski snorted. "A beginner's title? We've all already got that."

Rosca stared. Before she could retort, Dium and Adnesi lifted her once again and paraded her away.

They replaced her on the floor as the watchman ushered them from the ring so he could prepare for the next competition.

As they returned to the fighter's hold to grab their belongings, she skipped and sang old, childish songs with her brothers. Nothing could stop the high of the moment. Nothing had ever felt so perfect and complete.

***

That night, sitting around the dining table, her father smiled at her, but distance clouded the look. As though the celebration of the day brought to light haunted memories.

Her triumph faltered. Her adopted brothers, his blood sons, looked nothing like Deb Rez. In features, yes. They shared the shaggy dark curls, broad noses, and chiseled jawlines, but his expression held something more. A smolder like fog, which obscured every thought with a mask. His eyes attested to wars outlived, with the fire of a champion melded into the golden iris. As though he hadn't only survived his battles, but taken the spirit of each brave, fallen brother, and carried it with him. For all that he'd had given to her, he could never duplicate that furnace of experience that molded him. The discipline formed through the loss, victory, and hard work found in an adventure.

I don't care if it takes a lifetime, I will accomplish something. The viciousness of her sudden oath made her pause. Post-fight aggression, more than likely. Still, the promise gnawed at her insides, yearning to burst out. *I will do it. I will find my adventure. I will prove my worth.*

Chapter Two
Shot

Although the ecstatic cheers of a thousand islanders still rang in Rosca's ears, life resumed normally that Monali. Perhaps a little too "normally", since Monali marked the start of a new tempa, or eight-day period, and a return to work after a few blissful free days.

Groaning, she staggered from bed to dress. The gold encased looking glass reflected a yellow, puffy bruise underneath her eye, and a small cut on her cheek. They blended into her hazelnut-colored skin, and only the sunrays of dawn streaking through her window revealed them. Her lips twitched in amusement. It wasn't bad compared to last sparring, when her pink lips had looked as though she'd made out with a thornbush.

She ran her hands through the soft blackberry waterfall of hair. It flowed down to mid-back, spiraling and frizzing because of yesterday's braids. Her lean form looked like a ten-year-old's body, rather than a fifteen's. She sighed in exasperation. Already short and thin, losing weight for the fight had destroyed the small curves her body had started developing. They would return, but how long? She imagined her mother wagging a finger at her. *Boxing stunts a female figure, Rosquevalarian,* the visage used her full name to reprimand.

Maschiach, please don't let Mother be right, she prayed before common sense kicked in. The debna couldn't be right. Plenty of female boxers had figures to spare. 'Course, they were heavyweights. She grimaced.

Slipping into a green, velvet dress, she cinched it with a braided leather belt, and doubled over to lace up the boots. A pang flared in her ribs, and she hissed sharply. "Everyone cheers you in the ring, but no one cares when you gotta put your boots on," she quoted softly to herself. Bits of books or songs tended to pop in and out of her head like minnows scurrying in the shallows. Sometimes it seemed as though the world only made sense if you could put it into words. But other times, like in fighting, words could never depict reality.

With closed eyes, she pictured Lilith's head jerking back from a jab. Confidence blossomed in her chest.

She opened her eyes. "And back to duty. Like Ski said, they all got the Banli Boxer title." Disappointment pitted her stomach. "Time to focus on the next fight. I'm gonna be champion. I want to be champion." Sometime later today, when the aches of yesterday and the exhaustion of today had settled in her bones, she'd face a bag and a deb would yell at her to hit harder and faster. Then, she'd need that reminder more than ever. "I *want* to be champion," she hissed one more time, but the thought of this evening's training loomed ominously. "Ugh. I'm going to be late. I don't have time to argue with myself."

She stuffed her work clothes into a leather bag. In the castle halls, groggy-eyed fighters in baggy clothes tramped past cursing the first day of the tempa. Two full rest days meant little when you spent them getting puke-faced drunk. She smiled to herself. A servant girl hardly older than herself, stared out a stained-glass window, a rag held limp at her side. "Morning," Rosca dipped her head. Starting, the girl jumped to work as though the greeting was some subtle reprimand. Rosca flushed head to toe, wishing she could crawl out of the aristocratic clothing keeping the girl wary.

At the end of the long gray hall, a closed walnut-colored door announced her destination. Shut? "Shel it!"

Master Felki would kill her. She could say she had to turn back for a book, but she used that last tempa. What if she invoked Deb Rez's name. He could have called her in for some extra chores or… who was she kidding. The deb would never interfere with academics, and he'd made that clear to all of her instructors.

Mind racing, she inched open the door like it could shatter at a moment's notice.

Master Felki stood on the top rung of an overextended ladder, shuffling through the bookshelves. Centered in the library, a ten-foot-long table held a myriad of papers, maps, and books used for their studies. Her brothers and the other noble deb and debna children already sat in their places. The long line of them turned and watched as she raced to an empty stool between her older and younger brother. It squeaked as she plopped down, but Master Felki took no notice.

A sigh of relief escaped her.

Dium wriggled his eyebrows at her. "Late again?" he mouthed.

Dread hollowed out her stomach. "Don't you dare!" she hissed.

"Master Felki," her brother called, still staring her down. "Rosca's late again. I vote you make her do fifty push-ups. I'd say 100 but we'd be here all tempa."

Before their lessons master could catch her, she dug an elbow into his ribs.

He howled like a minsk-head.

The man turned around; a scowl plastered on his dark Valsquelian features. The young scholar had come from the plains from across the sea, like most dedicated to seeking knowledge. Yet, for all his intelligence, he still didn't know the island's native language. Rosca whispered to her brother in Ikuela. "Ti gidget."
I'll get you back.

Dium rubbed his injured side. "Prib li." *Try it.*

"Trader's tongue, please." Master Felki rubbed a large, ink-stained hand over the shaved scalp.

Her experience with that tired tone warned Rosca not to push his patience. The owl-eyed teacher could go from a sleepy sloth to a raging boar faster than Dium could race on an island-bred stallion.

Master Felki descended from the ladder and handed out the thick volumes resting in his bulky arms. "No hitting, punching, clawing, biting, or cursing. It's time to settle down and focus. If you can," he added in a dry undertone.

When he got to Rosca, he paused. "Debna, you know the rules. Or should considering how often you test them."

"Yes, Master Felki." She ducked her head. "Twenty lines of poetry?" She drowned any glee in her tone. Poetry calmed her down and time writing lines meant more opportunity to sit curled by a fire rather than doing beach sprints with Father.

"No. I think you've almost copied the entire volume at this point. Clearly, it's not a strong enough punishment." His eyes rolled over the study.

Grimacing, Rosca tried to follow his gaze, but nothing stood out. Limestone and shale bricks patterned the walls with cool browns and yellows. Twenty feet of richly stained oak bookshelves held texts and boxes. Behind her, an empty fireplace sat between two twelve-foot windows which overlooked the fishermen's district and open sea. Not the most practical for keeping in heat, but something about seeing the dancing flames and starlit waters at night made the room her favorite study spot.

"This place is messy." He ran a hand along the rectangular table and showed off a dirt coated finger. "All this needs dusting. And the floors are muddy. There're pen feathers on the chairs, and books everywhere but the shelves. The table needs buffing with oil. I assume you know how to buff?"

She nodded, making a mental note to ask a servant for instructions.

"It should take a few days. You can start today."

"Start…? You can't mean…?"

"Do you prefer I tell your father you were not only late today, but every day of last tempa?"

She shut her jaw and dropped her chin in submission. "No, Master Felki." Had it really been every day? It'd just been little things, like doing her hair or savoring breakfast. How did it add up so quickly?

"And Dium?"

Protest flashed in her brother's eyes, but he ducked his head in acknowledgment. "Yes, Master Felki?"

Iron cheeks drew tight. "The world is ruthless enough without having your own brother tattle on you. You will join Debna Rosca."

"But I'll miss training!"

"So will I." She dug her nails into the table edge. "And I have a fight soon."

"So you can miss it together. Or I can have another talk with your father about your maps test." He raised a brow at Dium. "Then you'll have to miss anyway, and you'll be writing lines for several days. Any more questions?"

"No, Master Felki."

The corners of the master's lips twisted into a smile. "Good, I'm glad. Now we can start. Children, open to page forty…"

Rosca tuned out his words as she grabbed her book, her scroll paper for notes, and a feathered pen out of the inkstand. Laying out the materials, she pretended to read. Of all the times to miss training. She had the biggest fight of her life in less than a tempa.

If she failed to become Champion Contender because of this... Sucking in her cheeks, she blew a puff of air through her nose. Her fingers curled around the edge of the table, crushing the feather pen in her grasp.

"I'm sorry." Dium's whisper coaxed her back to reality. He held his book in front of his face, pretending to read but regarding her with a frank stare. "I didn't think he'd make you skip training."

The rare earnestness roused her compassion. "It's fine."

"It's not." His attention darted to Master Felki, who rambled in detail about the island's overthrow of kings, and the establishment of a council of debs as though all his students weren't the children of council members and distinctly aware of their place.

She cut in before he could continue, keeping her tone low. "As Father says, 'If you get knocked down, life doesn't wait for you to get back up.'" Chest tight, she forced a shrug. "I'll train extra tomorrow. And when the time comes, I'll determine how I fight. No one can stop me from giving my all."

Respect flashed in his eyes. "If I didn't lose all my money at your last fight, I'd bet on you."

"But I won? Oh." She punched his arm. "You minsk-head!"

At a raised brow from Master Felki, they quieted, and he resumed the lesson.

A single thought tickled the back of her mind, until she couldn't stand it. She hissed at her brother, keeping her expression neutral and a wary eye on Master Felki. "I need to win this fight, though." As the lessons master paused his lecturing to search for another book, she turned to Dium.

"Why?" His thick brow arched until it disappeared under the black curls.

"I want to get out of here. See the world. Make something of myself like Deb Rez. He started in a dirt hut in the middle of

Valsquelian slums, and now he lives in a castle. In the fight capital of the Eastern Realm!"

Master Felki slammed his book shut.

Rosca started. Had he been talking to them? She scribbled nonsense on her paper. The dry pen left it blank. Feigning frustration, she dipped her pen in the inkwell. When he didn't address them, her breathing evened out.

Transfixed on a pile of books at his feet, the lesson's master poked through them. "Can't find anything in here. It's like a blind rat organized this room."

Dium snorted. "Yeah, you."

Master Felki's hawkish nose pointed their way. He opened his mouth to speak, but a student called from the far end of the table.

"Master Felki, can you show me the different regions of the sea again? I found two, but I'm not sure about the rest."

Rosca tilted forward to shoot a grateful look at the girl. She winked in return. "Janel, I owe you," she mouthed.

As the instructor walked away, Dium tucked himself behind his book again. "How is winning going to get you away from here?"

"You know how the deb is. He respects you all because you've won a Championship tournament."

Dium stiffened.

"Am I wrong?"

"No, but… he loves us, Rosc. You don't need to win—"

"I'm talking about respect, not love."

"Sometimes, I think you think they're the same." His dismal tone made her squirm.

"I do not. Respect is earned. Love is free."

He shrugged, hardening his features to a mask of indifference. "You didn't answer my question."

"It'll be easier to convince Father to let me go if he trusts me."

"Sounds to me like you just want people to respect you before you disappear. The rest is just an excuse."

Crimson heat spread across her cheeks. "Well, 'course I want respect. I can't just leave without proving myself here first. If I did, it'd be like running away. I'd be a coward. But I don't want to stay boxing all my life. I want more. Adventure, travel, something new."

"Proving yourself?" He guffawed loud enough for Master Felki to give a disapproving glare their way. "We're a family. Not jungle animals."

"Love without respect is like a fish without water. Eventually the relationship will die." She tapped the desk rhythmically.

He shook his head. "But you can't base a whole relationship off you acting like some great champion so everyone loves you. You're not Father." The tight jawline relaxed, and his brown eyes melted into pools of amber. "You don't need to be."

Leaning back, she scrunched her nose. "I don't want to be a deb. I'm still a female. I got my own dreams. Why would I want to be a grizzled old fighter? I just want…" Shel. What was it? Respect? Love? Adventure? "More."

"You want to be impressive."

"No," she barked the denial too quick to be believable. His eyebrows shot up. Holding in a groan, she checked to see that Master Felki remained at the other end of the table. He didn't seem to notice them. "I don't know who I want to be. I just want to be better."

Arrowing his eyes so the burning pupils hid underneath the thick lashes, he flared his thin nostrils. "The helski does 'better' mean? Better than us? Your family?"

She rolled her eyes. "No. I want to grow. Do something more than what everyone else does! I want adventure, you minsk-head.

Adventure and…" and romance. She threw back her hair. No shel way would she tell him that.

Something hard thumped the desk in front of them. Fists ready, she started to her feet.

Master Felki had dropped a bucket full of metal book ends on the table before them.

Grim as death, he raised a brow at her. "Don't forget to polish these when you clean."

"Yes, sir."

Master Felki turned away.

Dium nudged her with his shoulder and muttered, "I'll cover for you so you can go to training. But you owe me."

A massive pressure rolled from her shoulders. She sagged in her seat. "Thanks." Gratitude melted the ice between them. "If I ever do leave here…" she hesitated as his head shot up. His cheeks tinged red like they always did when he tried to keep his mouth shut but the emotions wanted to slop over. "I promise to say goodbye. And to come back. And maybe bring you along."

He gave a tight nod then turned to his book.

He didn't believe she'd leave, but he'd see. One day, she'd just go.

***

The afternoon sun stretched out Rosca's shadow, distorting the shape of her bundle until it looked like a giant's. Wincing her way down the dirt path, she dreamed of her goose-feathered mattress in her room. The dry ache in her head had made map studies more daunting than usual, and the useless shapes still swam in front of her. At least thinking made moving more bearable. Anything to escape the hours of sitting.

Gritting her teeth, she broke into a jog. She couldn't be late again. The hill's swift decline deposited her at the edge of the fishermen's district, and the smell of saltwater and ripe seafood enveloped her. Scrunching her nose, she reached inside her bag to make sure she hadn't forgotten her serving maid's outfit. Her richly embroidered dress wouldn't work well when she had to scrub pots and pans and run about serving hungry sailors.

Deb's daughter or no, she'd begged her parents for the position helping her uncle at his inn. A chance to earn something of her own, she'd called it. In reality, it was one step closer to the adventure she craved. Maybe she couldn't pick up and sail away just yet, but she could listen to stories from those who did. She would plan her travels for one day and make connections with those who might help. "Afterall," she told Dium at the start, "sailors have ships. And ships mean adventure."

Her brothers still protested her job, calling her a minsk-head for piling on extra to-dos, but they picked at everything she did. Anyway, she'd have her laugh when they ran out of wages. Deb Rez made it clear that they must make their own way in the world. It was the right of a man.

She, on the other hand, would inherit enough to live on. But she'd give them her share. She'd rather work for Uncle Dobson. Despite his grouchiness and stringent rules, he told stories better than any she knew. And his honesty breathed fresh air into the dead life of politics her parents played.

Her jog turned into a run as she went down the hill towards the traffic-filled streets. People bustled about their business, locked into their tasks for the day. Swerving to avoid a cart and horse, she received a disgruntled old man's curse and smirked. The extra challenge of dodging and ducking the tradesmen, fishermen, and carpenters exhilarated. She might tell Deb Rez to add this to her training. It was great footwork. He'd probably just give one of his infamous *what exactly goes on in your head?* sighs. She sailed over a puddle, hiking up her work skirt.

A pair of young girls yelped and jumped out of her way, scattering like startled hens. Rosca chuckled.

The inn came into sight, and she skidded to a halt. If her uncle caught her racing like a wild horse, she'd hear of it from her Mother, Debna Le. As she ambled on, a pair of boys stared then pointed at her, their fishing spears resting on their shoulders.

Cheeks heating, she ducked her head. Being Chief Deb's daughter attracted more attention than flies to a carcass. Or perhaps they'd found her pretty. She discarded the thought. That usually came second.

Thatch-roofed cottages, held precariously together with broken-down ship parts and fish nets, lined her peripheral. At the street end, a once brightly painted inn towered over all. Men, women, and children milled about outside, gutting their latest catch, chatting, or vending goods. Less than thirty paces away, rows of wooden piers berthed small rikkey ships, fishing skiffs, and a few lucrative trading barques.

Hanging from the wooden rafters of the inn's porch, a sign reading *Sailors' Solace* creaked in the wind. She stepped underneath it, the clattering of plates and raucous laughter greeting her from inside. Gazing up at the sun, she let loose her breath. She'd arrived just in time.

Someone exited the inn, bumping her backwards. She teetered on the open porch side. Regaining her balance, she yelled after the careless person. "Watch it."

The woman turned back with a drunken sneer. A Valsquelian by the looks of her. Her beauty struck Rosca, and jealousy flashed like a firefly. Curly, lustrous black hair flowed out from under a strip of red satin, wrapped around her forehead. Skin dark as ebony and clear as the night sky shone in the afternoon sun. Un-Nilealien and distinctly careless garb, a black leather vest squeezed a loose, white blouse. Tight brown breeches ran into knee high black boots, made from something other than leather.

Dragon skin? Rosca's heart raced. *Don't be ridiculous.*

Over the woman's shoulder poked a quiver and longbow. On her exposed collarbone rested puffed, scarred skin in the shape of a "P". The branding for pirate. Noting Rosca's gawking, the woman growled and pulled up her shirt to hide the mark.

Rosca clamped her mouth shut and tore away her stare. A pirate? Here? But the Nilealian penalty for piracy was death... And those clothes... Rosca stared at the leather vested back of the retreating woman, her red silk head wrap had a loose tail which fluttered in the wind like a cloak. Her fine jewelry flashed through Rosca's mind, and she shook her head in disbelief. Many travelers wore expensive silks and golds, but only pirates put them together in that haphazard, chaotic yet enchanting mess. Like somehow, it was meant to look like that and that made the look complete. She rubbed together her fingers, mumbling to herself. "A praeti would be sure to detain her." Weren't criminals supposed to be clever? She may as well put the brand on her forehead.

The woman disappeared around a corner. Disappointment flooded Rosca. She took a step to follow but stopped short as a man stumbled into the open street cursing and yelling.

"Shel the minsk-headed witch!"

Widening her eyes at the vulgar language, she noted the man's wiry build, hand clutching a clay jar, and twitching moustache. His long black coat and breeches made spotting a weapon impossible. He doubled over, hacking, then took a swig from his drink. "I'm no dog! The... the witch doesn't know me. The raschuka!"

A pair of kids raced in front of the man, lost in a game of chase. Growing in agitation, he shook his fist at them. He gnawed his lip and foamed like an oversized, possessed rat. People swerved to avoid him.

She would be late. Unable to tear her eyes away, she stayed riveted to the spot. Her senses tingled. Something was about to happen.

The drunk gnashed his teeth at the children and ripped his tunic in two. His hairy chest puffed as he roared.

Tension shot through her. She instinctively balled her hands for a fight. A series of scenarios flew through her head, and she assessed her chances of restraining the crazy man. Slim. Very slim. His hulking, bare shoulders hunched over a lithe body. He had a good three feet on her in height. Even if she hit him with all she had, she wouldn't stop him. Especially not in his state. He probably wouldn't even register pain.

The kids scampered out of range and a praeti a Iecula approached the scene. Rosca relaxed as the civil protector addressed the situation. Surely the island could deal with one minsk-head, and she needed to get to work. She shifted her feet towards the tavern door, still staring.

The drunk reached towards his belt. Her heart filled her throat. The praeti rambled some pointless speech to the disrupter. Couldn't he see the danger?

"Hey!" Rosca called. As the praeti turned to her, the man raised a knife which flashed in the sun.

She dropped her jaw, fumbling over how to warn the praeti. The man drove his knife towards the city protector's heart. A screech erupted from her throat.

Before he could deliver the death blow, an arrow pierced the drunk's hand. The weapon crashed into the dirt. A howl like that of a wounded animal filled the streets. Chaos broke loose as people scattered.

Rosca's heart pounded till her throat throbbed. Taking a step back, she scanned the square. Who had shot that? Replays of the gray tip impaling the small target spun through her mind. One second, nothing. The next, a perfect shot. Who in the helski had shot that? An image of the pirate flashed through her mind. Had she held a bow?

A gnarled faced grandpa, a buck-toothed fisherman, and a whale-sized street vendor all crossed her vision. None of them armed. None who would have that kind of training or presence of mind. A flash of red silk disappeared behind a row of vendor's stalls. The pirate!

It had to be the pirate. "Shel." Unhinged, her jaw hung limp. "What a hit."

From within the inn, she heard Uncle Dobson cursing her name. She weighed the consequences of running after her. Debna Le would make her quit in a second if she heard she saw a pirate, much less chased one. The deb may even agree.

Bouncing on her toes, she searched the crowd, but the woman had vanished.

Duty tugged at her, and she inched inside.

Uncle Dobson gave her a surly snarl. "Late again. Debna or no, I'll fire you just the same as any other. Learn your place."

Caught in a replay of the exciting moment, she grinned as wide as her lips would go. Even her uncle's use of her formal title couldn't distill her spirits. "There was a crazy man in the street going on about nothing and a pirate…" She paused, heat flooding her neck. "I mean a woman…" Great. That secret lasted all of ten seconds.

"A pirate?"

Too late now. "Yes. A female one. She saved a praeti and—"

"A female one?" His twisted temple unwound. His potbelly shook as he hooted and slapped his knee. "Girl, I always did say you had an imagination to beat a ship bard." Growing serious, he placed a calloused hand on her shoulder. "But don't be tellin' such tall tales in here. You'll cause trouble, yah hear? Ain't nobody gonna sleep or drink in peace with talks of pirates."

She shrugged her uncle's hand off in defiance. "I'm no liar. She came out from this tavern. Surely you saw her."

"Aye, I reckon I know who you mean. I'll admit, the girl had an air to beat all. Walked with real pride and mean-eyed, pretty though she be."

"Yes!" Rosca danced on the uneven boards as though they burned her feet. "And she was dressed just like a pirate. A *real* pirate."

Uncle Dobson scrunched his nose further up with each word. Abruptly, he swiped his flat hand in the air. "There are no pirates in Nileal." The man's tone split her excitement in two. "Jist cause you dress so, don't make you so."

"But—"

"I won't hear no talk of it."

"So you didn't immediately think pirate when you saw her?" She waved her hand as though she could shove the obvious truth into his small mind.

"I've lived on the sea my whole life and seen plenty that looked a way but wasn't so. Plenty that didn't look a way and was so. But I ain't never seen a female pirate." He left her to puzzle out his riddle.

She bounded after him. "First time for everything, ain't there? Isn't there?" She corrected herself automatically, her mother's chiding sudden in her thoughts.

"That's what I tell Maschiach every day when I pray you come to work on time."

Scowling, she resisted rolling her eyes.

"Git!" The man clapped his hands together, the sound rising above the din of patrons' voices.

Muttering, she dashed off.

With a sense of chagrin, she grabbed a tray of ales from an overburdened serving maid. He hadn't even asked if she'd won her fight, the old grouch-tooth. At least he'd shoved off her pirate theory. A bit insulting, but necessary. She didn't need him reporting to Mother and adding more shafts to the quiver of reasons why her parents hated her working here. This tavern was her best chance of seeing the pirate again.

She had to meet her. To know her story. How had a female gotten branded as a pirate? Why was she here? Just one conversation, then she'd report her. If needed. One pirate couldn't do that much damage. Not in Nileal. They were the fight capital of the Eastern Realm for Maschiach's sake.

Chapter Three
Home

Heading home, new complaints had joined her sore ribs, and the dryness in her head had grown into a splintering headache. Her wrinkled hands smelled like soap from doing the dishes. Protesting joints and knotted calves made the inclined walk home feel hundreds of miles long.

The gathering darkness cast a drowsy curtain over her thoughts. She fought it, glancing about and tuning into the noises around her. She clutched the dagger strapped on underneath her tunic. Anything could happen. Today proved that. A pirate and an attempted murder all in one. Maybe Nileal had some adventure after all. She smirked, calling to mind the curly-haired, charcoal skinned woman. A Valsquelian pirate. The one place no one expected a pirate to come from. But a pirate had no land. They followed the pull of the sea, no ties to anywhere. Excitement spun in her chest like fallen leaves in the wind. She could imagine it. No ties. No one to get mad 'cause you were out late or treat you like you were a toddling infant every time you made a mistake. True freedom.

But to become a pirate? Killing and plundering? Maybe the weak deserve what they get, or maybe violence is the law of the insane. Either way, she didn't have the heart for that kind of bloodshed. She knew that much about herself. With a sigh, she slipped through the back training fields of her home and approached the kitchen entrance embedded in the castle wall.

Wild rose vines framed a chestnut door. Light green ivory draped the top, hanging from a stone ledge. In an uncovered window, a single candle flickered with the soft breeze. The warm welcome to her home pushed away her troubles.

Inside, the recognizable voices of the cook and servant discussed tomorrow's breakfast. Rosca banged on the door, and they bustled her in.

"Another long day, aye?" The cook's knowing tone soothed Rosca's headache.

"Not too bad." Rosca attempted a smile, but a yawn won out.

The cook gave her a sympathetic look before returning to an overboiling pot hanging over the fire. The motherly woman had her own worries to attend to. Rosca slipped into the hall.

A light spilled from the study. She stopped to glance inside. Father was still up? Was he waiting for her again?

She slipped inside and took the seat opposite him. "I'm home."

He ignored her, staring at the book as though lost in its pages. "I'm glad."

You don't have to keep pretending to read. She bit down the words, a sliver of appreciation slicing her annoyance.

Lifting her eyes, she stared at the bookcases running from ceiling to floor, filled with stories and information from as far as the Molatineez Mountains. She examined the title of the deb's chosen story. *Rylheim's Rally-Cry.* "How's your book?"

"Uh-huh." He cleared his throat. "Boring, very boring. But it's good for me. I'm expanding my horizons, as your mother would say."

She stifled a chuckle at the pain in his voice. "Pretty sure you would have to actually read it for that to happen."

His head shot up. "What do you mean?" Gray specked eyes narrowed in suspicion over the crooked nose.

She rolled out the knots from her shoulders, throwing him a teasing glance. "You've been on that same book since I started working. You're not reading, you're waiting."

Clearing his throat, he set down his novel. "Not all of us are little speed readers like you. Some of us take time to enjoy the literary essence of..." he squinted, "of books. Don't be so condescending."

"Mm-hmm." She stroked her chin, mocking his studious façade.

He scowled, but a smile twinkled underneath the baggy eyes.

Lapsing back into silence, she once again pictured the pirate, but discarded the image as though he could see into her thoughts.

Her father shifted back in his chair and studied her. "How was work?"

Guilt soured her mouth, and she swallowed in discomfort. She studied the dancing flames of the fire. Their reckless jumps and flips eased the tension. Shrugging, she untied the ribbon holding back her curls. "Same old. Some guy tried to intimidate me into giving him free food, not that he needed any. We had to search the storage just to find a chair big enough to fit him."

Deb Rez rumbled with laughter.

The deep sound sent rivers of warmth over Rosca's heart.

He tilted forward. "What'd you do?"

Massaging her scalp, she shook out the long curls. "Let him know I carry a dagger."

Worry flashed across his features. Pensive faced, he steepled his hands. "I doubt that'd scare off most men. You need to be careful looking for fights. I know it's my fault. I trained you after all, but real life is not a controlled boxing match. Hardened sailors and soldiers won't take a little girl with a pointy metal stick seriously. The world's dangerous. I'd feel better if you stayed home. You don't need the money."

Inwardly sighing, Rosca gave him a smile he couldn't possibly resist. "Fair enough. But being the daughter of war hero and Chief Deb Rez sure has its benefits. Even if a customer tried something, I'd have the whole tavern rising to protect me." It wasn't flattery. Most Nilealians took her father for a wild, unquenchable fire harnessed into a human, bear-like figure. A bit dramatic, but people usually were when it came to their heroes.

With the texture of old, reliable leather, his face crinkled into a pleased self-assurance, as it always did at the mention of his people. "Many, many years I have served the citizens of Nileal. Never once have I found them ungrateful."

Rosca snorted. "Even when they tried to get you kicked out of the council?"

He guffawed. "My enemies tried to defy the desire of the people. But that is not how we work. That's why we overcame. Because the people believed in me and I in them. Now look at us. Look at where servitude gets you. True servitude. True loyalty." He gestured about the luxuriously decorated room.

Statues, one of Rez himself, stood about like a white marbled host of servants awaiting orders. Lavish artifacts filled the space, hand-painted plates from Limur, wool-spun quilts from Valsquel, furniture of ghensig wood, and paintings as large seven feet depicting waterfalls and forests.

"Sometimes," she lowered her head, not wanting to see the pride slip from his gaze when she made her confession. "I forget about all this... I mean that other people don't have this. And that we're special. Unusual. It just feels..."

"Like a part of life." He surmised.

She nodded. "I don't mean to be ungrateful, but..." She chewed the inside of her cheek.

A frown twitched on the brown lips. "Sometimes I think I've doomed you kids by giving you so much. But then…" Stopping, he took a long breath.

Awed by the pain in his voice, she searched his expression.

"Then I remember what I lived through. My family. All the fighting, cursing, and manipulation…. No security. No safety. I wouldn't wish that on my enemy, much less my children."

Resting her chin in her hand, she sighed. Would fear always keep him from letting her go? Would she ever find a way to leave? To adventure?

"Listen." He leaned forward and placed a hand on her shoulder. "The best things in life do not cost money. They cost courage and strength. You'll find your own life, but it's more than this. It is not what someone else has built. Someone else can take this away."

Hope bloomed in her chest. He understood. At least partly.

"You never realize how fast life can change. Until it does. There are people who would give anything for what we have, including their spirit to damnation."

She nodded solemnly, but wondered, who would dare? In the west, men dreamed of the brawn and agility possessed by the Banli warriors. Their kingdoms could not reproduce what decades of tradition had bred. In the east, the island Iecula, on which their home Nileal sat, reigned as king over the other tribal lands spotting the sea. Not a soul had so much as threatened war with them in a hundred years. Except pirates. The murderers once had no qualms about midnight raids, but even those had dwindled since her father became chief deb.

Unbidden, the Valsquelian's earlier bow shot replayed in her mind's eye. Excitement coursed her veins. The guilt returned, splitting her thoughts until a roaring headache seized her.

With a hug goodnight, she retired to her room, where ships, adventure, and pirates haunted her dreams.

Chapter Four
Preparation

The promise of dawn hazed the grassy hillside with a morning glow. Rosca tramped behind Ski across their mother's back garden to their training center. "It just feels like another training. Doesn't feel like we're on the edge of a competition."

Ski whistled, jumping over a patch of leafy greens the Debna had planted. "Speak for yourself. I'm starting to get excited."

As though the words had released a million butterflies in her gut, she cupped a hand over her stomach and nodded. She was going to be sick. Waiting was worse than fighting. What if she got knocked down? Dium would never let her hear the end of it. Was she really ready? Shel. She hated this. Always the same doubts. How could anyone guess if they're ready? "I'm excited," she said lamely, clearly unconvinced.

"You'll be fine." Ski waved a hand, dismissing her heavy tone. "If you're really ready, you'll know. You won't be nervous." He shadowed a few punches. "I'm ready."

Okay. So she wasn't ready. But he didn't need to know that. She straightened her slumped shoulders and added a light-hearted bounce to her step.

Grunts and thuds of fighters resounded from the pavilion. Rows of columns supported a gable roof. The lined pillars sprouted at the top like overgrown ferns with masoned, leafy branches spilling out in star points. Detailed recesses of lions, battles, forests, and a king's ancient throne lined the lilt-stone base of the roof.

Her brother's furtive steps rushed her along.

Her fists clenched, the butterflies returning with dagger-wings and slicing her insides. Licking her lips, she cleared her throat. "Who are you going against?"

"Goliath."

She winced. How was her brother not scared? "Goliath? That boy could enter his hands in a footrace and win."

"I know." His sharp tone stilled her tongue, but memories of the young giant popping in with a deadly six-punch combo, then retreating before his opponent could react played in her mind.

"And you?"

"Lelina." She tried to level her voice, but it spiraled with worry. Lelina. Four years older and the favorite of everyone she'd talked to. Boxers were nothing if not blunt.

Ski stopped and spun to face her. "They're letting you fight Lelina?"

"Letting me?" She snorted. "May as well 'let me' throw myself off a cliff." She shrugged as though her heart hadn't just shriveled like dried mango. "I'll win." She hoped.

Ski put a hand on her shoulder. "We both will. You know why?"

The slump in her shoulders returned. "'Cause we're gonna sneak rocks into my gloves?"

"No. Because we train like a pack of helski hounds are at our heels."

A genuine smile overtook her. "True."

They walked on.

"The deb wouldn't let us go if we weren't ready."

Ski snorted. "He would. Ishels fight. It's what we do. It would reflect badly on him if we didn't compete. I mean look at him, he's even pushing you to be in the ring. You're a girl!"

Temple wound tight, she caught her breath. "I forgot. You can't say anything nice about him in your presence. Even if it's true."

Ski kicked a clump of grass, shoving his hands into his pockets. "I just don't worship the ground he walks on like everyone else."

"I chose to fight, and you know that." She glanced at him, but he pretended to study the bright horizon. Despite his show of superiority, the veins in his neck twitched with anger. "Begged him to let me." She leaned forward to catch his eye.

Ski ground his teeth loud enough for her hearing. "A real father would never put his daughter in the ring. He's Chief Deb first. Always."

She bit her tongue, and they lapsed into silence. Like her, he had come from Valsquel to live with the deb and debna when their parents disappeared. Unlike her, he acted as though this made them their own family, separate from their uncle, aunt, and cousins. It didn't matter that Rez and Le had raised, sheltered, and adopted them as their own. To him, they would always be Deb and Debna. Uncle and Aunt on a good day. And it seemed to grate on him that she called them Father and Mother. But what did he expect? To her, they were.

Maybe he was just trying to protect her. But why did he have to be such a minsk about it all?

When she entered the gymnasium, a cheery grin lit Deb Sergio's pock-marked face. "Miche wu, chilita i chey." His thick knuckles, white with dead, calloused skin, reached out for a fist bump from both, which they returned.

Rosca's smile turned genuine. Chilita, or little curly-haired girl, had been his name for her since childhood.

Behind him, rows of leather and burlap bags hung from a trellis. When the sun sank low, it would play with the red grain of the nama wood, making ruby sunbeams dance on the dirt. This earned the center the name "Asium", or red in Ikuela.

Rosca searched the room. "He's not here?"

Ski grabbed his gloves from inside the same box. "Who?"

"Father. We were supposed to work a new combo today. He said—"

"You're surprised?" He cut her off, holding out his glove for her to lace up.

She obliged with a glare. "Don't be a minsk-head."

An *I-told-you-so* smirk curved his lips. "Don't say things you'll regret."

"I regret nothing I say." She met the hard, pine-colored eyes.

"Maybe you should."

"So you deny being a minsk-head?"

"Takes one to know one."

She squeezed the lacing on his glove till his arm paled, then tied it off before he could protest. "Other hand?"

He waved her off. "I'll find someone who doesn't want to cut my arm off."

"Suit yourself." Spinning on her heel, she pushed through the crowd to find her own gear.

Fighters from nearly all ten weight divisions crowded her family's training facility. The deb held responsibility for some three-hundred boxers in addition to soldiers, retired Debs, one active deb, and servants living on his land. Most of the time, it felt like it.

She skirted several fighters doing bag work. What was the point of having a private facility if everyone and their third cousin could use it? A woman had claimed Rosca's favorite bag, faded and dented in spots where she threw her most valuable, most precious combos. Even with a thousand acres of training grounds and bags taking up most of it, people insisted on stealing her stuff. Huffing, she picked a different bag.

The first speed drill warmed her arms and lulled her mind to stillness. By the second, she had to resist the urge to switch to power shots. Anticipation mounted within her, ready for a release.

In the corner of her vision, a figure grew larger and larger. Deb Sergio took up watch near her, waiting.

She switched to power shots. Slip right, upper-upper. One, two, pull back, two, three, two. Mechanical, she ran through the combos.

"Call that a punch? I know you're a debna but try not to hit like it."

Rosca grunted as though that would convince him she was trying. Why couldn't he find someone else to pick on? She'd just won her fight. Clearly, she was doing something right.

Deb Sergio crossed his arms. "You're tired, Rosca. Your punches are sloppy."

She straightened each one's course but, feeling sluggishness in every fiber, held back on power.

"Shel. What happened? You go party last night or something?"

Her ribs burned with bruises. She may have won her fight, but Lilith had left her mark. Hadn't he seen that? Didn't he realize that? Fury enveloped her. Speed picking up, she dodged and slithered around the bag like a snake, then threw a one, two double-hook.

"I heard you were fighting Lelina? You think she'll let you hit her like that without responding? It's all you. Either make her respect your punches, or you may as well offer yourself up as a boxing bag."

She pushed off her heel to harness power from her legs. Muscle and rotation worked together to create a hit that thudded with power.

In her peripheral, Deb Sergio smiled. "You shouldn't have shown me you can do that. Now I want every punch to sound that good."

Sucking in measured breaths, Rosca drove each shot into her imaginary opponent. Yells of effort escaped her. Her muscles trembled. She moved around and made a show of footwork. Gah, why did she feel like mescucha today? Digging into the bag, she listened to Deb Sergio's drill commands. One minute of speed punches to head. One minute to body. Power right. Power left. Gasping, she prayed for the torture to end, then cursed her weak mind.

When Deb Sergio allowed for a quick break, relief swallowed her aches. She rushed to grasp the long wooden ladle sticking out of the nearest communal water bucket, but Ski shoved her aside. He stretched his sips into eternity, and her patience finally snapped.

"Just take all day, why don't you?"

"Oh, I will, thank you." With a mischievous grin, he purposely sucked the water in slow drops.

"Don't make me punch you. I'd hate to see what gettin' beat up by a girl would do to your reputation."

"Yeah, right. You can't even reach my face."

She attempted to uppercut his gut, but he blocked it with his elbow and, dropping the ladle into the bucket, wrapped her in a headlock.

"Let go!" Fury burned her cheeks as she twisted and elbowed his ribcage. When that didn't work, she stomped on his foot. He loosened his hold. She wiggled out and kneed him between the legs. With a yelp, he crumpled.

"Told you to let go."

Leaving his moaning body to the chuckling Deb Sergio, she grabbed the ladle and took a long, satisfying swallow.

"That's cheating!" Her brother glared, pink creeping into his cheeks.

"And what is fighting a girl six years younger than you?"

If he answered, she didn't hear it.

Yelling stole her attention. She scanned the gym. The woman who had taken her favorite bag now attacked it with ferocity. A grave expression tightened her dark face, and the sound of each hit reverberated in the gym.

Rosca stared. The pirate! Surprise and delight interlaced. Heart thumping, she raised her hand to point at her, then dropped it. Minsk-head. Was she going to call the pirate out in front of the whole gym? Still chiding herself, she took a few tentative steps in the woman's direction then froze. What would she say? *Hey, it's cool you're a pirate minus the killing and pillaging part.* She rolled her eyes and settled for studying the woman.

No longer in her seafaring garb, but wearing traditional boxing gear, the woman looked like another regular fighter. Or would have if she wasn't the only other female in the gym and gorgeous.

Like Rosca, she wore long black breeches and a short-sleeved gray tunic. Their faces copied each other's angular structure and high cheekbones. Although the darker woman possessed a mature, curvy figure and the sun-kissed wrinkles of a seafarer, their similarities sent chills racing up Rosca's spine.

Ski nudged her elbow. "Lelina's here."

Rosca's heart dropped. Pirate forgotten, she spun to where he gestured. "She doesn't even train here. What does she want?"

"Probably a face off. You know how she is. She nicknamed herself 'Bruta' for Maschiach's sake. Brute!"

Rosca tore her gaze away and walked back to her bag. "Well, she won't get a rise out of me." Despite her words, the nineteen-year-old's smushed, boar-like face floated in her mind.

For years, people bullied Lelina for her ugly looks. Now, she used it to sell her fights. Before each bout, she entered the ring on all fours, barking like a dog. And she had warrior blood in her. Banli blood. Compared to her, Rosca was shark chum. Rosca hesitated, watching her opponent.

Lelina caught her eye and spun in the opposite direction, pretending not to notice her.

Fine, then. Rosca whirled out her combos, growing in speed. The hairs on the back of her neck prickled. "Bruta" was watching. Simplifying her punches, she avoided any combos she planned to use in the fight.

Lelina approached Rosca's bag. Her large figure loomed left. A chill washed down Rosca's spine.

"Training won't help." The big girl goaded. Even resting at her side, the girl's biceps looked flexed.

She could take her boasting elsewhere. She hadn't wanted to acknowledge Rosca. Rosca sure as helski wouldn't acknowledge her.

Pivoting, Rosca dug another combo into the bag. A series of satisfying smacks filled the gym.

"That's it?" One of Lelina's cohorts chuckled.

A pit opened in Rosca's stomach, but she grinned. "Guess we'll find out at the fight." She let out an eight-punch combo.

Lelina stepped closer.

Rosca refused to look at her, but curiosity froze her movement. She quit punching and waited for the big girl to state her piece.

Lelina whispered, her hot breath swarming Rosca's ear. "You're nothin' but a set-up fight. Your father's name gets me my fame, and you get a chance to share the ring with a real fighter. That's all this is about."

Calm blanketed Rosca's pulse. She didn't need to say anything. Bruta wouldn't be here if she wasn't scared. She met the girl's pinched glower with one of her own. The silence stretched between them.

Lelina crossed her arms. Tattoos of skulls and triangles curled around them. The mosaic of sharp lines expected on a Banli man, not a young girl, cut and stained the skin. "By the time I finish rearranging your face, even the mutts will yelp at the sight."

The irony hit Rosca before her resolution to keep quiet. "At least they don't mistake me for their sister."

Fury framed Lelina's snarl. Tension rippled in the air. Rosca's abs tightened. Cocked ready, her arms took on a life of their own. When the girl refrained from starting a brawl, Rosca smirked. Bruta hadn't come to start a fight. Besides, with a face like that, she'd probably heard it all before.

Stillness had iced all movement as the crowd watched the girls. Deb Sergio burst into the scene with a look that could have set fire to stone. "Lelina, get out. And all the rest. No pre-fight drama."

"Fine." Lelina tossed her wiry ponytail. "But your father's guard dog can't protect you in that ring."

Rosca lurched forward, but Deb Sergio jerked her back. He held her arm vice-like. "Let it go. I've been called worse."

Her stomach dropped, but she relaxed, and he released her.

They left.

"That was dramatic." Humor danced in Ski's tone.

"You good?" Deb Sergio's expression dropped into one of concern.

Rosca faked a nonchalant shrug, head spinning with the girl's accusations. *Father's fame. A set-up fight.* Her heart hammered. No. She was a fighter. She was!

She took a deep breath before responding. "I'm good. She just likes to make a show."

Ski snorted. "Clearly."

Rosca resumed her work-out, her blood pounding in her ears. She would earn respect. From Lelina, Deb Rez, Deb Sergio. Everyone. By the end, it'd be enough. She wasn't just her father's daughter.

Two hours passed. Then three. The morning cool changed to midday heat. She'd have to make up culture studies. Master Richson would be angry, but, unlike Master Felki, he wouldn't do anything. He feared Deb Rez.

She jabbed, hooked, and uppercut with the same hand. The *thud* of each in the rapid series sang to her.

Deb Sergio approached her, shaking his head. "You can't let it get to you so much."

"Nothing's getting to me," she lied.

"Go home. You're wearing yourself out. Rest."

Pulling off the gloves, she nodded. "Yes, Deb."

The path home had more hills than flat earth. Ambling over one, she kicked a loose rock in the path. Satisfaction filled her when it sailed right and hit a nama tree. The motherly girth of the tree provided a spot of shade, and she rested for a moment under it. If the deb had been there today, Lelina would never have thought to try her. She leaned against the trunk, refusing to acknowledge what it meant that Lelina knew the deb wouldn't be there. "He's a busy man," she reminded herself. But how many times had she seen him in the last month? Other than when he waited up for her and that could as easily be duty as— "Stop it." The empty blue horizon stared back as though annoyed with her for bringing a dark mood into the beautiful day. "I'm letting Ski get to me. He does care about us. He is a good father. It'd be suffocating to have him there every second." She dug her nails into her palm. Besides, she could handle herself. She wasn't as weak as they believed. As Lelina believed.

Exhaustion broke the dam of protests, and she sighed. Ski was right too. She rested her chin on her chest. Deb Rez pushed them more than most fathers. But didn't love make you want to respect those important to you? She fiddled with the chain of her gold necklace. The sapphire gem stared back at her. "I want him to respect me. I'm not trying to be 'impressive,' Dium." Screwing her face into a sneer, she imagined her brother as he looked in their earlier debate. Intolerably cocky with his set jaw and dead stare.

Guilt wrenched her gut. Would she know the difference? She scratched the surface of the gem. Was there a difference between being impressive and being respected? Sunrays cast a dancing light on the hard surface. The deep blue twinkled like a wave-capped sea. She smiled. "No matter the storm, the waves will calm." The mumbled adage lightened her ponderous spirit.

"The sea. Everyone's their own man in the sea." Like the pirate. Slamming a hand to her forehead, she jumped to her feet. "Shel. I forgot all about her. Shel Lelina." She threw up her hands in frustration. "Whatever. As it is." The wind picked up, whishing her curls into the air. She spun to face the view.

Below, her home sprawled over the grassy valley. Made of blanched stone, a short wall surrounded the debna's manicured garden. Blue, red, yellow, and green flora made a quilt of the land. A tamed wilderness. Loathing rose in her breast. "Why do we have to control everything? Can't we trust things to find their own place?" Pacing, she stopped to kick the nama tree.

The mighty trunk leered at her, like a king on a throne. Her hands itched with a sudden urge to climb. She gripped the first branch. Racing up, she chose a nook at the top and straddled it. "Father would banish me if I became a pirate." She tasted the word with caution. Father. Always flipping between Father and the deb. Never set on if she belonged to him or not. When had that happened? It'd just been Father in her youth, hadn't it?

She rested her head against the scratchy bark and concentrated on picking leaves from the branches above. "He'd be right to banish me too. Iecula doesn't need another King Dahl." It'd been hundreds of years, but Iecula's last king gave sanction to the pirates and their treacherous deeds in exchange for plunder. The corruption had torn their island so far in half, she wouldn't even call it a civil war. War implied armies and brotherhood. This more closely resembled caged animals tearing out each other's throats. Eventually, it led to the uprising of a Banli Brotherhood and the dethroning of kings forever.

But what did hand-me-down tales have to do with today?

The woman would come back to the gym, and Rosca would get to know her. She would see if she meant any harm. Just because she was a pirate didn't mean she was a horrible person.

Anyway, Rosca wasn't scared of her or Deb Rez. She could handle crazy people. She did it every day at work. She wouldn't be some spoiled debna minsk-head that went running to her father for help. But it was her duty to figure out why the woman was here. If the pirate tried anything, it was on her. She was her responsibility now. With these justifications, she put her conscience to sleep.

***

Rosca tossed from right to left, left to right. The bed cozied her sprawled form, but rest evaded her. First heat, then cold, blanketed her body. Thoughts of the tournament kept her eyes wide, and heart rate elevated.

A full day remained before her fight, but two had passed like nothing. Fighters didn't usually take such long breaks in a tournament, but this year too many people signed up to keep the old format. Just one more fight and she would qualify for the final ten. She just had to get past Lelina.

But Lelina wasn't a fighter you just 'got past'.

Unable to endure the whirling anxiety any longer, Rosca sprang from bed and dressed for training. She snuck out to Asium. Cloaked in nighttime mystery, the familiar gym almost intimidated.

Cool night air loosened the constriction in her chest. Maybe she couldn't stop the war inside her head, but she could do something to give herself a better chance at winning.

Shuddering under the weight of a single punch, the bag vibrated in front of her poised position. Double-jab, cross, slip, cross, hook. Throw a few jabs to re-center. A one, two combo. Again. Again. Double-jab, cross, left hook, uppercut, pivot.

"Someone make you mad?" The laugh came from a petite figure just entering and dressed for training. The pirate! The woman tied her hair up. A closer look at her features revealed a scarred jawline and care-worn face.

Rosca froze, unsure of what to say. What was this woman doing? It wasn't even the third hour of the morning.

Without another word, the two drove away at the bags.

After about thirty minutes, Rosca perfected a new combo. Her sore limbs reminded her that sleep was also essential for athleticism. She slipped off her gloves and sat on a wooden crate that contained extra boxing gear.

The steady beat of the woman's punches stopped, and Rosca looked up in surprise.

The pirate approached her. "Hey, how 'bout a fight?"

She raised her brows. "You want to spar?"

"Isn't that why we're here?"

The allure of beating a pirate quickened her pulse. Rosca opened her mouth to agree, then froze. The d— Father would kill me if I got injured before my fight.

The pirate's alert eyes scanned her from head to foot. "More of a show than a fighter then, ain't you?"

Her challenge washed over Rosca like a bucket of cold water. With a shrug, Rosca looked down at her wraps as she unwound them. On the inside, her rough hands had calluses from gripping brooms and scrubbing dishes at Sailor's Solace. Running her finger over the coarse texture, she hoped the woman would leave her alone.

"I find it hypocritical you call yourselves an island of warriors."

She was baiting her. Rosca examined the ground, pushing out a long breath from her nose.

"Even your horses live pampered lives with castles as grand as any king. I have yet to see a hardy soldier, beddin' in the woods and at peace with his state. They all sleep on goose feathers here, with their mothers two doors down in case of nightmares."

Rosca's head shot up. "I know what you are. A pirate. You know nothing about honor or respect."

"Maybe not." The older woman tilted her head and scanned her with calculating, disappointed eyes. "But I know what it takes to survive. I've had tempas with more adversity than your so-called fighters have had in their entire lives."

Rosca curled her toes, careful not to show emotion in her face or hands. "Anyone can fight. It takes honor to live a steady life." Her voice faltered. It just wasn't the life she wanted.

The pirate's airy laugh echoed in the stillness. "If honor leads to sittin' on one's fat rear and having servants drop desserts in your mouth all day, then I am glad I do not have it." Thinning her features into a scowl, she stared through Rosca, as though reading each hope trapped inside her racing heart. "The sea holds enough shine for me and fighting enough satisfaction."

Rosca reeled back as though struck. They were the same. The heat of a battle was their home. Steadying herself, she rewound her wraps. "Okay."

"Okay?"

Rosca shrugged. "You insult my family, my country, and me." She grinned. "Let's fight."

The pirate's smirk startled Rosca with the similarity to her father's. She tucked away the thought and approached the center of Asium where a round splotch of dirt was marked off. The pirate followed.

Rosca ducked under the ropes of the practice ring. Jumping about on the balls of her feet, she waited as the woman joined her.

"Headgear?" Her opponent held up the bundle of leather.

Rosca grabbed it. "I fight to be a Banli Champion Contender in two days. Father will kill me if I get a brain injury before my fight."

"No promises." Neither worry nor comfort showed on the woman's face as she adjusted the leather straps of her helmet.

Rosca twisted her own for reassurance. The padded leather ran from the chin to an extra-thick cap up top. It felt like having a skinned pig-turned-pillow glued to one's head.

Running her finger on the cool, hardened clay of the mouthpiece, Rosca took a deep breath and put it in. Time to fight.

They touched gloves and retreated. Circling, they trained their gazes on the other's chest, watching for action. Rosca advanced on the woman and threw jabs to gauge the distance between them.

A counter overhand responded and connected with her right temple.

Dazed, Rosca instinctively slipped side to side, and the woman's slew of punches missed her. She shuffled out of the pirate's reach.

But her opponent did not relent. Onward, the woman's feet carried her charge. Unrefined steps, but quick and effective.

Rosca dodged until her opposition grew sloppy. She threw a hard, counter-straight, followed by two left body shots. Their thumps filled her chest with satisfaction.

A smear of red flashed across Rosca's vision. The pirate's nose bled.

With a feint that threw Rosca off rhythm, the woman successfully set up a vicious right hook to the temple, in the same spot as her very first hit.

Rosca's head spun, and a warm feeling erupted in her chest. Slipping, she jabbed instinctively, keeping distance between them.

The pirate didn't fight with the clear-cut technique of a boxer, but her onslaught never faltered. Never quit pressuring the younger girl. She used a jab-cross-left hook to advance.

Rosca took them, then countered with her favorite combo, body jab, right to the head, left uppercut, power right. Inside each other's range, they brawled. Each blow given meant taking one in turn. She counted the combos. At six, she tired. At ten, she burned with exhaustion. At twelve, she gained momentum.

In one victorious moment, she let loose her favorite combo. Jumping out, she evaded the pirate's return blows. By the third successful time she did this, she had to hold down a grin. Perhaps she had a serious chance.

The pirate landed a double jab-uppercut-left hook.

Gnat-sized stings flushed the right side of Rosca's face. She danced away, controlling the distance with feints and slips.

Whooshing out deep breaths, she steadied her mind. Her hot cheek puffed up, pushing against her eye. In her blurred peripheral, she saw an incoming hook, ducked, and side-stepped. Her legs deadened, but she pranced on.

Continuing to force retreat, the woman jabbed and uppercut.

Rosca bobbed and weaved.

Thrown off by the there-again, gone-again head, the woman shot a power right punch and missed. Seeing her opening, Rosca pounded into her opponent's side with vengeful uppercuts. But the body shots from the pirate had sapped her energy. Her arms trembled. She stopped throwing and shoved the woman into the ropes.

They stared at each other. Blood dripped from the pirate's busted nose and her left eye had swollen slightly. Sweat coated her. Rosca didn't flatter herself with thinking she looked any better.

"Wait." Coughing, the woman leaned over the ropes and emptied her guts on the ground. Heaving, she wiped her mouth. "I may have overdone it at the pub last night."

Rosca snorted. The way the woman had stumbled out of the tavern the other day, she wasn't convinced the bow shot through that looney's hand hadn't been made minsk-faced drunk. Which just made it that more impressive. But how many times could a woman get wasted in a tempa?

Rosca spit her mouthpiece into her glove and straightened. "That's enough."

"I didn't say I was done." With a dry laugh, the pirate took a few unsteady steps forward.

"Fine." Rosca replaced the clay piece onto her teeth, calling the woman's bluff.

Her opponent flared her nostrils, annoyance in the dark eyes.

Straightening, the pirate wiped away the expression with a smile. Tearing off her gloves, she held out her hand. "I'll give you the match. Your father has shaped you into quite the weapon, but had it been a true fight, with kicks and steel, you'd be dead."

"You're not giving anything." Rosca ignored the offered hand and exited the ring. "I took it."

"I'm Hel—" The woman unstrapped her headgear and followed Rosca onto the bare earth. "I'm Ray, by the way."

Rosca pretended not to notice the blunder. Pirates didn't shake the noose by announcing their arrival. Most of the criminals she'd met working at Sailor's Solace went by so many names they'd forgotten the one their mother gave them.

"You haven't trained mixed fightin', have you? The way you duck and sit heavy on your front foot... I seen a million times where I could've taken you out with a knee." Ray tried to spit out her mouthpiece, but nothing came.

Rosca had a feeling it lay somewhere in a pool of puke. "Not much reason to practice. I don't have time with boxing, lessons, and work. It isn't as though I plan to go into the militia."

"What's wrong with the militia?" Ray wiped the blood from her face on her handwraps, then slowly unrolled them.

Laughing, Rosca threw her gloves and gear into a pile.

The woman's somber face pinched tight.

"Oh, you're serious?" Rosca paused. Of course she was serious. She was a female pirate. Gender rules didn't mean fish eggs to her. "I don't want to go to war to fight with men four times my size and eight times as strong. My brothers beat me up enough."

"But you're a fighter in spirit. I saw it. That's the thing about boxin', you can't spit rookah."

"Spit what?" Rosca raised a brow.

"Lie. 'Tend to be something you're not."

"Oh. Mescucha. We say 'spit mescucha'."

Ray nodded as though she didn't hear. "You respond well to pressure. When I caught you with that hook, you didn't panic. You adjusted, bobbin' and weavin' more. That's a fighter's mentality. And you're tough. You ate some of my best shots. You don't belong here in a castle. You're no debna."

Pride ignited in Rosca's chest. Unable to meet her fiery stare, she flopped onto the cold ground. "I don't know where I belong yet. I'm only fifteen."

"All the more reason to start now. You have talent and a solid base. By twenty, you could be fightin' whole armies with your hands tied."

"Hah!" Rosca rolled her eyes. "Do they train you in flattery on your ship or is it a survival skill?"

Something akin to tenderness softened the woman's expression. "Maybe someday you could fight with me. Sail the world. Find real adventure. True fights. None of this staged, fake stuff you do here."

The insults rolled off Rosca's back as she considered the idea. Dreams usually submerged beneath life's duties flocked to the forefront. Imaginings inspired by things she'd only heard of swirled in a chaotic blur. Mountain ranges dipped in white, lands undiscovered, wild exotic beasts, titles won through adversity. Rosca the adventurer. Goosebumps peppered her forearms. But a pirate? She'd be disowned.

From the corner of her eye, Rosca saw Ray's expression fall into a thoughtful daze, preoccupied with musings of another world. Another life. One that could sweep Rosca away just as easily. Afterall, she'd beat her boxing. Certainly, she could handle whatever Ray did.

Ray caught Rosca's stare and snapped to life. "All I ask is you let me train you for a while. And help me get food and lodgin' while I'm here."

"There it is. Your price." Rosca rolled out the stiffness in her shoulders. The stress of the past few hours dribbled down her back like pitch. Couldn't they have this conversation after she won her championship and got some sleep? "Everyone's got one. At least it's out in the open now."

"My coachin' is worth a lot more than a bed and stew," Ray snapped. "I'm just in the mood to do favors." She rubbed her hands together. "Don't you wanna prove yourself? Don't you wanna show people you have what it takes? Not just as a boxer, but as a true fighter? Take a chance."

Rosca peered at her, misgivings filling every pore. Her body tensed as though balanced on a precipice, and the slightest breath could send her tumbling down either side. "Why are you so interested in me?"

"Because you're gonna be someone great. I already see it, and I want to be there to say I knew it from the beginnin'."

Hope burst within Rosca. She chewed the inside of her cheek. Someone at least thought she could make it. Thought she might do something beyond the mundane. As fast as the inspiration came, it faltered. Who was a pirate to see potential in anyone?

Flushing, Rosca picked at some spare splotches of grass and watched the distorted shadows cast by the flickering torch flames. A pile of dust and greenery shifted between her thumb and forefinger. Replacing her hands at her sides, she met the pirate's austere gaze. "I've had training in mixed fighting."

"Show me a kick."

With a groan, Rosca rose to her feet and faced a bag. Throwing a double-jab, she twisted her body, landed her right shin on it, and immediately retracted it. The bag swayed from the impact.

"Hmm." Ray pursed her lips, her thin, dark brows inching together.

"What does that mean?" Rosca's voice pitched higher than she meant for it to.

"It means you didn't rotate your hips fully, your speed is decent at best, and you seemed off balance. Do two."

Biting her tongue, Rosca tried again. Another one-two combo to establish rhythm, and she threw three right kicks.

"Hmm. Well, if you're happy with that." Ray stood to go.

"Wait! Okay."

"Okay?"

"It's that bad?"

"Worse."

"But you'll train me?"

A mask of indifference slid over the beautiful features. "If you insist."

Chapter Five
Waiting

Rosca pressed her knees together so tight the bones bruised, but she welcomed the pain as a distraction. Fight day had arrived.

Zafiere's holding room contained knots of boxers, their coaches, and teams discussing strategy and warming up. The clay walls made her think of the island caves and caverns she loved to explore. Large and open, the space reverberated with energy. Above their heads, thousands of voices booed and cheered in turn as spectators celebrated or heckled the other Banli Boxers.

Her brother Dium shadow-boxed restlessly, as though he was the one about to fight, not her. "Zafiere's full as a deb at a dessert bar tonight."

"Funny." Rosca tilted back her chair. "I don't remember hardly anyone at your fight."

Unbothered, he bobbed and weaved with a grin. "Even better. It's all the fun and none of the pressure."

"Yeah, right. Like you could do without a crowd. You need people to cheer you on just to relieve yourself."

Adnesi's chuckle echoed her father's.

Scowling, Rosca wiped her sweaty palms on her boxer's shorts. Why hadn't Dium stayed in the stands with Mother and the little boys?

The five Ishels lapsed back into silence. Even the ever-energetic Dium leaned against the wall, still, if only for a second.

Rosca dug a nail into her leg. Bile tasting of fish and oatcakes coated her tongue. She now regretted her earlier nervous snacking. Surrounded by her father and brothers, everything blurred between reality and the anxious battle taking place in her head. Lelina must be as nervous as she was. This was her Champion Contender fight too. Something about picturing her opponent, head between knees and shaking with fear slowed the pounding rhythm in her eardrums. She gulped the stale air like spring water.

"Lelina will try to bully you using her power, but you can take it."

Jerked into reality, she looked at her father to show she understood his words, though they barely registered in her head.

"She loves that power hook, but all you got to do is duck it. Just like we practiced. Once you duck it, immediately come back with a combo. I don't care which, as long as it starts with an uppercut and has at least four punches to it. Dium, go ahead and start wrapping her hands."

Dium set to gathering the gear from where he'd thrown it on a table.

Her father watched with a far-away expression. "Do not give her space to breathe. She's aggressive. You know how you win against an aggressor?"

"You duck?" Rosca let Dium grab her hand and wrap it in cloth for protection. He raised an eyebrow at her, but even as she said it, she knew she'd answered wrong. Shel it! She was too shel nervous for a test. Could they just get this over with?

"You be more aggressive." Deb Rez's stern tone silenced her inner protests.

"Right." With a nod, she dropped her gaze to Dium's fast-moving handiwork.

He jerked her hand forward for a better grip.

It didn't hurt, but she squealed anyway. "This isn't a race."

"If you're gonna complain, you can do it yourself." Dium'd already started wrapping up her other hand, placing extra padding on top of the knuckles and tying it off with skill.

"Fine. I just don't know why you go so fast."

"To make it interesting."

Ski turned to his younger siblings, his narrow mouth frowning. "Dium's good at his job, Rosca. He could do this in his sleep."

"I better be able to." Dium didn't take his eyes from the cloth wraps. "I've done it enough."

Rosca bit her lip. All three of her older brothers, Adnesi, Ski, and Dium, had already earned their juvenile champion chain. The cheap metal flashed around their necks, prized even beyond the gold jewelry their family could afford.

But she wasn't her brothers. She lacked Dium's instinct for technique, Ski's speed, and Adnesi's power. All that had brought her here was a stubborn streak and consistency. As her father said, she was a boar in a glass house. She saw what she wanted, and she became what she needed to be to get it. No matter the cost. And this time, she wanted to be free. To be trusted. Respected. Her knee took on a life of its own, bouncing up and down like a grasshopper.

If only her brothers' athleticism would seep into her. They could skip practice for tempas and come back as sharp as when they left. But she took a few days off and returning felt like a trip to the dungeons. Everything ached, and her body forgot how to move.

Light-headed, she smushed her forefinger and thumb together to pull her back to reality. Knots slithered and curled in her gut until she thought a snake might pop out of her throat. Her stomach rumbled.

"You hungry?" Her father frowned in displeasure.

Or maybe he was just thinking. It was hard to tell when someone only had a maximum of five facial expressions. Angry Father. Mildly pleased Father. Proud Father. Fight-face Father.

"Rosca?"

"What—? Oh. No. I don't want to eat before I fight."

"You still have two hours. A snack won't hurt."

Two hours? Another shel two hours of this wait game? Hopefully, she didn't puke up her nerves before then.

Taking the silence for her consent, Rez rose. "I'll grab you an oatcake. It'll fill you up, but it's light enough it won't hurt."

"No more oat—"

He walked off.

Adnesi and Ski circled her, stern expressions chiseled onto their features. Rosca didn't dare look at her two brothers, knowing they'd read the fear on her face like a scholar reads books. Dium tore off the excess material from her hands and stood in front of her chair. Great. Now she had all three on her.

"I was nervous too." Adnesi spoke first, as always. "This is a big fight. The qualification for the championships. These nerves are the worse."

She pretended to inspect her wraps. "They're a little tight, but I'll make them work." She faced them, daring them to defy her nonchalance.

"Rosca, you look like you're going to puke." Dium's grin pushed into his deep-set eyes until they disappeared under laugh wrinkles and black lashes.

"I might. I'll make sure to aim for you."

He shrugged. "Just don't overthink it. Like always."

"Easy for you to say! You already won a champion tournament, and you're only a year older than me. If I fail—"

Dium cut her off with a wave of his hand. "Yeah, yeah. You'll be the only one of us to do it. You'll drag the name Ishel through the dirt. Personally, I vote we just kick you out of the family."

The irreverent mocking of her fear allowed the ball in her chest to uncoil. She took her first full breath of the day, then used it to kick his shin.

"Ow!" He jumped back and growled.

"You're going to be fine." Adnesi pulled Dium to the side and kneeled before her. Kind dark eyes met her own. A terrible urge to cry filled her. Large, muscular arms covered in intricate tattoos grabbed her forearms and held up her hands in a fighting stance. "You have not come this far to give up on yourself. Despite the mescucha Dium loves to spit, we're all proud of you. How many girls are competing tonight?"

She breathed in deep. "Ten if they all show."

"And how many were there in the beginning?"

"Nineteen."

"Nineteen out of what, hundreds of guys?"

Rosca nodded, heat creeping up her neck.

"And how many of those girls are debnas? Rich girls who could be spending all of their father's money and refusing to work at anything?"

"To be fair, she does spend a lot of Father's money." Dium's goofy smile dropped five years off his age.

Too grown to stick out her tongue, she raised a brow. "And you don't?"

"Rosca." Adnesi squeezed her arms tighter, and she snapped to attention. "You know what the sign of a true fighter is?"

She shook her head, too nervous to think of anything.

"They love something so much, neither pain nor fear can stop them. You're here because you love boxing. That makes you a true fighter. A warrior."

Dium clasped her shoulder. "You know I'm just kidding, Rosc. Adnesi's right. It's in our blood to love fighting."

"No." Calm, Adnesi stared at Rosca with a seriousness that touched her soul. "It's in our blood to love things pure-heartedly. With everything in us. When you're given love like that, nothing's left but to fight for it. So fight!"

His words sunk into her bones. She loved the minutes in the ring almost as fiercely as she hated the walk up to it.

Dium had been wrong. She had been wrong. She wasn't here to earn anyone's respect or keep a family name clean. She was here because she chose this. Because something in her needed this. Needed a reason to wake up, to try harder, to push back. She was here because, win or lose, she was a fighter.

Chapter Six
The Fight

Rosca ducked a hook and hammered an uppercut into Lelina's liver. The girl stumbled back, and she chased her down, maintaining distance with her jab.

Lelina's thick brows furrowed. She slipped and scraped Rosca's side with a double-right. The girl racked up points as she zapped Rosca's body with a gust of light punches. Shuffling away, she dodged Rosca's power shot.

Rosca fell forward with the momentum of her own punch. She pivoted away from Lelina's one, two combo. They hit air then chest with such delicacy that only the blur of fists told Rosca she'd been punched.

Rosca jabbed to close the distance, then fired a power right. Repeating the punch, Rosca bludgeoned the girl's skull. Fear shone in Lelina's piggish eyes. Rosca drove in for an uppercut kill, but the gong sounded. Before Lelina could escape, Rosca stepped up till their noses almost touched. "If this is your set-up fight, you don't stand a chance at becoming champ."

Lelina snarled, but her silence proved the words had hit.

Satisfaction flooding Rosca's breast, and she returned to her corner.

Deb Rez grabbed her shoulder, and she jerked her gaze upwards. "One more round. She's up in points. You're not winning this without a knockout."

Rosca hung her head, too tired to hide her disappointment. Anger nipped at her heels, tempting her to storm away. "She hasn't even hurt me." She found his steady eyes with a pleading look. "She's touching me with a lot of punches, but I've blocked most, and the rest lack force. I've caught her multiple times now. Doesn't power count for anything?"

Grim-faced, he shook his head. "This is juvenile boxing. They're looking at volume, not damage. I see what you're doing. You're waiting. Looking for the best punch. You're thinking like a boxer."

"But I'm going to lose."

He sat silent.

She twisted her heel into the floor. *You didn't teach me to go for volume,* she wanted to accuse. *You taught me to fight like you.* Swallowing the words, she set her jaw.

The watchman called for the fighters to take their starting positions. A hand pulled her back as she tried to obey. Frustration tightened her actions as she spun on the interferer.

Dium stared back. "Forget about points. You determine how you fight, remember? So fight like a champion. Fight like it matters. No one can take that from you."

He was right. Shame licked her spine. With a look she hoped said everything she didn't have the time to say, she rushed to the center of the ring. The gong sounded.

Lelina drove in with a series of jabs and uppercuts that darted like hummingbirds.

One touched Rosca's chest, then several hit her sides, though her elbows blocked them.

Lelina released a straight left and dropped her right hand. Rosca caught the jab and delivered a right power punch to Bruta's jaw.

Rocked, Lelina fell back, arms at her sides, eyes glazed.

Rosca flurried out punches until the watchmen stepped in. He held up his fingers, counting out eight seconds in front of Lelina. At seven, she snapped to attention. He pulled back her eyelids and pointed her towards the sun. If the pupil didn't dilate correctly, he would stop the fight. Supposedly. Apparently satisfied, he released her.

They met in the center and touched gloves. Rosca threw several jabs, but Lelina steadily retreated out of range. Rosca cut her off, and hit her with a one, two. They thudded against the girl's head, but once again, Lelina scooted away.

She was running scared.

The gong sounded. Ice slipped into Rosca's soul. Not scared. Lelina knew she had won the first two rounds off points. She'd thrown away the third.

Tears sprung into Rosca's eyes. She should have knocked Lelina out or gone for points over power. Hanging her head, she couldn't meet the stares of those in her corner.

Lelina offered her hand, already ungloved.

Rosca tried to shake it with her heavy mitt. Numb, she barely registered when the watchman raised Lelina's hand in victory.

Chapter Seven
Spiraling

Chuckling, Deb Rez leaned forward to poke the fire. The resulting heat dispelled the biting draft hanging about the family room's edges. Centered in the middle of the cotto ali fimili, a tiled square sunk into the ground and cradled an iron frame six feet long and wide. Blazing with full girth, a fire danced inside it, and long, thin sheets hanging from the ceiling tunneled the smoke up into the night air.

Rosca's slumped silhouette shimmered into his mind. She'd hardly raised her head since her defeat with Lelina. She hadn't set foot in Asium until today, and it'd been four tempas. He'd never seen his daughter take a loss so hard. He'd nearly lost faith she'd return. His stomach clenched. But she had. Thank Maschiach. She'd found her hope again. Something tumbled loose inside, like lungs being drained of mucus. He inhaled.

From her rocking chair beside him, his wife lowered her sewing and raised her brows in an unspoken question.

"You won't like it." He challenged her with a sly wink.

Her beautiful Banli eyes, slanted like arrow tips, burned for a moment. "Rosca is training again, isn't she?"

He squirmed in his seat. "I knew you wouldn't like it." Why could that one look push him back to his boyhood? As if he hadn't faced armies of killers before. But no. Five foot four inches of liquid-smooth skin and rich tousled hair had stolen his heart. No army could do that. If only she wouldn't squeeze that stolen heart so much.

She raised her fabric and pierced the needle through it with unnecessary ferocity. "I'd hoped that girl Lelina had knocked some sense into her." The orange of firelight haloed her round face.

Rez replayed the night in his head, torn between a grimace and a praise. "When Rosca stepped into that ring to fight Lelina, she looked like she wanted to melt through the floor."

His wife kept sewing.

"But she didn't run or cower. Le, the way she went after her, the way she didn't back down… That's a true fighter. She lost by points, but the truth is, Rosca fought like a warrior. I've seen many people get the perfect technique, footwork, and timing, but only a handful can claim a fighter's spirit. She should have won. And those are the hardest fights to lose." Pausing, he steepled his hands in front of his lips and bounced his knee.

Le grunted.

He pressed his palms together in grateful prayer. "She proved herself a far better boxer than that girl. She was thinking, picking her punches with purpose and power. And Lelina, for all the hype people talked about her, did nothing but touch Rosca with as many punches as possible before shooting away like a startled cat. All light punches. Nothing with meaning." He spoke in a low whisper, careful not to get carried away in his praise. Attending lessons or pastimes, his children sprawled out over the fur covered couches or floor. They gave no sign of hearing his conversation, but years of fatherhood had taught him better than to assume. "At least I'm training her. I can protect her here. Rosca's got a restless soul. If I don't push her, she'll go look for challenges somewhere else. And the real world isn't as kind as her father." He steepled his fingers to his lips, studying the iron ornament of the hearth before him.

"Go look for it?" She knotted her brows, eyes full of knowing. "You mean like your siblings did? Like you did?"

He grunted his assent.

Le sighed. "Well, I knew all that about her before she set foot in a ring. But Rosca did not think it such a victory. How long has it been since her fight with Lelina?"

Rez interlocked his fingers and squeezed. Four tempas. Four tempas of hanging her head and moping over her failure. He'd bribed, commanded, challenged, and almost begged for her to return, but she had just watched him with those distant, shame-filled eyes and shook her head.

But not now. "Today she came back." He steadied his tone so it wouldn't betray the anxiety wrapping his thoughts. "That's all that matters."

"Maybe to you." His wife yawned, gazing out the window at the night sky. "She's growing up, Rez. Maybe boxing isn't for her anymore."

He refused to answer. To have this fight again.

Silent seconds ticked into minutes, signaling the conversation's end. He soaked in the comforts surrounding them, any thought to avoid his wife's comment. The room made him think of a bear's cave, a place of hibernation and restoration before the sunstruck's call to hunt. Here, his family could burrow away with books, writing, games, and crafts, and hide from the responsibility and attention which tended to shadow their steps.

The room encased them in silver-white stones, cut in rough-hewn squares and piled in neat lines. Over their heads, rich, dark brown beams finished with a glossy lacquer ran parallel to each other. Between these, four rectangular skylights exposed them to the night. Through their openings, crystal moonlight shone down and danced with the wispy smoke. A line of door-sized windows faced the cliff drop-off into the fishermen's district. Beyond the little town, the sea nestled their island home in her wild arms.

The nippy nighttime breeze carried the scent of ocean freshness and made him grateful for the warmth of the fire. A boar's skin lay on the ground, the face and tusks appearing toyish with lifeless, black marbles in the eye sockets. A bit ironic. It hadn't seemed toyish when it charged him.

"Psst!"

The sound drew him to look at his daughter. She approached them from her corner of the room, pointing to her mother with a smirk.

For a moment, an unreasonable fear gripped him. But she had sat too far away to hear them, and they had whispered. He followed the direction of her gesture, and relief seeped in.

Le's work lay in her lap, her head hung, and she snored for all the family to hear. Amused, he gave Rosca a knowing wink.

"Me and Ski..." Rosca scooted up to him.

"Ski and I." Le blinked and squinted the sleep away.

A chuckle escaped him. "Leave it to your mother to wake up just to correct your grammar."

Le ran her fingers over a fresh stitch. "If you're going to speak the Trader's Tongue, you should do so properly. Otherwise, people may think you're ignorant and take advantage."

"They'll already think she's stupid because she's a pretty young girl." Rez pointed out cheekily. He loved to watch his wife teach their children, especially when she grew a little angry. It made the red in her bronze cheeks deepen.

"And because she's a minsk-head." Jack chimed in from the floor where he and Mar carved swords and compared hilt designs.

Rez cocked a brow at the boys. How much had they paid attention to the last twenty minutes?

"Language!" Le barked. She turned her frown towards Rez. "They can assume as badly of her as they want, but not because she gave them a reason."

"I completely agree. It's important to speak the Eastern Realm Language properly." Rosca forced a too-wide smile, a crisp formalness lacing each word.

"You mean ewl?" Mar corrected.

Rez gave a worried glance to his wife, who nodded at him in encouragement.

He narrowed his gaze. He knew that nod. That was the *you got this* nod, which left him alone. Jack and Mar, his two youngest sons, scooted closer, expectation written on their small faces.

"Thank you." Le resumed sewing as though she couldn't sense the request poised on Rosca's lips.

Rez leaned back, clasping his hands over his sturdy belly. "What do you want, Rosca?"

Determination brightened her countenance. "Ski and I would like to take the horses to the west side of the island these free days and spend the night in the woods there. We don't get to go often." Rosca stared at him, hope in the half-smile that rounded her soft cheeks.

Rez cleared his throat. Le acted as though she didn't notice the conversation or his silent cry for help. "Just you two?" He studied her carefully, but Rosca seemed honest as she spoke.

"Yes. According to Lippy, the waves are much better for broadboarding on the west side."

Rez cast a questioning look at his son, who walked up as she finished speaking.

"Lippy works with Rosca," Ski explained shortly.

"And that's her real name?"

His son shrugged.

"But we have waves." He tapped the arm of his chair. "Why don't you go here?"

"I want to see something new. Ski will be with me. It'll be fine."

Doubt tugged at him. "What about your training? You just returned. This isn't a good time."

Triumph shone on her face as though she'd been waiting for this question. "I won't miss any training. I'm going to box in the morning before we leave, and the next day is a Soonmae. I don't train on Soonmaes. Plus, I'll still do something active. We'll ride and broadboard. It takes a lot of core strength to ride waves. You gotta spin the board and—"

He waved her down. He didn't need a full description of broadboarding, and Rosca could go on for hours once she got started on a topic. Definitely his most talkative child. "Ski?" Rez addressed his son. "You will take care of her?"

"If I have to."

"Okay. I trust you both. Just make sure you are back for a good night's rest on Soonmae."

"Thanks, Father!" She hugged him. Scooping up her books, she skipped from the room.

He sat back in his chair, soaking in the warm glow her smile always gave him. Daughters were so much more thankful than sons. Why didn't they have more girls?

His wife fastened a reproving glare upon him. "Rez."

Squirming, he nodded curtly.

"Don't you think you should have checked with me first?"

He repressed a groan. "You're sitting right here. You could have said something."

"You're the leader of the house. I won't interfere if I'm not asked."

He snorted. Never stopped her before. With a sigh, he folded his arms over his chest, ready for a fight. "Do you truly care, or are you just trying to make a point?"

"I care!" She clenched her fist. "Our daughter does not always need to be gallivanting off. She is a young lady and must be recognized as such. This boxing, these adventures? It's too much. She must have more propriety. More training to be a lady."

He shook his head. "She's an Ishel. A fighter."

"She isn't a boy." Le's work bunched in her grasp. "You can't sit here preparing her for a life she'll never get to live."

Rez stiffened. "You think she'll stay if we don't give her this? Rosca is not a daughter you cage. She'll burn up every bar if you do."

"I am not saying she cannot fight, but if she does not also learn to be a lady, then she will be an outcast for all her life. She'll never marry, and she'll fall to the lowest place of society."

"Rosca is not you! She doesn't mind being an outcast if it means she can do what she wants."

"And you would support a lifestyle of such selfishness? To just 'do what she wants' and ignore the world?"

"It's not selfish to work at what you love. It's selfish to withhold your gifts from the world."

"Believe it or not, our daughter has more gifts than punching people in the face."

"Yes, but that's the most interesting one."

Le threw her hands up in defeat. "It's like talking ewl to a deaf pig."

Rez massaged his temples. "Your moods make me feel like a pig trying to understand ewl."

Le pinched together her lips before hissing, "Rosquevalarian is used to luxury. Eating what she wants. Doing what she wants. Having the nicest things. You cannot expect someone to give that all up and still live a happy life. You're leading her on. Filling her head with dreams of grandeur that will not come true. No one wants to see a girl fight. No one will come to watch a woman champion. She cannot make a living doing such things, and we will not always be here to protect her. She must grow up and take her place whether she likes it or not."

"Place?" His tone mounted. "The little raschuka from down under speaks to me of place? Did I not elevate you from streetrat to debna?"

Pain flashed on her features and guilt twisted in his chest. He wished he could take back the Ikuela cuss. The word rarely came up in polite conversation. Yet it proved his point. She had done nothing to improve her status except say yes to his advancements. He had done all the work of changing their social standing and gaining the respect of the people.

Furious, Le seemed like a snake ready to strike, and her words held a poisonous anger. "Do not jibe at me. You know I speak the truth. If I am wrong, then come at me with rationale, not insults."

"Why can't Rosca be independent? Why must she marry? She could be a famous warrior. A real warrior. She's so smart, and now she's becoming disciplined. She could do great deeds, win battles. Rosca is a born leader."

"If you believe that, then why do you not teach her to be a soldier?"

"Soldiers are not leaders."

She slammed a fist onto the arm of her chair. "And fighters are wild!"

"The mental toughness will serve her more than anything. She doesn't have to be a soldier. She could be—"

"If you really loved her, you would do what's best for her. She must be trained to host parties, dress appropriately, flirt—"

"Flirt?" His voice thundered. "You would have a... a coquet? A bird that sings pretty tunes at your window, but claws at your back? To invest in what the world would praise and ignore discipline and strength?"

The debna rose. Her figure towered in the room with a still, quiet anger that held the force of a stormy wind. "As long as we live in this world, Reznaldo, we must teach our children to play its game. I will not have my daughter an old maid, still suckling at the protection of her parents because we failed to show her reality. You would doom her to poverty and back-breaking work, which would bring gray hair, sorrow, and an early grave. You would suck beauty and youth from her and fill her with the harsh, grave countenance of a man."

Rez rose to meet her. "There is beauty in a loyal and disciplined heart that outer looks cannot compare to. I would have her great and gray over fun and frivolous."

"And I would have her happy!" The debna's eyes glinted with the tears of a mother weighed down by anxiety. A noble layer of wrinkles crested her brow underneath strands of silver hair. He resisted the urge to push them back. Her boldness had been his companion for many years. Perhaps she had not worked her way to the top as he had, but the very strength that had singled her out to him in their youth still vibrated within her, deep and alive, supporting them all.

He softened. "So would I."

An eternity stretched before them. Rez steadied his thoughts with long breaths.

The debna sucked in her heart-shaped cheeks. "Do you not trust me?"

He paused, fixated on a single flame of fire, twirling and jumping. Free. His forehead tightened in concentration. A sigh escaped him, and his fist unclenched, hanging limp at his side. "I will tell her she is to spend her time under your guidance. She will quit the Sailor's Solace after these free days."

"Rez..."

He didn't heed the warning note. "After these free days and that's final."

***

Dawn reached orange and yellow tendrils over the waking city, casting golden glows on the thatch rooftops scattered below. Rosca sped ahead of Ski. Not even the heavy knapsack could slow her. Each step down the hill brought her closer to adventure, closer to Ray. A smile spread across her face.

"Rosca."

She ignored her brother's exasperated tone.

"The harbor isn't going to burn up in the next fifteen minutes. We'll make it on time. Quit running."

"I know." She mapped their route in her mind. Down the hill through the market stalls littering the fishermen's district, and to the docks. There the pirate would be waiting.

"I can't believe she got away with laying anchor in the main harbor." Ski's long legs carried him past her, and she jogged to catch up.

"She didn't." Rosca conjured an image of the *Lady Scarlet* from two days before, when Ray had taken her on a special tour. The ship eclipsed any she'd ever seen. Her black and brown hull puffed out like the chest of a champion. The double mast boasted of speed while the sleek build promised agility. "She's laid anchor on Filmore's Beach, but they're using a few borrowed skiffs to transfer everything needed for tonight."

"Filmore's?" Her brother stopped short, and she bumped into his back. He faced her. "That's the island blind spot."

She dipped her head. "Yup." The curve of the island hid the sandy stretch from prying eye. To spot a ship, you'd have to climb 180 or more feet of rock face to Alarog's point or hike through the woods fringing the fishermen's district. Few cared to do either.

"But how did she know to anchor *there*?"

"I told her." Rosca eyed the wisps of clouds, squeezing her thumb and forefingers together. "I told her, and she moved her ship."

His searching gaze turned acidic.

She pretended not to notice.

"Rosca, what other secrets have you given away to this pirate?"

Rosca twisted her boot into the ground and glared at him. "She's not some pirate, she's Ray. She wouldn't hurt us."

His cold laugh shriveled her soul.

Rosca stepped back, curving her lips into a sneer. "I'm not telling her everything," she protested, although several spilled secrets now flew to mind. "I know she's still a pirate, but she trains me. She cares. If she wanted to attack us, she would have done it already. I'm the chief deb's daughter. She could have killed or ransomed me, but I'm still here. You know how many people, who aren't pirates, I wouldn't trust myself being alone with? She isn't looking for power. She's just in love with the sea and adventure, and, in the process, has made some minsk-headed choices."

Ski's color drained, and a stony seriousness hardened his mouth into a thin line. Bending down, his sharp nose flared its nostril hairs in disgusting display. "You're blind, Rosca. That woman is after something, and if you're this sold on her, that tells me she's after you. I can't believe I didn't see it before. You have to let her go."

Rosca reeled back. "You don't know what you're talking about. I came to my own conclusions. She's never asked me to trust her. Never defended herself."

Straightening, his expression screwed so tight he looked ready to burst. "After tonight, you say goodbye to her, you understand?"

Her fists clenched. She tucked her chin. "And who's going to make me? You? Fine. Then I'll tell Father you've known about this for tempas. That you've been lying and aiding pirates right under his nose."

Ski stiffened and blinked. "Better caught now, then some disaster outing us in the end."

She crossed her arms. "The only disaster that could happen is Father figuring out what we're doing tonight."

He chewed his lip. "Just promise me you'll tell me before you do anything minsk-headed."

"Do you want the list daily or by tempa?"

His snort of laughter eased the tension.

Encouraged, she plowed on. "I'll stay alert. I'm not going to let her talk me in to anything without knowing it's right. I promise. Besides, you're with me. What could happen?"

Scrubbing his face with his hands, he moaned. "Let's just go and get this over with. We'll take it all one night at a time."

Relief flooded her head to toe. She turned so he wouldn't see her beaming and skipped ahead. "Let's go. We've wasted enough time. Di's meeting us, right?"

"Yeah, but you know not to run off looking for him."

"I'm not a child."

"Yes, you are. And if Father finds out we lied to him, you'll never make it to be anything else."

She ignored him, breathing in the fresh sea air. Hadn't Father himself said don't rely on what he'd given her? She was building something for herself. Maybe it was disobedience, but he'd understand. An exhilarating blend of fear and excitement sizzled along her nerves.

Ski crossed his arms. "Do you think anyone will mention to Father if they see us? He's going to know something's up when we aren't broadboarding on the other side of the island."

"People aren't nosy here like in the market district. They mind their own. Besides I think they're more afraid of a pirate than Father."

"You think they know who Ray is?"

She rolled her eyes. "If they're not minsk-heads. She's smuggling in sesaquilles for Maschiach's sake. It's kind of hard to miss seeing beasts the size of a horse swimming about. Besides, who do you think is coming to these races? People must be willing to pay, or she wouldn't be risking her neck to sneak the creatures onto the island."

The mythical sesaquilles, or fish-horse when translated to ewl, showed all horse above water. Beneath the waves lay the sesa, or fish, part. Their unnatural four flippers and rubbery underbelly made the superstitious Banlis brand them evil creatures of Alarog, the king under the sea. Something about breeding sea and land animals apparently invoked curses.

Even their father bought into the old legend. The council he headed forbade import of the creatures, though many of the beasts already lived near the island. Father didn't have the heart to slay them, so they roamed free. A few extra wouldn't stir up too much notice. At least, they wouldn't once her and Ski finished their part of the plan.

Ski's disgruntled glower looked like an old man's. "I don't see why she can't do this without our help."

Ignoring him, she trotted down the hillside, pulse rising. Four tempas of training mixed fighting with Ray had built a bond between them that would never break. Something about the pirate felt like home. The woman was halved, like herself. Half Valsquelian, half world adventurer. Half fighter, half feminine. This world didn't have a place for halves. But the sea did. Pirates did.

Dium greeted them at the docks. A purple bruise ringed his eye.

Rosca winced. "You win?"

"Yup." He smiled. "The tournament continues tomorrow. I fight in the afternoon." Rapture shone on his face as he watched the pirates ride sesaquilles or float in lifeboats to release the captured creatures. They had hitched the water beasts to the ship in long lines, like a two-pronged tail, in order to transport them to the island.

"Let's go!" She slapped his back in support, and his grin widened.

"Rosca!" Ray swaggered to the Ishels with a cool, easy gait, as though all the world waited for her arrival, and she would savor every second of it. Her wild curls billowed out from under the tight red silk, framing the gold hoops dangling in her ears. Smoky black eyes, smeared with charcoal face paint held both exhaustion and excitement. Even at her mystery age, her cheeks glowed with unmarked, smooth skin like the rounded, small nuts from nama trees. Her toned arm reached out, a rawhide string dangling from her slender, weathered hand. "I thought you'd appreciate this. More than these cuas anyway."

Breathless, Rosca took the ornament and a smile stretched wide. Looped and knotted onto the brown string, a silver token held the image of a skull over crossbones with tiny scarlet eyes. This would be fun to hide at home. Discarding the sarcastic thought, she thanked the pirate with an appreciative smile.

"Can I?" The pirate took the necklace and loosened the string. "I don't imagine your parents will appreciate it quite so much." She winked. "You wear it low enough, no one will tell."

"Thank you." Rosca donned the gift and fiddled at its intricate image.

"Now," Ray's sharp tone indicated business, and Rosca's brothers snapped to attention. "Ski and Rosca, you two will—"

"Be making rounds to pay off the praeti for the race," finished Rosca, then blushed at her outburst.

Ray nodded in approval, but annoyance flashed in her gaze.

Rosca clenched her teeth. Why couldn't she keep her mouth shut?

The pirate handed out a yellow, short parchment. "Here's a list of each location. Don't make your mission obvious. I provided extra coins in case you need to stop somewhere to avoid suspicion. Look around market stalls, grab food, whatever but don't let on. And remember the agreement. Each praeti must repeat the terms before we pay. Do you know them?"

Rosca's stomach curdled, but she recited the threatening lines. "By accepting payment, you're entering contract with captain and crew and swearing to ignore all illegal activity involving sesaquilles. This includes but is not limited to unhitching sesaquilles and bringing them in from ships, town gossip of racing the beasts, and race night noises." She paused.

Ray's brows lowered menacingly.

Taking the cue, Rosca numbed her mind as she finished the speech. Nothing would ever make saying this part easy. "If the race and those involved are discovered with the result of confiscated sesaquilles, imprisoned pirates, death, or incurred fees, then those under contract will be held responsible and slaughtered, along with their families. This is in exchange for the lives damaged." Rosca rubbed her thumb against the rawhide string of her necklace. "I changed it a bit, so it'd sound like a real contract."

Grasping Rosca's shoulder, Ray simmered with laughter. "Sounds like a real professional did it. I didn't know you had brains behind those hands."

Fumbling for words, Rosca squeezed the necklace. Unease gutted her. She refused to linger too long on the contract's meaning. Agreement or no, Ray wouldn't dare such a trick, but, without the threat, the praeti might try something worse.

Rosca glanced at Dium. If he didn't find objection to the words, why should she? Noting her stare, he cocked his head in question before turning his attention back to the sesaquilles. He hadn't heard a word said.

A whinny pierced her eardrums.

Dium dashed past her, lunging into the water. Amidst the sesaquill chain, one beast strained and fought violently as five pirates circled and struggled to cast lassoes over his thick body. Panic grew as did the ruckus, and the men cursed and yelled.

"What in the helski—?" Ski stepped to follow his brother then stopped at the dock edge.

Dium had closed half the distance between himself and the ship before the wiggling fish-horse slipped his bonds and captors and took off to open sea. Meeting a man astride a sesaquill, Dium gestured wildly until the pirate slipped from his ride and handed him a lassoed rope. Mounting, Dium sped off after the free beast.

Rosca ran up to Ski, her heart pounding. "What is he doing?"

"Trying to catch the shel creature." Ski spat. "He's going to get himself killed."

"If the pirates couldn't keep it under control, he can't."

Ski clenched his jaw.

With one swing, Dium slipped the rope over the proud, arched neck. A screeching neigh echoed on the waters. The sesaquill pulled back, flippers coming up and down, making splashes and ripples in the sea. A chill laced Rosca's spine. She forgot to breathe. One hit from those stone heavy fins would crush Dium's skull. Even if it didn't, the blow would send him unconscious and spiraling into the sea. Maybe this was Maschiach's punishment for lying to her parents.

Dium forced his own steed back until the rope pulled taut. Other pirates, atop their own mounts, circled in to help. Within minutes, they mastered the beast, and Dium returned to the man he'd taken the sesaquill from. Dismounting, he slipped into the sea and swam to shore while the water-treading pirate gathered the fish-horse's reins.

Her fear melted into awe as he trudged in from the waves, shaking and pale with the cold. He drew himself up and met Ray's twitching expression, which toggled between scorn and admiration.

She looked him over. "You could have been killed."

Dium shrugged, a smile chasing away his stoic look.

A laugh escaped Ray. "How'd you learn to ride like that?"

"I work at the stables when I can. Help break horses and the like. I knew he would bolt. I could see it in his ears and neck."

Ray nodded. "Impressive. You should race."

Dium's ears pulled forward, and lines creased his square brow. "Wha…race sesaquilles? Like as a rider?"

"Why not?"

"Well, I…" He straightened, his shivers dissipating. "Yes. I'd like to. But I don't have a sesaquill."

She waved a hand in dismissal. "We'll fix that."

Rosca beamed at her brother. He'd talked of riding sesaquilles for years. Now he'd race one. She wiggled her brows in congratulation, and he dipped his head, his face bright with excitement.

Ski's disapproving glare broke her triumph. She shrugged at him, and he turned away. A childish urge to stick out her tongue arrested her, but, at the sight of the pirates, she mastered it. He just didn't understand business like she and Dium. Ray opened up opportunity after opportunity, and they'd be minsk-heads to ignore them. Pirate or no, she made things work in her favor. In their favor. It took strength and leadership. Suppressing a ridiculous smile, she sidled up to Dium for a fist bump. Her stomach fluttered. Tonight's race would be something she would never forget.

Chapter Eight
Intervening

Abandoning propriety, Dium ran through the fishermen's district. He had half an hour before Ray expected him back to prepare his sesaquill. Just getting that break had proved a battle. He all but pitched a tantrum to get her to release him, claiming he needed wool pants to ride in the freezing water tonight. When he returned without them, there'd be questions, but he could worry about that later. Family came first. This was his duty.

He spotted Rosca's long, blackberry curls before they disappeared into the crowd. Thank Maschiach she had stayed close.

He sprinted after her, Ski's lanky frame nowhere in sight. "Rosca!" He shouted, sick of running.

She spun. "Dium?" Her surprise melted into annoyance. "We only have a few more hours to pay off these..." cutting the confession short, she glanced around, then stepped out of the street into a vine-covered alcove. "Why are you here?"

"I needed to know you're not planning what I think you're planning."

The crimson blush running brow to neck confirmed his suspicion. She stared at the top of his head and crossed his arms. "You already know what I'm planning. To put on a sesaquill race. You're planning to be *in it,* so what's your problem?"

Taking a deep breath, he leaned over to force her to meet his gaze. He hoped he looked half as intimidating as Adnesi did when he intervened in Dium's foolishness. "I mean running away with Ray. You're not a pirate, Rosca. I know you. You don't have the stomach for it. You cried when we saw that boy sent to jail for stealing, remember? Think about the threats you're sent to deliver today. Killing praetis' families? Are you insane?"

She pushed him back. "It's easy for you to say." Choking, she paused before rattling on. "You're not a girl. I have no place in Father's world. My future is ballgowns and debna training. I… I don't want to be stuck. I can't just be a debna."

"You're more than a debna, Rosc, but Maschiach put you here for a reason." The sternness slipped away, and he knew he couldn't match Adnesi's tough love warnings. But that didn't usually work with her anyway. He grabbed her shoulders. "*Look* at me. It will destroy you if you try to become Ray. If you even think about getting on that ship, I will find you, hogtie you, and carry you back myself. Don't be a minsk-head. You know better." How was that for tough love.

Tears dripped out as she nodded.

"Promise me?"

"I promise." She swung her arms around him and buried her wet face in his chest.

Relief swept through him. He rested his chin on her head, then kissed the top of it. She was going to be okay. They would find their own way.

Chapter Nine
The Race

"It's a proper Banli celebration."

The expectation in Rosca's voice burned in Ski's ears. He ground his teeth, peering out from under the hood of his cloak. When no sign of Father or anyone who might report to him showed, he flipped it back, still wary of the enormous crowd. "This is insanity."

Dium side-eyed him but did not respond.

Ski's nails cut into his palm. Suddenly, he grabbed his brother's arm and pulled him back, away from the beach filled with bonfires, pirates, and partiers. "Go home. You have a fight tomorrow. You need to rest."

With a glare, Dium pushed his brother off. "I'll be fine. I can do both."

"Why risk it?" Ski barked, ever muscle fiber shooting with fear. "Let it go. It's just one night. We should all be home. Safe and warm—"

"And missing out." Dium's steely tone hardened with conviction. "I'd rather find out for myself what life holds."

"You're a fool."

Stubborn determination framed his younger brother's features. He didn't have to say another word for Ski to understand. Dium would not turn back.

"Fine." Resigned, Ski threw up his hands. He shouldn't have expected him to listen. He shouldn't have to convince him in the first place. How did he end up with this responsibility?

"Rosca. Ski. Dium." Ray approached the group holding two brimming mugs. One of her men, featureless in the dark, held two more.

Ski accepted the drink with thanks. It was the first useful thing the raschuka had done.

"No, thank you. I don't drink." Dium shook his head.

"Very well." Ray held out the beverage to Rosca who looked from Dium to Ray, idol to idol, as though unsure which to listen to.

Ski guffawed. "You may as well drink it, Rosc. Not the dumbest thing you're doing tonight."

"Oh?" Ray tilted her head.

He grew hot. She didn't usually spare him a second glance. Most of her attention went to his two younger siblings. "If Deb Rez catches us here, we're dead. Well and truly dead."

"If that's your worry, then you can take a breath. I have one of my men watchin' him now, just for your three's sake. Accordin' to my man, he's snorin' up a storm while your mother finishes some late-night needlework. You got nothin' to worry about." Her twisted smile leered at him.

The hairs on Ski's neck prickled. How had she infiltrated their home? Their security? How clever was she? With new respect, he studied her slight frame. "Thank you."

She nodded. "Dium, go get ready. Race starts soon. You'll be one of ten on the track. Three laps."

Dium hurried away.

Ski rushed after him. "Wait up, Di. I'll help."

"You're going to leave Rosca by herself?" Dium snorted.

Ski dodged a raucous group who were drowning their grilled fish with mugs of ale. "She's fine. Not like she'd listen if I was there."

Brightly painted markers connected by long ropes traced a track in the water some thirty yards from the shore. At the start, nine riders prepared their beasts, and two pirates held Dium's.

Dium hopped in the water and Ski followed, yelping at the sudden freeze. With broad, fast strokes, they swam up to the waiting crew and animals. The pirates worked to cinch the smooth black saddle, crafted from eel skin, tighter around the creature's belly. The sesaquille's round, smoky blue eyes smoldered at Ski, glinting in the darkness. Its thick boned head tilted, and mist rose from its nostrils. It danced like it could sense his ulterior motives. Fresh sweat poured down his forehead despite the icy water.

Ski paused, unable to swim farther. No wonder people believed the creatures had spiritual powers. The mass of muscles striated taut in the moonlight. A thunderous sound erupted as the creature slapped the water with its gray fin. His brother mounted, and he shook off the ridiculous notions. It was now or never. If he could just get Dium to quit, it'd be worth it.

The dim lighting and cover of water made his job easy. Slipping a knife from his belt, he sawed at the saddle's girth. Fingering the band, he hooked his hand under the thin remaining strand. It would snap with the first lurch. Good enough. Guilt webbed in his mind like an inky net, but his brother had to learn. He couldn't go around risking his neck, when all his siblings would have to pay the consequences. When he had to pay the consequences. After tonight, he never wanted to see that blasted pirate or this track again. Forcing a smile, he slapped his brother on the back. "Go get 'em."

Dium straightened and adjusted his grip on the reins. "Wait. Should I be doing this?" Nerves edged his voice.

"No." Ski's heart leaped with hope. "For once in your life, be a chicken. Be smart."

"Forget it." Dium smiled, but it lacked its usual self-assured mischief. "You were supposed to tell me to quit acting like a tiweekah." He turned away.

"Okay." Ski imagined himself home and safe, and pushed that enthusiasm into his response. "Not like you ever listen to me, anyway." He swam back to shore.

The night air cut through his soaked breeches as he waded out of the water. He cussed and searched the beach for the shirt he'd thrown. Even if falling didn't convince Dium to give up this hare-brained plan, he'd still get what he deserved, an icy dunking and an embarrassing tumble. Spotting a glint of white fabric, he plucked his clothes up. Familiar voices emitted from the shadows. Looking up sharply, he scanned the scene.

Facing the water, their backs to him, Rosca and Ray stood lost in conversation. They waited for the race to start like so many now crowding the beach. Careful to blend in with the few strangers around, Ski inched closer to catch their conversation.

"Why not come with me?" Ray's mothering tone made his skin crawl.

"I couldn't," Rosca squeaked.

He dug his nails into his palm. He should have told Deb Rez. This was his problem. Now, if she ran away… Oh Maschiach, he was dead. The shel raschuka! Why did God curse man with sisters? With such shel responsibility. He may as well try controlling the ocean.

"You're a fighter," Ray cooed. "An explorer. The sea has been the home for such people since the beginning of time. I know you know this in your heart. I know you feel it in your bones. I see the way you look to it. Look for what will never come. Unless you leave. Unless you chase it."

Ski took a heavy breath. Then another. Rosca did not speak. He inched forward, freezing when she broke the silence.

"I've been placed here. For some reason. I love my family, and, though I'm young, I think they need me." Her voice cracked. "But I wish I could go. I wish I could sail."

"Another time may not come for you. Are you willing to stay here forever?"

"Forever." Rosca choked on the word. "I will not be here forever." Iron melded the statement. "I cannot. But neither can I go now."

"It's your choice. Your own fault." Frost laced the pirate's response. She spat, and Ski retreated into the shadows, trembling.

Why did she care so much? As though Rosca was her own child, not a stranger?

An uproar broke out among the water. He squinted into the night. Cries of "Dium!" filled the beach. His brother had fallen from the beast.

Ski's gut churned. What had they got themselves into?

***

Rosca waited for Dium to reach dry land before handing him a shirt and coat, a gift from Ray.

He waved her away, his shoulders tensing high.

"What happened?"

"The shel saddle fell off. Just broke! Someone said it'd been cut, but I don't know. The whole thing was just a stupid idea. Maybe it's my punishment for sneaking around."

She rolled her eyes. "Then what's mine? I started this whole thing."

He kicked the ground, flinging a sand cloud into the air. "Rosca, there's… there's something I need to tell you."

Blinking, she wiped her face. "I'm waiting."

"I overheard some pirates gossiping while we were getting ready today. They said there's a black cloud in the water on the west shore. A current. Coquerielle's Current. They were scared it'd reach over here before the race, but Ray told 'em not to worry."

Quiet, she waited for him to laugh it off. To crack a joke. Of course Ray said not to worry. Coquerielle's Current was a legend from nightmares. A sailor's tale. He couldn't truly believe it had come to their home.

"Rosc, you know the stories same as me. That current is run by Alarog— evil itself. And it only comes where it's invited. I think Ray invited it."

White hot anger flashed up her spine, stiffening every disc. "Dium, you're crazy. Ray is not a witch. That current isn't even real."

"You don't know that."

Her top teeth ground bits of powder off her bottoms. Wasn't she supposed to be the one with all the crazy fantasies?

"Maschiach's real," he gestured to the sky, "and Alarog's real, and dragons, and… there's a lot we don't know about the world, Rosc. Look, I don't trust her, okay? That's the long and short of it. I don't trust her."

"Well, I do," she snapped, and spun to face the starlit sea. The crescent moon beamed down, casting silver rays on the waves. They called to her. For a moment, she considered dashing into their beckoning embrace. Shuddering at the strange impulse, she turned back to face him. Her anger disappeared as quick as it had come. "At least, I did. Forget the current, Di. Maybe we shouldn't be doing this."

He started, and his lips tightened into a grimace.

"Not the racing part." She waved him down in exasperation. "Or the associating with Ray part," she added in a pointed tone. "The lying to our parents and breaking every Nileal law and tradition in one night part."

"Oh." His broad shoulders shifted down as he stared at the path leading back home. In the silence, a mask slid over his features.

Exhaustion spilled into Rosca's limbs, as though she'd been lost in a dance, and stopping brought the realization that every muscle ached. She collapsed to the ground. Longing pulsed in her chest. "I can't believe it's wrong to want adventure. To want to fight beyond the roped off regulated matches. I love boxing, but it doesn't feel like my lifeline anymore. It's like it prepares me for life. I just don't know what life. With Ray, I thought maybe I could get a glimpse."

Dium sat down beside her. "I know what you mean."

Gratitude flooded her. Ski would have already asked how many drinks she'd had. But Dium saw things like her.

He drew lines in the sand. "I don't like lying either. I don't want to. I just want to race sesaquilles. What if I never get another opportunity like this?"

"And what if we drown our conscience?" The words slipped out before she could stop them. Every prick of guilt she had fought to keep down burst like fireworks in her chest. "I don't want to be a liar. But neither am I made to follow rules."

Dium leaned back. "Rebelling creates as many problems as being a follower. Either way you're a hypocrite 'cause you're reacting to someone else, 'stead of acting with your conscience. You should know that by now. You're fifteen."

"You're so cocky sometimes. It's not like you know everything there's to know about life."

"Of course I do. That's a big brother's job. Who else is going to tell you when you're being a minsk-head?"

She punched him playfully, then stared at the glorious ship haloed my dim moonlight.

Dium shoved her. "You'll get your chance for adventure, Rosc. But it'll be the right way."

The disappointment knotting her gut unraveled. She dug her fingers into the cool sand, peace blanketing her soul. Everything would be okay, right?

Chapter Ten
Goodbye

The cotto ali fimili appeared barren without the blazing fire or other family members. Her father gestured for Rosca to sit, and she tentatively took the armchair opposite him.

"Rosca, your mother and I have come to a decision, and you aren't going to like it."

She curled her hands over her knees, digging the jagged nails into the linen skirt.

Cool, he considered her with a sharp expression, and she forced the tension from her posture.

"It's time you train to be a debna. That means less free time and additional lessons in etiquette, manners, diplomacy, and the like."

Rosca's jaw hurt from clenching the muscles. Her father's set tone told her he expected an outburst, but she determined not to give it to him. Even if his every word stung like a dagger point.

"You're a debna, Rosca. And someday you'll appreciate that fact, but for now it's enough you accept it."

She balled her fist.

"Debna Le will guide you throughout this. You'll spend your free days with her, and as you learn to be a lady, you'll see why it's worth it."

"But I don't have time to work, train, be a debna, and do my lessons." Collecting herself, she steadied the whine in her voice. "I need to sleep at some point."

"Which is why you'll have to quit work."

Her fingers squeezed the chair like a laguli eel constricting its long body about some helpless prey. First, Ray had disappeared into the night, leaving nothing more for her than a letter. Now this. If only she had known her parents' plans before the ship sailed away. Her hands quivered, aching to punch, counter his attack.

"Rosca, I know growing up isn't any fun, but it's necessary. It's your duty to be a debna."

Her trapped anger boiled over. "You promised I could work as long as I could balance it with my lessons and boxing. What kind of man doesn't keep his word, but lets his wife- *a woman*- force him into her own will?"

Her father's mouth sunk into a frown. "You know nothing of marriage or raising children. Respect the wisdom of your elders. It's time you learned. Whether or not you like it, daughters need their mothers. And if I hear of you making such comments to her or her friends, I'll personally see to it you never set foot in another training gym."

Rosca's heart shuddered in her chest, and her lip, catching the motion, trembled. "You beast!" She sprung to her feet.

He rose and took a step in her direction. Instinct kicked in. Her long legs carried her through the castle and out the back door. Past Asium. Past lines of archery targets. Past Banli Boxers and militia men alike. No one stopped her. No one saw the dark thoughts pursuing her. Under the cover of the nama trees, she slowed her run.

Just the sight of their impenetrable trunks, some thirty-seven feet in diameter, gave her new strength. Waist-high ferns brushed her legs as she waded through the greenery. Their leafy tops blurred between her hot tears. Many said the dense forest was older than the reign of King Dahl, and each tree sprung from the spirit of a warrior.

Perhaps she'd get attacked by a wild boar and die here. Then she could become a tree and show all of them. But would her spirit sprout life here? Father claimed she had a warrior's heart, but now he wanted her to be a debna?

Could she blame him? What great deeds had she done in her life? Nothing. Absolutely nothing. If Maschiach took pity, she'd probably become a fern.

Miserable, she stumbled on.

***

Ski watched his sister as she raced past him and several others, training archery. Rushing headlong into a group of men, she almost collided with several of them, but didn't slow down.

"Who set her on fire?" commented an archer as he pulled back his string and released an arrow.

Ski chewed his lip. Had his parents found out about the race? Would they surrender their own children to the praetis? The island protectors hunted down pirates and their associates like sharks after blood. He had to find out. Replacing his bow on the archers' rack, he sprinted after her.

He found her ranting and swinging her arms about like a mad woman amidst the namas.

"Rosca, what happened?"

His sister's contorted face shot up in surprise. When their eyes met, she softened, and tears burst forth. "Father said I have to quit the Sailor's Solace for debna training. And Ray left!"

Ski sighed, relief flooding his core. Deb Rez didn't know. Ray was gone. Now they could get back to normal. At least until his siblings pulled him into some other genius plot to bring disgrace on them all. Thank Maschiach. Even if He was the one to put him in this situation in the first place. How could God let a pirate onto their island? And, to add insult to injury, give him such troublesome siblings? "You're sure Deb Rez doesn't know about the sesaquilles?"

Rosca nodded. "Yeah, we're good. Father isn't one for tact. If he knew anything, he'd have confronted us." Wrinkling her nose as though catching a whiff of something rotten, she cried out. "It's all her fault! Father wouldn't do this, but she is determined to make me a simpleton. A debna? I have higher aspirations than spending my life inside complaining on balmy days and calmly serving tea to gossips and weak-minded old ladies."

Ski spread out his hands in a question. "She?"

"Mother!"

He resisted the urge to cover his ears. For someone who loved being one of the guys, Rosca could squeak out a very pitchy female whine in her tantrums. She paced about again, stomping on fallen branches.

Rubbing his temples, he leaned against a nama tree. "She must sense you've been up to no good. It's womanly instinct."

"It's infuriating. I'm not her daughter— I'm a groomed horse! A minsk-head debna-in-training. I'll show her. I'll be the most troublesome, inappropriate debna ever forced into a dress. When I'm through, she'll beg me to stay away."

"Don't you feel guilty? Don't you care that you've been lying for tempas?" He stepped forward, towering over her small frame.

She hung her head, but a defiant gleam cast mahogany shadows in her gold eyes. "Of course I do. But I thought..." She looked up. "Ray offered for me to sail away with her. But I said no. If I'd known they're set to turn me into a true debna, I'd have said yes."

"Would you've?" Disbelief summoned disdain, and he guffawed.

"Yes." She pounded her fist in her hand. "Shel it, I would have. I'm not meant for this life."

Blood boiling, he pointed at her. "This life is safe and steady. Most girls would kill to be in your place. You're a shel ungrateful minsk-head and nothing more."

She reeled as though struck, then snarled back. "I don't want to be safe. I want to be great."

A humorless laugh escaped him. "That's just what someone who's always been protected would say. You have no idea the sacrifice this life takes. You know what I have to do to be a deb? Hours of tactical meetings, physical training, fighting, militia service… And you think afternoon tea is hard? At least someone in this family has the foresight to teach you your place, so when reality hits, you aren't knocked out. It isn't Mother's fault you're a girl. At least she is willing to prepare you for it."

His sister slammed her foot into a stump.

Taking her silence as a concession, he crossed his arms. "Grow up, Rosca."

As he turned to leave, something hard pinged his back. "Why don't you grow up?"

It hadn't hurt, but he clenched his fists as he spun around.

A second branch poked out from her hand.

"Watch your mouth. I'm still your elder. I deserve respect."

"You're a hypocrite. You want to talk to me about taking your place but don't even like your own. You may do what's required of you, but it's all with a snide comment or a sneer." Dropping the stick, she stepped forward. "You hate responsibility. I even wonder if you hate us sometimes, you're so frustrated with taking care of us. Not that you do."

"Watch your tongue!" Striding forward, the scenery blurred. With harried breaths, he grabbed her shoulders and shook till her head jerked back. "You have no idea how hard my job is. I never should have been here. We're supposed to be home. In Valsquel. With our actual parents. You don't even remember, but they loved us! More than reputation or power or anything else. They wanted us." He didn't realize he'd slapped her till her rosy cheek and warm glare met his gaze.

Why did she cry so much? She'd taken worse hits. "I'm… I'm sorry, Rosc."

Looking younger than ever, she trembled head to toe. He jolted back when she grabbed his hand. "Ski, look at me. They love you. They're just imperfect."

He stiffened. "If they loved us, they would have left us until our parents returned."

"They weren't coming back." Her voice shook with grief. "They'd been gone for over a year. Nine months longer than what they said. We would have starved." Her lips pressed into a hard-set line.

"And what if they came home? And saw that we…" his voice cracked. "…we left. What if they're looking for us?" A tear slipped down his face. He pulled his shoulders back and gritted his teeth. Shoving his pain into a mental box, he touched her swelling cheek. Embarrassment washed through him. "I'm sorry, Rosc."

"I need you, Ski. Please, don't be angry. I need my big brother."

Resolve filled him. "If our parents were here—"

She crossed her arms, pulling back. "I have everyone I need."

She didn't understand. Didn't know how much they had loved them. Enveloping her in his arms, he placed his head in her soft, thick hair. Perhaps he should have accepted Ray's deal. But it was too late now. She'd sailed away, and, with any luck, she'd never come back.

Chapter Eleven
Jump

Three Years After Ray's Disappearance

Above the three Ishels' heads, the imposing lion statue guarding Nileal's entrance roared in frozen ferocity. His white lok-wood face melted into a blanched stone gate, the iron bars of which swung wide for travelers. Vivacious, pink buds flowered and climbed wooden trellises bolted to the wall. A number of city guards stood at attention, two on the ground, and several more marching mechanically behind the parapet above their heads.

Dium's critical gaze ran up and down the scene. Taking in each detail, he sketched out the picture, glancing back for confirmation of the likeness.

"This is boring," Adnesi, the oldest of the three at twenty-one, complained.

Dium resisted rolling his eyes. Of the many grand qualities his brother could, and would, boast of, sitting did not make the list. Of course he would think a warm sunstruck morning of relaxing at the Nileal's garden entrance to the city and observing passersbyer "boring." He, on the other hand, found it peaceful. Especially since few other than the city guard had the will to brave the heat.

Adnesi sighed and leaned back. Although he'd inherited many features from his Banli mother, like light olive skin and round cheeks set in a broad face, he most resembled his father. Both men possessed ripped, intimidating figures. Wherever they went, people acted self-conscious or even skittish. As though meant to balance their appearance, they also shared friendly grins with a magnetism which people loved. Adnesi had copied his father in growing his wavy, black hair out till it reached the middle of his back. As usual, the sides were shaved, and he'd twisted his hair into dreads.

"Maybe you're bored because you haven't worked in almost a month." Dium tilted back his thin face, acutely aware of the way his cheekbones and jawlines jutted out. In preparation of Rez's annual Nileal ball, a servant had shorn back his thick, inky hair till only an inch remained atop his head, exposing his sharp face lined with permanent loftiness. He preferred his long hair to hide the sharp bones, but his mother had insisted on the cut, and he hadn't cared enough to argue.

Although shortest of his grown brothers, his full nose and angular facial structure created a cocky, self-assured look. Opposite of the imposing, boar brawn the rest of the adult males in the family possessed. Despite all this, he prided the muscular, defined body he'd worked so hard for. Short or no, he made sure to train every inch of what he had, then trust growth to years.

Adnesi jumped up, and Dium paused his sketching to watch him.

His brother picked a stick off the ground and pretended to use it as a sword. "They gave me a month of liberty."

Dium guffawed. "Why? You didn't get cut again, did you?"

Like most debs, Adnesi had chosen to go into the Nileal Ambassadorial Force, or N.A.F., as his career. A force formed to protect not just Iecula, but West Salme, Uluah, and the other nearby islands of the Speckled Region. They protected trade ships, warded off pirates, and hired out warriors as needed.

Adnesi thrust the fake sword forward. "Not that it is any of your business, but no, I did not get cut. They give me a free month every year. You know this."

"I don't believe you." Dium resumed his drawing.

"Besides, what do you mean again?" Adnesi swirled the stick in dramatic twirls and cuts, slicing his invisible opponent to bits. "I got injured last time. I couldn't do much good with one foot."

"And the time before that?"

"Wasn't my fault they only needed a few soldiers for the mission."

Squinting, Dium filled in the outline of the pathway and forest leading up to the city gate. "And no wonder you weren't one of them. I suppose it also isn't your fault you broke ten bowstrings in two hours, lost all your knives in a bet, or, my personal favorite, shot an arrow through your commander's hat?"

Adnesi threw the stick down. "I'm sorry, but seeing how you, my little little brother, was able to somehow dodge the deb militia tradition, you can't talk."

Dium smirked to himself. Adnesi only doubled the "littles" like that when he had nothing else to say, but the words lost their sting long ago. "You should have chosen boxing."

"Maybe I should have."

But neither of them would have lasted in a different career. Dium tapped his fingers on his leg. Adnesi had played war since before he could talk, while he himself had trembled at the thought of a nomadic soldier's life, away from home. The boxer and the soldier. It's like they were meant to be deb's sons.

"Look," Adnesi gestured off into the distance, down the road leading to Nileal's entrance. An approaching dot morphed into a figure, then sprouted a feather plumed hat and golden boots. "What is that minsk-head wearing?"

Dium grimaced as the man marched up. His lavish, richly styled dress shirt sported purple silk sleeves and pearl buttons. A black leather belt, clearly made to hold in the overspilling belly, cinched in spotless white breeches. Completely unpractical for the dusty road. Misgiving tightened Dium's throat. The generous, odd show of wealth brought back unwanted memories.

Without a word, the two brothers agreed on a plan as the man stopped in front of the city gate. Dium shoved his sketchpad in his bag and drew a saber and whetstone. Leaning against a tree, he soaked in the satisfying *hiss* stone and blade created as he sharpened. Perhaps the intimidation tactic was childish, but the man deserved it for dressing like a flagrant raschuka. Besides, that sense of misgiving mounted. Perhaps he'd get some answers.

Wary-eyed, the newcomer stepped forward, examining the men's unwashed clothing and lazily displayed weapons. A sneer tilted his nose. Scars ran down the lopsided face and amusement flitted in the expression as he slowed his gait. His composure spoke for him, confirming Dium's suspicion. This out-of-towner, dressed in enough finery to outdo a prince, knew how to brawl. And from the mean look in his eye, he expected to win.

Dium cocked an arrogant brow, challenging the stranger. Once, you would have had to kill a man to get them to wear such attire. Now-a-days people quickly sold their dignity for style or popularity. Or maybe the outside world had always been so minsk-headed.

Standing between him and the entrance, Adnesi polished his knife with his shirt, a lazy eye fixed on the man.

Feather-Plumed growled as he approached the gate. "Some other time, boys." The pompous traveler drew a jewel hilted sword. "I'm not in the mood."

Adnesi made an elaborate bow and scooted out of his way. "Of course. Nileal always welcomes *visitors*." He emphasized the last word, letting that speak for itself.

Dium snorted, but stepped aside. They had no real grievance against the man. He doubted his brother shared his own worries. To his knowledge, Adnesi never knew about Ray or her goons. His brother had no reason to watch for their return, anxious lest a knife should find its way between his shoulders. Not that Dium had done anything to her. Except steer Rosca away. And she couldn't know that, right?

The last of the feather disappeared behind the hill. "That was a pirate." Adnesi noted grimly.

Dium's stomach sank at the unwanted confirmation. "Maybe not. Father said Nilealians were getting high and fancy. Maybe it's some overdressed fighter." He faltered. He didn't believe that. Pirates were known for two things, flaunting wealth and brawling. This man had hit bullseye on both counts.

"Hmm." Adnesi tapped his chin, uncertainty in his tense expression. A grin broke the mask. "You know what they call us over in Uluah, don't you?"

"What?" Dium took a deep breath. One pirate meant nothing, right? Nileal was a port city, after all. Criminals trickled in. They couldn't go chasing each one.

"The pretentious peak of a spoiled nation."

"Ay, I'll take that. Better than Valsquelians. Even Father says they think we're a bunch of brainless brutes playing around with gold and silk like its dirt and cloth."

"Hah, they would join if they could. Pretty sure Valsquelians think everyone needs to pay tribute to their righteous rears just for blessing us with their existence. Too bad we don't do charity for minsk-heads."

Dium cracked his knuckles. The peace of the morning had dissipated. He rocked back and forth, as restless as Adnesi now.

His brother sheathed his knife. "Let's go cliff jumping."

"Without Rosca again?" Dium raised a brow. "She'd kill us."

Adnesi huffed. "You know what our problem is?"

"You mean in addition to being related to you?"

"Everything we do has to be a family event." After a pause, Adnesi asked, "So, jumping?"

Dium threw up his hands. "Fine."

"Great."

"Can I come?"

Dium directed an annoyed stare at the speaker. He'd been so quiet, Dium forgot the youngest Ishel brother accompanied them on their walk.

Mar-Iecula, more often called Mar, waited patiently for his brothers' verdict. From under smooth lids, his black-lashed eyes stared up at them with expectation.

"You got money for food?" Dium picked up his fallen stone and sheathed his saber.

"Just enough for me." The boy crossed his skinny arms defensively.

"Well, if it's enough for you and a snack for me, you can come."

Mar scrunched his baby-fat nose into a disdainful line of wrinkles like a plump caterpillar. "Dium, you're nineteen borrowing money from a nine-year-old. Have you no shame?"

"Nope."

"Fine." Groaning, the boy accepted the defeat.

With a small detour to purchase the tasty island snack known as chalips, they set off towards the cliff range that crowded the coast outside Nileal's city walls.

The empty, dirt road felt tranquil compared to the bustling city life just behind them. A breathy chill in the air silenced them. Even the chippering of birds quieted to a distant song. After a while the dry earth turned lush with foliage. Great hills steepled before them, dressed in nama, fruit, and silver lesp trees. The group livened as the dense canopy of branches, leaves, and lesp needles blocked the scorching sunrays. Their path, trod a hundred times before, steepened with each labored step.

Abruptly, the green grass turned to hard rock, and they climbed to the cliff tops. Straining their necks to look up, they eyed Alarog's point, a 200-foot peak named for the evil sea king.

"I dare you to dive off that." Dium pointed and looked meaningfully at Adnesi, who rarely refused a dare.

Adnesi shook his head, still fixated on the natural tower. "Not a chance. I'm not stupid. You know three kids got killed last year jumping that. They fell on some rocks. And even if they hadn't, they were falling fast enough to break their necks."

Dium grinned. "I know. I just wanted to see if I could get rid of you that easy."

Adnesi rolled his eyes. He pointed to a narrow pathway walled in by pure rock which opened to a protruding ledge. "Let's do the same place as last time. The bottom's clear."

Disgust curled Dium's lips. They always went there. But what else could you do when you had little brothers trailing your every move? He could risk his own neck, but Mar would follow.

As they emerged from the caverned walkway, Dium sighed at the stretch of sapphire, gold, and turquoise before them. The clouds drifted farther and farther out to sea, and the cool breeze pushed past in languishing wisps. He almost reached for his sketchbook, but charcoal wouldn't do the scene justice. To their right, the ocean's reckless crashing beat upon the sun-blanched base of Alarog's point, coated in seaweed. Noonday rays made the stretch of crystal water glitter with promise. Not a speck of land broke the horizon where sea and sky flowed together as one, making a glassed-in bowl of strange wilderness. A perfect picture of reality and reflection, indiscernibly mixed into a new world. A bittersweet sensation filled Dium's chest as he looked about. Such beauty was too good for this world.

A whoop of excitement interrupted his reverie, and Adnesi barreled through the middle of his brothers and off the cliff.

Neither had expected the violent movement. Mar, who barely weighed as much as a quarter of Adnesi, fell to the ground with his big brother's shoving, too close to the edge for Dium's liking.

"Minsk-head." Mar snapped, shooting to his feet with an embarrassed glower.

Dium thought of a few worse words to describe the careless man.

Running off the cliff edge, he sank feet first into nothingness. The fall sent spikes of adrenalin from head to toe. His muscles twitched with lurches of fear and enjoyment.

His heels hit water. Lower and lower, he sank until the momentum died. For a frozen Motherent, he floated in suspension. Then he flipped and kicked down to the depths. His hands reached forward in search of something. His fingers wrapped around the muddy clay, and he piled handfuls of fish poop and gunk into his shirt, which he had folded like a sack. Armed, he pushed off the ground and returned to the surface.

Adnesi had already scaled about five feet of cliff face, but Dium set after him, one hand gripping crook and cranny to climb and one hand cradling the gunk in his shirt.

Concentrating on his ascent, Adnesi's oblivion shattered as Dium massaged handfuls of fish poop into his long hair. Howling, Adnesi turned towards his brother, and Dium rewarded the movement by throwing mud in his face and smashing it into his dreads.

"You—" The insult died on Adnesi's lips as he lost his grip on the slippery rock and fell below.

Dium found a small ledge for stability, then pushed off, back flipping into the sea.

Treading water, he yelled, "Watch where you're running next time! You almost killed Mar."

Adnesi swam closer, his long arms speeding him along. "You're more dramatic than the debnas." Adnesi punched his brother.

Dium kicked his stomach underwater, and they wrestled for several minutes.

Another splash paused their fighting. Dium spun in time to see Mar's brown hair resurface. The youngest boy attacked both, lunging forward.

The fight kickstarted hours of jumping, wrestling, and slinging mud, leaving them exhausted but grinning ear to ear.

The three collapsed on top the cliff.

"Just one more time?" Mar begged, prodding his brother with his barefoot.

Splayed on the rock and dirt, Dium sat up and shook his head. "I'm resting."

Adnesi pulled a long brown stem and roll of taboc from his knapsack and gestured to Dium. "Smoke?" He filled the pipe's bowl and lit it.

"Ooh." Sitting up, Dium accepted the gift from his brother, white tendrils of the remains of Baska taboc floating in the clean air.

"Can I?" Mar walked over.

"No chance." Adnesi tackled his little brother.

While the other two wrestled, Dium sank into daydreams of his last sesaquill race. The animals Ray had snuck in three years before for profit now served for their entertainment.

Lin, a newcomer to the island, and Janel, Dium's oldest friend, helped him breed and race the animals right under the praetis' noses. Not that the civil protectors cared. Not when Dium slipped them such a pretty sum of his bets each month.

A puff caught in his throat, and he coughed. "This is stronger than usual."

Adnesi took the pipe from his hands. "Shel right. One of Rosca's friends brought it for me. An old sailor, you know the type. Said he traded a month's worth of sesaquill feed for it."

"Rosca hasn't tried it, has she?" Dium propped himself up on his elbows, guilt and worry knotting his brow.

"You're downright hypocritical." Adnesi rounded his mouth into a fixed "O," breathing out a near perfect smoke ring. "But no. She won't touch the stuff. Says it hurts her lungs."

Dium raised a brow. "It does."

Adnesi screwed his face into a skeptical ball. "It won't even give you a buzz or high."

"Yeah, I don't mess with mescucha that gets in my head."

Adnesi waved him down. "Neither do I. It's got a rich, smoky flavor, that's it. It's not bad for you."

"You don't think anything is bad for you." Dium rubbed his sore feet, tired of the bickering.

"Okay, it's about as bad for you as Rosca's cooking."

Dium chuckled. "You know Rosca told me she made tuna salad yesterday and forgot to put in the tuna?"

Mar snorted, and Adnesi barked out a laugh. "Sounds 'bout right."

Dium shook his head in disbelief. "It's in the name. How do you forget?"

His older brother raised and dropped his shoulders. "It's Rosca. The girl lives more in a world of her own than this one. Always dreaming and talking about leaving home and seeing the world, which I get, but…"

Mar jumped in. "But we're talking about the girl that got lost in her own backyard at fifteen."

"And," threw in Dium, "caught a wild snake, brought it in the house, and forgot where she put it."

Adnesi shrugged as though his sister's idiosyncrasies could no longer amaze him.

A staggered pattern of cracks and ledges caught Dium's attention. The cliff face shot above their heads like it would touch the clouds, then stretched out in a jagged, wild show. His hands itched to touch it. Standing, he approached the rock. Its massive body checked him, and he looked down at the cerulean blue below.

"We're high enough, Di," Adnesi warned.

He smiled at the challenge. Now, he had a reason to climb. Reaching up, he locked a hand over a knob in the rock, warm from the sunstruck sun. A shuffle behind him told him Adnesi had risen to his feet. He scurried up and out of reach.

"Fine," his brother called. "Be a minsk-head. I won't bury you."

He wouldn't jump, he decided halfway up. But he couldn't leave without seeing the top. By the time he reached it, his arms burned, and his head ached with the elevation. Laying out on the rock, he gulped the fresh air, the sky spinning above him. When it stilled, he stood to look around. Misty clouds crowded his view. A second more and the wind blew them on. He caught his breath. Miles of gray rock face webbed with silver and sand-colored lines curtained the mighty sea. The lush green ivy faded into the rock from here, shading it green.

Pure ecstasy shot through him. Nature was the only drug he needed. This was living. Leaning back like a wild man, he howled into the open air.

Peering back down, fear latched his heart. Among the crystal blue and frothy waves, a brown-and-white speck nested in the water. A ship? His heart sank. There was only one reason a captain would anchor here, hidden in the shadow of this secret cove. "Pirates." He ground his teeth. "Shel it. Can't they just leave us alone?" He reached to pull at his hair, forgetting it'd been cut. "I have to tell Father." His bare toes dug into the hard ground.

He'd planned tonight to perfection, Janel and Lin filling in any holes he'd left. While the island partied hard at his father's castle, he and his friends would race sesaquilles on the outlying beach. If he told Deb Rez pirates had landed, he'd be sent to the head praeti to deliver the news. Everything would be ruined.

No. Lifting his chin, he set his jaw. They'd put too much into this. His mind flashed back to Ray and his time with her crew. "They didn't hurt us then, and they've no reason to do so now. We're too powerful for a raid. Helski, the Banlis may enjoy the pirates stirring trouble. We're always looking for a fight." A grin broke through. "I'll tell him tomorrow. When we're done celebrating and ready to deal with the problem." Satisfied, he took one last glance at the sails and descended.

Shaking from exertion, he jumped the last seven feet, rolling onto his side.

Adnesi and Mar chattered as though he'd never left. Stretching out on the ground, he watched them and rested.

"You ever notice how the farther down the Ishel line you go, the crazier we get?" Adnesi smirked at Dium.

"Hey, I'm the youngest." Mar protested, puffing his cheeks in a pout.

"Exactly." Adnesi pointed the pipe stem at him.

"What do you mean?" Dium lifted his chin, furrowing his brow.

"Well, Ski's got his intense moments, but he's a pretty practical guy, right? I would probably be crazier, but the militia evened me out. You," he pointed the pipe at Dium, "are where we get interesting. You hold onto grudges like a dead man's sword grip and have more sarcastic comments than a fish has scales."

Dium put a hand behind his head and stared up at the leaves shaking in the breeze. "You trying to write a book or something? You're starting to sound like Rosca."

"No. I'm just pointing it out. After you, we got Rosca, who always wants to do good but somehow always chooses wrong."

"A hazard of being human, I suspect." Dium reached for the pipe.

Adnesi released it without a glance. "Then Jack, who's the stubbornest wild man you'll ever meet. You remember when he would cling to the undercarriage of the cart every time Father traveled? He refused to let him leave."

Dium chewed on the pipe stick, trying to picture the scene. "Oh yeah. It got so bad Mother had to lock him in the pantry till Father left. And he was only five."

"Well, at least I'm normal." Mar stretched out and looked at each brother with a too eager expression.

"Nah." Adnesi shook his head. "You're the worst of us all."

Mar flapped his arms in agitation. "I am not! When's the last time I did something crazy?"

Dium put up a finger as though counting off. "Let's see, you once tried to poison our cook's cat—"

"I was six! And that shel cat hated me."

"Watch your mouth." Dium smacked his brother's head playfully. "Oh yeah, you lost your temper and cussed Father out last tempa."

Adnesi held up a hand to pause his brother's speech. "Which should have gotten you thrown into the sea with rocks tied to your feet. You got lucky."

"Lucky? Father made me clean the servants' communal privy. Wheelbarrow after wheelbarrow full of human dung and piss." The young boy shivered. "Maschiach knows what diseases I could've caught. I'd rather be thrown in the sea."

Morphing his features in a sagacious expression, Dium nodded. "If you're gonna talk mescucha, you best know how to handle it too."

"Anyway," Mar's young face tilted up in pride, "it's not as though I'm the kid who got into a fistfight at a ball and knocked Debna Remalu into a pool."

A hearty chuckle rumbled in Dium's chest. "It was worth it. I've never seen an old lady pitch a tantrum like that. Plus, I won the fight, and Roj is no slouch in the ring."

Roj, part-time Professional Champion, part time city bully, had all but called Dium a cheat for winning so many sesaquill races, claiming nobody could get so lucky on an island-bred mare. Dium's sesaquill, the man had insisted, must have been imported from a breeder who specialized in race-sesaquilles. Dium hadn't meant to start a fight, especially since the accusation wasn't ungrounded. But then the drunk brute had set his sights on Rosca. Dium's fist had found its way to the guy's face of its own accord.

"Well," Dium looked from brother to brother, warmth filling his soul, "If we're crazy, I'll take it over normal any day."

Chapter Twelve
Suspense

Visions of an angry mother scolding the boys for their tardiness hurried Mar's steps.

Dium's yelling paused his march, and he spun to look back to see what caught his brother's attention.

He sighed. Adnesi had stopped to stare at some bird nesting in the tree above. Perfect. Now Dium would have to tease him about it, and they would fight as usual. That didn't bode well for his plan to sneak some pre-party cake and avoid Mother's long-winded lectures. His feet danced with impatience. He should just leave them.

"What's wrong, Di? Scared you won't have enough time to fix your hair?" Adnesi approached the two with a grin.

Mar crossed his arms. "He's not the one with fish mescucha in it."

Level with them now, Adnesi went for a tackle. Mar jumped aside.

"You sound jealous." Adnesi chuckled. "Come on. Even you know I got the good hair in the family."

The boy grimaced. "I have no desire to look like a female. Your hair's almost as long as Rosca's."

Backing his younger brother's jibes, Dium swished his head back and forth mockingly. "Oh, my locks. My beautiful crown. Oh, don't tell me that's a tangle!"

Adnesi raised a brow at Mar. "You wouldn't know a female if she came and kicked you where it hurts."

Dium huffed. "That's because if someone looking like a female comes at him kicking, he assumes it's you."

Silent, Mar prayed they wouldn't start wrestling.

Instead, Dium took off in a spontaneous race, booting up the dry, yellow dust of the road. He called over his shoulder. "Come on Adnesi, or you won't have time to wash those luscious locks."

Their racing didn't last long. Nileal's city gates lay open to a crowd of natives, tourists, and immigrants milling about in the usual free day bustle. Tramping over the sampietrini stone, the boys shoved and bumped into stranger after stranger as people thronged the streets.

Mar elbowed his way through a wall of men. Fight days were the worse, but since one happened almost every set of free day, the square usually held an overflow of traffic.

The towering doors of the city's athletic stadium lay wide open. The Nial v. Lin fight must have just ended, and the attendants were heading home. Usually, the local boxing tournaments took place at night, but today they'd held it earlier in honor of Deb Rez's party.

No wonder there was a crowd. Father said that the stadium Zafiere could hold three-thousand people and, by the looks of it, Mar'd wager that it had been full. Its magnificent structure rose like an ancient power, and guarding its entrance stood two chiseled eighteen-foot lilt-stone boxers ready to face off. Under furrowed brows, tenacity shone in the bright, blanched eyes. The stonemason had captured the determination which blazes a fighter's expression as though he spent years studying the look.

Zafiere and her fights drew in spectators from all of Iecula's neighbors. Some from the Speckled Region, the dotting of islands surrounding them, but also from the large countries of Valsquel,

Limur, and even as far as Kenst. Garbed in animal furs, the fair skinned, bulky Limurians laughed and gibbered in their short halting language. Kenstians made a show of themselves with tight, elaborate clothing. Like most port cities, their metropolitan culture created an energetic, loud, and opinionated people. Full of post-fight energy, a group shadowboxed and roared in laughter at some private joke. Even a few thin-faced Valsquelians grew alight with the adrenaline the atmosphere held.

"Hey!" Mar called to a strange man passing-by. "Hey!" he called again, and the man paused.

"What is it?" The man looked down on him as though he'd performed some great act of self-sacrifice by stopping.

"Who won?" Mar demanded, distracted by the man's overflowing nose hairs.

"Lin." The stranger's jaw hardly unlocked to allow him speech, and he stiffened even further. "I'd bet good money on the other."

Anxious for a full account, Mar bit down the temptation to inform the man he hadn't asked about his poor betting skills. "How'd he do it?"

"Hook to the temple. Knock out." The stranger escaped into the crowd.

"I knew it!" Adnesi exclaimed as the man walked away. "Man, that guy Lin is an animal. He came to the Asium last tempa to ask Father for advice."

"But isn't his trainer Deb Faram?" Mar chewed on his cheek.

"I don't think he has a trainer." Dium resumed walking and his brothers followed. "He just fights under Deb Faram's name cause you got to put a deb's name down or they won't let you compete."

Mar slowed his gait. "If he's getting advice from Father, why not use his name? I don't like people using Father's advice without his name. It's wrong."

Adnesi frowned at him. "Deb Rez is the best of the best. You must earn that right of association."

"He only takes fighters that have a few wins under their belt," Dium explained with more patience. "Lin just came to the island maybe a year ago. This is the first time he's fought at Zafíere. He's good, but untested. And a little unpredictable. He's got a temper."

"But he won," Mar pointed out.

"Lots of people win."

"How do you know all this?" The eldest brother gave Dium a curious side-eye.

"Lin's my friend." Dium shrugged. "He races sesaquilles with me."

Adnesi grunted. "So why didn't you go?"

Snorting, Dium gestured emphatically. "I'm not spending my free day watching him. I can see him spar in the gym for free."

The dim skyline of Banli mansions filled Mar's view. A jolt of excitement and expectation ran through his body. Party time had almost arrived.

"Look out." Adnesi pointed to a sour-faced messenger shoving his way through the human blockade. His crimson vest had an image of parchment stitched on the front to announce his role.

Crinkling his nose, Mar shifted out of the man's path. "Miley." Bile filled his mouth with disgust.

The wiry man tripped over an elderly lady's walking stick but drove on. She stumbled. Mar steadied her with a low growl in the man's direction.

Unaware of the boy's attention, the messenger drove on, violently pushing aside two children play-boxing. "Move! Important news for Debna Le."

Perking up at the announcement, Mar exchanged a worried glance with his two brothers.

One of the children previously play-boxing kicked Miley's behind. They roared with laughter as he fell forward, dropping his parchment on the muddy ground. Recognizing one of the boys, Mar aired a boxer's hand sign meaning, "Nice work." The boy smiled and the two mischief makers disappeared.

"Alright, let's see what this nosy fool wants with Mother." Adnesi hooked an arm under one of Miley's and Dium took the other. Together, they hauled him to his feet and into a quiet alleyway. Mar picked up the parchment and followed.

Squirming, the messenger's paper-thin face spun back and forth. "There is no time to be wasted! I must see—"

"Miley!" Adnesi barked with full command. For a moment, he appeared like one of the lilt-stone statues of the Banli Boxers. Mar puffed his chest. Someday he would be as big as him.

"Adnesi." Miley straightened as the men released him. "I'm sorry, but this news is for your mother and her alone."

Dium leaned against the alley wall, using his knife to clean dirt from under his fingernails. "I wonder how my father would feel about that?"

Miley spurted like a boiling teapot. "It's your father that voted in the law. Only the one whom the message was sent to may receive the message. The terms are quite simp—"

"Yes. We know." Adnesi's boar-like brow darkened.

"You could at least say who it's from." Dium cocked his head. He lacked Adnesi's towering presence, but the cunning glint in his hooded eyes and drawn, golden cheeks made a noble show. The king of mischief, as the family sometimes called him.

Miley pressed his lips into a bloodless line, his nose flaring in contempt.

Dium's features hardened, twiddling the knife in deliberate spins.

Miley cowed. "Your sister handed it to me from a jail cell. That's all I'll say."

"What!" Mar turned his attention to the parchment he'd picked up from the dirt, only to have Adnesi rip it from his grasp. He grabbed after it, but without a hope of recapturing the prize.

Laughter shook Dium's lean frame. "The minsk-head. What'd she do now?"

"Do not read my message." Miley screeched like a baby bird. "It is forbidden by your father himself."

Adnesi's ears drew forward in a tight scowl. With decisive care, he handed Miley his message and stepped aside. "The law is the law. Go."

Agape, Mar threw up his hands at his brother's quick compliance. "But—"

"We'll find out soon enough." Adnesi silenced him. "Go on, Miley."

Skittering around them, the messenger dashed off, his spindly legs bounding over the sampietrini stone.

Mar resisted the urge to race off after him. All the way home, he sensed Adnesi had slowed their gait on purpose to increase his suffering. He couldn't help recalling his father's lectures on self-denial and delayed pleasure like a lion might muse over a bowl of collard greens.

Chapter Thirteen
Arrested

The cold stone walls and darkness of the damp cell contrasted the midday sun burning outside. Just a few hours before, it had smothered Rosca and her younger brother in unrelenting heat. Funny how just a few hours turned everything upside down.

Sitting, the girl ran her finger over the dirt floor. They'd almost made it. Her finger paused as her throat tightened. Best not to think about it. That life was never meant to be.

Restless, her younger brother chided her. "What a lousy fighter you make." Jack kicked the ground, sending a cloud of dirt into the air. "They cornered you in three seconds."

Rosca leaned her head against the cool cell wall. "That's real condemning coming from the twelve-year-old who squealed like a ruskag pig just cause a praeti grabbed you."

"I thought it was Father." Jack's defensive tone boomed in the near silence of the jail cell.

Rosca searched for her brother in the dim lighting. The outside torches caught the tips of his curly black hair, but she couldn't see his face. Jack was tough, but Father was tougher. A hot defiance rose in her chest. Really, what could he do? Kick them out? They were trying to run away. Shel Chares. Shel being a Deb's daughter!

Chares, a praeti friend of the deb Rez had caught her boarding a smuggler's boat, and Jack following to say goodbye. Now that the civil protectors had confiscated the boat and thrown the captain in jail, no one would ever aid her in escaping the island. The punishment would outweigh the risk. She was stuck, with Jack caught in the middle of her mess.

"Jack, I'm sorry."

"Don't be sorry yet. We'll have plenty of that when we get home."

Rosca eyed her brother's shadow with a fondness that tickled her heart more and more recently. Of course she'd get sentimental right before trying to leave. She choked down a sob, then cleared her throat so Jack wouldn't suspect her of crying.

It was ironic. When she came to live with the deb and debna as a child, everything in her only wanted to belong. Now, she couldn't outrun being their kid when she tried.

A hacking cough announced the return of the guard. He walked the lines of the cells every ten minutes or so. She placed her head against the wet stone and prayed.

A rattle of keys interrupted her. In seconds, she and her brother had sprung to their feet.

A sneering voice greeted them as the guard opened the door. "Debna Rosquevalarian. Deb Jack. Debna Le has paid your fee. You're free to go." He screwed his face as they passed, like smelling something rotten.

Jack gave the man a sour look. Rosca bumped the back of his head in reprimand. "He's just doing his job," she hissed.

"Fine, but he doesn't have to stare at us like we're rat droppings while he does it."

Rosca stopped in the middle of the hall. The glowering expression of a short, plump woman met her. Age had crept up on Debna Le steadily, but she wore it well. As though it testified to a life wisely lived rather than being something to lament. The muscles in her jaw tightened as she pursed her lips into a disapproving grimace. In tight rows, her hair hung down her back in thin, hard braids. Rosca tugged her own, styled in a similar manner, but with a thickness that felt soft to the touch. Both of them females in a family of pragmatic men. Both of them debnas. Many times, the older woman was Rosca's only anchor, only reference point in the sea of male opinions. How did they end up such opposites?

"Debna Le." The moist gray walls felt like they would crash in on Rosca at any moment. With a deep breath, she lifted her chin, but her stare stayed on the woman's collarbone. The guards had not left.

"Rosquevalarian." The woman's hickory-colored cheeks drew tight.

They're watching, Rosca interpreted her mother's taut stance. They would expect a groveling apology from the offenders. Or at least a curtsy. Some sign of deference and guilt. She froze, torn between stubbornness and just counting her losses.

"You ready, Rosca?" Jack pushed her from behind. "We got to mentally prepare to meet Father."

Her mother's lips twitched. "Yes, let's go home."

The carriage ride home lasted three eternities. Coated in sweat induced by heat and nerves, Rosca ambled inside. Nobody spoke a word until they had reached the cotto ali fimili.

With a look of placid command, their mother folded her hands and examined both of her children. Rosca met the invasive gaze with a stout stance. Perhaps in public, it spoke of virtue to show deference, but here they must share an equal ground. To apologize now, just because she got caught, would be worm hearted.

"Rosquevalarian Ishel, see me in my study. Now." The two started to follow her, but her mother spun on her heels abruptly. "Did I say Jack Ishel? To your room. At once!"

With a wince, he scurried off.

Her mother swung open her study doors like a bitter north wind. "Ridiculous! Absolute minsk-headed— Did you even think what might happen to Jack? To you, if those smugglers were something more than what they professed? I know we don't permit it here, but the slave trade is very much alive and booming. God knows the life they may have forced you into."

Rosca felt heat rush through her body. "I was careful—"

"Careful? Careful? Hah. When you climbed the east tower with a bedsheet for a rope, *that* was comparably careful. This was an atrocious disregard for common sense, thought, or dignity. On top of it all, you endangered your brother!"

Indignation thundered within Rosca. "He followed me. I would *never* invite him on such a thing. You know how stubborn Jack is. If I left him, he'd still find a way to come, and that'd be worse. He wasn't going with me. Just seeing me off." She added, her voice betraying her misery. Her defense was weak. She saw that now. What if Jack had gotten grabbed or hurt? It was one thing to put her life at risk, but his?

Her mother sighed and knuckled her forehead, every second aging her features. "I don't understand, Rosque. I know you love us. I know you do." She challenged her daughter with a stare. "What... why...?"

"I wanted an adventure." She hung her head, wishing she could give her more.

"Oh!" Debna Le threw her hands in the air. Womanly grace vaporized as she all but bounded across the room and stuffed her finger in Rosca's face. "There will be no more adventures for you. Not until you learn to think of something other than yourself. No more fantasy stories, boxing, or tramping about the city with your brothers and their vulgar friends like a raschuka!"

"That's not fair!" Rosca's knees knocked. Her breath bubbled in her chest, refusing to release. She swayed. It was as though an invisible beast had entered the room and siphoned the marrow from her bones. She balled her fists, clinging to willpower in desperation.

Electricity sizzled in the air, like the smell of the beach before a storm, but she didn't care. She stepped towards the plump figure until her mother's finger touched her nose. "You promised as long as I stuck to my studies and trained to be a debna, I could keep fighting. Will you break that promise too? Just like you made Father break his promise about allowing me to work?"

Her mother flinched but stood her ground. "Promises are built on trust, and you broke that."

"Promises are built on the man or woman who give them. If you take it back, then you're a liar." Limp at her sides, her hands trembled. She racked her brain for a solution, a reason to stay in the ring. If she had to be here, she couldn't lose that.

But there wasn't a reason. She'd lost her rights when she tried to leave. She was a prisoner. Nausea washed over her. There had to be a way to convince her mother. Any way.

She took a step back. She would not lose control. "I respect you and Father too much to live my life as an ordinary person. If it costs me everything, even what I love, I will be great. I will find a way. I can't do that here. Not where everyone already knows me as the deb's daughter."

Le shrunk back, disbelief and acceptance written on her face in tired lines. "You don't know what it is to be great. If you did, you wouldn't have to leave to find it."

"Maybe you're right. Maybe it is here. But I don't believe it. I don't feel it here. I feel it out there."

Le rested a tender hand on her daughter's cheek.

Rosca flinched but didn't pull away.

"You don't need to prove who you are, Rosque. Just be it. What you are wrestling with is immaturity. You know it's time to grow up, but you're not sure how, that's all."

Rosca stared, a flurry of emotions flying through her chest. Guilt and hope wrung her heart like a wet towel. "How can I keep fighting the same opponents all my life and expect to grow? It's unbearable living in Father's shadow. The other debs fear him. Shel near everyone fears him. They're always guarding what they say, scared of offending him through me somehow. Other than Deb Sergio, no one thinks I can take a simple, 'hey your endurance is that of a beached whale and your punches resemble a dead snake with arthritis'—"

"Oh, mescucha!" Le rose up, fury written on her brow. "You have the best trainers around and they know it's their heads if they don't do Deb Rez's children right! When did you become so blind? So ungrateful?"

"It's my life. I intend to live it." Invisible strings tightened between the two women as Rosca mulled over her next words. As long as she was in trouble, she may as well say it all. "What's more I don't want to be married off or paraded like a puppy!" Rosca studied her mother. If only she could get her to agree to let her go, her father would follow.

"Rosca, please." Her mother took a deep breath, letting silence seep into the room. "I've given up."

"What do you mean—"

"I quit! I renounce my authority as a parent. Not that you'll notice. You never listen."

A pang filled Rosca's chest till she thought the pressure would crack her into a million pieces. The debna would never forgive her now. What had she done? This was why she hadn't said goodbye. No, she couldn't think like that. She had to.

Le hadn't finished. "If you'd try talking this through instead of gallivanting off into the sunset like a crazed, wild hog, we might have reached a civilized decision before the news of yours and Jack's arrest spread throughout the whole town."

Rosca hung her head.

"I blame your brothers and boxing, always pushing and prodding you to keep up. Rez, of course, blames himself, but as that man would take credit for a bird learning to fly, his opinion hardly matters. We had made a decision before all this..." She dropped off, as though forgetting Rosca's presence. With a shake of her head, she quipped, "Anyway, I doubt your father and I view the situation in the same light."

Bewildered, Rosca chewed her thumb to keep from interrupting. Her mother might decide not to tell her at all if she saw Rosca's impatience as impertinence.

"We had decided, after the ball tonight, we would send you to the Valsquel SOE."

Time froze. Rosca dared not move a limb as though she could shatter the glass moment. The Valsquel SOE? The one place... She killed the joyful thought before it could take root. She must have heard wrong.

"You will study there." Le's dry tone jerked her back to reality.

Certainly, she heard her wrong. It wasn't possible. The debna, letting, no, sending her away? She licked her lips. "The SOE?"

"Yes." Tilting her head, Debna Le cocked a brow. A smile tugged at her lips.

Rosca gulped. She could study literature, art, map-making, architecture, building, mixed fighting, and no one would think twice. No one would know her name. "I... I am to study at the SOE?"

"Well, we might send you somewhere else, but so few universities take girls. I believe it's your only option. That or settling into your role as a debna, that is."

The stupor ended as though her mother had dunked the girl's head in ice water. Rosca squealed. "Thank you!"

"Calm down, Child."

"Calm is overrated."

"I worry about you, Rosque." Bird-like, her mother studied her with unblinking wariness. "You seem intent on picking the hardest path to life."

"Pain is good," Rosca babbled, though she didn't know why. She and her mother would never agree on this. "Father sees that. He made a career of it."

Her mother's gaze narrowed. "Your father made a career of passion, not pain."

"Does not birth teach us pain is the way to life?"

"There is plenty of pain without you searching for it. A good fighter does not look to get hit."

"But neither does he run from it."

"You might have done some good to run more. I believe your brain has more scars than thoughts."

Rosca chuckled, then stiffened. Chills raced up her spines. She had run. She had run from honesty, from her family, from her duty. Was she a coward? Hot tears sprung into her eyes. "You were right. I should have talked with you both. I thought I was avoiding… I thought it would save our relationship."

"Rosca." Reaching out, her mother locked her in her arms and kissed her hair repeatedly. "You're a young fool, and I'll never be able to stop loving you. If you could scare me away, I would be gone. God knows you've put me through enough."

Rosca sunk into the embrace, soaking in the smell of vanilla and garden flowers that followed her mother wherever she went. "I love you.'

"You must be careful at the university." They pulled away. "Valsquelians are not overly fond of Banlis, or really, anyone from Iecula."

"But anyone can tell I'm Valsquelian by birth." Rosca pointed out as though the debna couldn't see the soft, voluminous curls of black hair, clear toffee skin, or small angular body and face all common to the inland plains of Valsquel.

"Mmm, yes. Well, you look a bit of both, even though you don't have any Banli blood. Maybe your mother was from here."

Rosca's heart leapt at the idea, but she dismissed it. Ski had called their mother fair skinned and blond. Few Banlis had either of those features.

"It doesn't matter," the debna continued. "You think like a Banli." She tapped her head. "I can't say I'm overly fond of Valsquelians myself. They're…" she crunched her nose. "…peevish and soft."

At this, Rosca fought to keep from smiling and pointing out that she married a Valsquelian. She placed a hand on the elderly woman's arm to pause her. "Don't worry. I'm not going to change. I'll always be Nilealian through and through. This city is my home."

Her mother nodded, a half-smile playing on her lips. "Well, change enough to grow up some, will you?"

Rosca smirked and shook her head. "I suppose I can try."

Her mother's delicate hand flew to her lips, and she jumped. "Oh! The ball. We'll be late. We cannot be late." Full of command and business, she shooed Rosca from the room, babbling as she did. "If you don't show up and at least pretend to have a good time after today's scandal, all of Nileal will think your father killed you."

"I wonder where our family gets its flare for dramatics."

Her mother flicked a pointed finger to the door. "Out."

Rosca opened it.

"Rosca?" Her mother's voice *ringed* like a bell.

"Yes?"

"It isn't a sin to want to grow up, but know your choices affect others, too. Great people never live for themselves."

"Yes, ma'am."

Chapter Fourteen
Confrontation

Rosca slipped into her room before anyone could ask any more questions. After closing the door, she leaned against it and stared at the happy haunt. Bookcases made up half of the circular wall. On the other side, door-size windows opened to look over the training grounds. Medals and ceremonial boxing gloves decorated the space between them.

Split. Just like her. A sardonic smile cracked her lips. Valsquelians and Ieculians clashed like water and oil. Her grin faltered. Why did she have to be the cup to hold both? She lowered herself onto her bed.

The prim, cautious, and studious Valsquelians lived in rectangular castles on stretches of plains rumored to have no end. In contrast, Iecula was a death trap. A water-bordered land full of reckless individuals who fought with fists, knives, even fruit for fun. Trained from toddling age to climb, scale, and attack like mountain lions. Yet, somehow, both electrified her veins.

She pulled a book from the shelf. Tapping the gray cover, she ground her teeth. She was not defined by where she was born or where she was raised. She didn't need to bow to any label. She was just her. Everyone else could get over it. The weightless declarations floated in her mind. On a better day, she would believe the words.

She rolled her eyes. This self-pity had to stop. She dropped the book like a hot coal and jumped to her feet.

Paintings, some bought, others done by herself, and plants decorated the space in bright colors. Yellow daffodils and sunflowers sprinkled it cheerily, while fat roses and daisies intertwined in windowsill flowerbeds. The motto of the debnas, burned into a namawood plank, sat on a shelf. **ALSON. SABINI. VERA. DAVIT.** In the Trader's Tongue, the four pillars of strong femininity translated to noble, wise, true, and life-giver.

Underneath, in smaller letters, lay an adage that dated back to the reign of King Dahl: *Of beauty. For beauty. Towards beauty.* Guarded by the towers of overflowing bookshelves, an armoire with an attached vanity desk, a chest, and a medium size bed dressed in silver linens furnished her room.

On the neatly made bed, her ball outfit twinkled with miniscule diamonds. She frowned at the glowing gown. The body she could appreciate. Strips of sheer tulle lay over a layer of maroon material which would cling and accent her curves, without revealing too much. The rich red color gave the golden specks dotting the front and skirt life. Modest, but youthful.

The sleeves, however, made bile fill her mouth. Gawdy, multi-colored gems ran the full length, some algae green, others mustard yellow, and, thrown violently in the midst of them, bright pink. Fiddling with her braids, she pursed her lips. "It didn't even match. Why would you ruin a dress like that?"

A parchment rested on top, reading: *Wear face paint- Mother.* A groan escaped her. "Always a new order."

"Did you say something?" Her lady's maid, an elderly woman with cracked lips and curled hair, peeped through the door.

"No, just talking to myself again."

"You do 'nuff yappin' when there are people about. Shouldn't you give it a rest between?"

Rosca rolled her eyes at the cheeky comment, but her mood lifted. "Nia, does Mother really expect me to wear this?"

"What's wrong? It's beautiful." Nia approached and ran her hand over the gown.

Rosca scrunched her nose. "It could be if a sea-sick rainbow hadn't thrown up on the sleeves."

Nia pinched her lips. "You're awful picky for a child that just got outta a cell. You best be grateful the debna is lettin' you have a dress. What is she thinkin', lettin' you go to a party after a stunt like that? Now, if you was my child, you wouldn't be sittin' for a month much less goin' to no party."

"I see the busybodies strike again. Gettin' into what ain't their business." She arched a brow at Nia, but the woman wagged a finger at her and *tsked*.

"Servants know everythin'. But don't worry about the sleeves. I know my job, and I do it well. Gimme two hours, and I'll have it ready."

Rosca snapped on a smile and kissed the woman's wrinkled cheek. "Take all the time you need, just please don't put me out in that."

Nia harrumphed. "I'll see you in an hour. You *must* bathe. Don't be late. You smell so bad Maschiach is holding his breath."

"God doesn't need to hold his breath. Scents probably turn into rose petals before they touch his nostrils."

"Git." Nia clucked and mimed kicking her from the room.

Rosca wandered the castle halls, nerves pooling within her. Blind instinct led her to Asium, as though a part of her knew she needed to work them out. A tingle went up her spine at the sight of the stone pavilion, which hovered over lines of punching bags. At least she wouldn't really have to give this up. The SOE had holidays. For a second, relief iced her inflamed thoughts. Then, a pit opened in her gut. Who would she be without training every day? Without the adrenaline? The challenge? Would she break like some of the sailors did when they retired from the sea? Could she really survive studying all day? She barely sat through her lessons now.

Oh mescucha! She'd been through these thoughts a thousand times. They didn't help. It was time to try something new. She reached into a wooden chest and pulled out some stinky wraps and ratted gloves. At least her hands wouldn't smell like she washed them in cat piss every day.

She stopped in front of the bag. Its dingy ropes creaked as the breeze rocked it. A plethora of memories haunted everything she saw. Wooden poles and nautical ropes squared off a section of dirt where she lost her first three sparring sessions. Fearful that her father would take the losses as proof training a seven-year-old girl was not worth it, she had spent hours in extra practice. After months of tears and fears draining her every waking morning, she won her first sparring.

Everything had always been an equal trade. When she began running extra miles, her father allowed her to spar. Forgoing social parties in exchange for extra resistance training had led to her first knockout win. Learning to rise early to shadow box had given her clarity and balance. All of it had given her irreplaceable bonds. So much of her life had taken place here.

And now she had to say goodbye. Deep sorrow pooled in her breast, keeping her hands locked at her sides as the bag sat motionless before her. Would people spit mescucha for her leaving? Say she couldn't handle it anymore? She wasn't a fighter?

Furrowing her brow, she tugged at her braids. It didn't matter what they said. She would use what fighting gave her, and that was enough. Courage. Strength. Action. She could choose who she wanted to be.

***

For the first time in tempas, quiet possessed the Ishel household. Dium almost turned around and walked back out. Anything powerful enough to quiet the ruckus of the mansion scared him. He turned to his two brothers as they ventured deeper into their home. Skeptical, anxious glances switched between them before the familiar creak of the pantry door led them all to the kitchen.

With a forkful of cake half lifted to his mouth, Jack froze at the sight of their three condemning faces peering down at him. "Oh, like you all don't sneak the cake pre-party." His nose scrunched defiantly.

"Where is everyone?" Dium peered around. A few cooks and servants hurried about, but his mother, usually downstairs with a list of last-minute orders, could not be found.

Jack shrugged, shoving down the cake. "I don't know, probably avoiding Mother. She's in a mood. I've been imprisoned in my room."

Mar's envious gaze followed the cake like a drooling puppy. Shaking himself, he shoved his baby nose in the air. "You don't look imprisoned."

Jack warbled a response with a full mouth. "Oh, I am very imprisoned. Quite stifling, those four walls closing in on you. If Father asks, I'm feeling very penitent for my actions. Perhaps you could even mention my eyes watering."

"Pretty sure that's 'cause of the peppers." Dium coughed and took a step back from the rows of spices above Jack's head. The burn of hot chili flecks drifted in the air.

"What'd you do to get 'imprisoned' anyway?" Adnesi pinched his brows down into a sharp V.

"Got arrested." Jack nonchalantly shoved in another bite of cake, but his ears wiggled with a suppressed a grin.

Mar jolted to attention, taking the bait. "You were in jail?" His voice held layers of awe and respect. Jack had just become his favorite big brother. Dium rolled his eyes.

Once he started, he couldn't stop. Jack's story spilled out with animation and detailed explanations. Before he could even finish telling about the lonely, damp floor of the jail cell, Dium had broken free to find Rosca, his steps brisk.

His march to find his sister took him through the armory halls and out the back. A short walk led to where the sun caught her silhouette as it sunk towards the earth.

"Hey. Hey!"

Ignoring his attempt to start a conversation, she turned out a set of combos ending with a vicious double left hook. Grabbing the bag, he moved it to break her rhythm. With a pivot and jab, she reset herself and the pounding continued, growing in speed and power. Impatient summiting, he pushed her to the ground with a teep-style kick to her hip.

"What do you want?" More tired sounding than angry, she threw off her gloves.

He helped her stand. "Just came out here to say you hit like a girl." Dium kept an even tone, but he searched her face and posture, looking for the answer before he asked the question. Adnesi would have ragged him for it if he were here. *Just ask straight up,* he always chided in annoyance. But her flittering gaze and lip chewing told him more than a million words could.

"Thanks. Got any more enlightening instructions?" Staring at her hands, she unwound the wraps protecting them.

"Oh, I have a lot of things I could say to you right now."

Her head shot up. Her eyes had sunk in, faded from their usual gold to muddy brown, but they appeared hard as a gemstone. "Dium, don't drag it out. You always do when you're angry. Trying to make the other person feel guilty or say something they shouldn't, but I don't have time for that. If you have something to say, just say it." She stood, lightning crackling in her expression as she faced him.

His temper spiked, pumping adrenaline through his veins. "I shouldn't have to say anything." He threw up his hands, then hit the bag. "Why didn't you tell me?" His yell shattered the stillness of the gymnasium.

She slunk back. "I'm sorry."

"I'm your brother!"

Her shoulders flinched. She lifted her chin, every face muscle tight.

"Even though you can be a real minsk-head sometimes, we are bound by blood to protect you, Rosc. We love you, though Maschiach knows why." He searched her face, but a stony mask spoke for her. She didn't need him or his approval. His throat tightened.

"Does it even matter now?" Her jaw screwed tight until the veins in her scrawny neck bulged. She *whooshed* a breath from her nose like a boar. "I'm back. Besides… you… you wouldn't get it. It has nothing to do with love. Or trust. I know my brothers have my back. I am more sure of that than anything else. You all are my champions. You've always protected me."

"Then why…" He closed his eyes, stroking his thumb on the outside of his balled fist. "You don't even seem sorry." He opened his eyes. "You have everything. A home. Security. Family. Name one thing you've been denied."

Two lines appeared between her brows. "I don't know." She watched the still swaying bag, barely giving the words the strength of a whisper.

The bashful tone drenched him like kerosene to a flame. He threw up his hands and shouted his frustration. She'd always idolized him. Feared his disapproval. But this? If she had the guts to run away alone, she could at least give him an honest reason. Pressure from his clenched jaw built at the top of his neck, and he twisted his head side to side with a crack. The urge to hit, kick, and fight electrified his limbs. Balling his fists tighter and tighter, his nails cut into his palm.

He focused on the line of bags. Deepening his breaths, he forced calm. No matter what she did, he could never hurt her. The mere thought released the tension in his chest.

She sniffled. Tears dripped down her cheeks. How was she still playing victim? A growl rumbled in his throat. "Your choices affect all of us, Rosc."

She wiped her eyes, bouncing with bundled energy. "I'm sorry. I should have said goodbye." Desperation mounted in her voice. "I should have told you. But I ran!" She growled like a wild cat and pulled at her hair. "I've never been as much of a fighter as you or Adnesi or even Jack. I got scared, and I ran."

Throwing back his head, Dium snorted and ran a hand down his face. "Oh God, this again? Your whole, 'I'm not as good as my brothers. I don't have a place here. I'm not a real fighter.' What? Are you blind? You're an Ishel, you minsk-head! You slug eating, slow-brained, three-legged cow. So you don't fight like us, too bad! You do other stuff like debna training and studying and reading. You don't need to be us. You're not going into the militia or becoming a pro-fighter. You're a girl!"

An open-face pleading met his outburst. "You're right. And that's why I had to go. I don't want to be you. But I'm not fit to be a debna either."

"But—"

She cut him off. "I worship you and Adnesi and Ski and Father…" She smothered the quiver in her voice. "If I had said goodbye, you all— you mainly— would try to stop me and I wouldn't have the heart to go. I know it's cowardice, but I have such a hard time telling you all no. It's like a spell. I open my mouth, and the words don't come. I respect you all *too much*."

"Respect?" His laughter held bitterness. "What about love? Loyalty?"

"Love and respect are tied together."

Was she really saying this? "Respect is earned. Love is free. That makes them different." How ironic that the one who'd first said that now forgot. "When it comes to family, love matters more."

She bristled. "But they're still bound together. Would you prefer I didn't listen at all? Didn't respect or love you or whatever the helski it's called?"

He snorted. "So respect and love mean doing everything someone says?"

"No, but—"

His chest constricted until he thought it would burst his heart. "There's no 'buts'. I didn't ask you to make an idol of me."

She reeled as though struck. Her petite form shook head to toe.

He studied the ceiling behind her, unable to watch her melt into sobs again. Pity and irritation seesawed in his chest. "Don't redefine words you barely understand." *Even if you once did.*

"Don't understand?" Her voice quivered in rage. She drew herself firmly up. "I'd do anything for this family… If there was anything to do! We just sit here… But I do love you all. More than anything."

"Not more than yourself." He slammed his fist into the bag. "Ray made you more desperate for respect than a bird for wings. Not that you required much pushing. It's pride, Rosca."

"It wasn't her."

Letting the quiet drag out, he waited for her to finish.

"I lost," she croaked, the heavy tone stretching across a thousand miles. "And I never came back. I never became champion. Not even a juvenile champion." As she released the last of the words, a final sob stilled her heaving chest and acceptance shrouded her features. "I don't fit in this life, so I must be made for something else."

He pulled at his hair, the three long years since she'd started her journey to become juvenile champion sped through his memory. Every year, she tried again. And every year, she lost. Last time, she'd made it all the way to the title shot. A few points difference, and she would have been champion. But that was the past. Neither of them could change it.

Only she could make her peace with it, and it was time she grew up and did so. "If you really wanted it, you'd try again." The naked truth set fire to the atmosphere.

Piece by piece, sorrow dropped from her expression. "Exactly." Iron determination steadied her voice. "I'm tired of trying. I thought… I was convinced that if I left without getting that title, it'd be like running away. That I'd never move past being a failure." Bunching her traps around her neck, she raised up onto her tippy toes then dropped back down. Her drying eyes refused to meet his. "But I can't take it anymore. I want to see the world. And I'm proud of what I've done with boxing. Proud of the effort I've put in. I just want something different now. Is that so wrong?"

Her voice shook. Stilling, she reached out to him, then snapped her arms to her sides.

One by one, he pressed his knuckles with his thumb. Tension shot out with each pop. How blind could one person be? "This isn't about boxing, Rosc. This is about us. Your family." Exasperation laced his tone with acid, but at least he'd kept from exploding.

He couldn't take this. Not from her. How did she not see? She didn't need some big title win or success. She had them. Her family. She had her home and fighting and a life. A beautiful, wonderful life.

An ache spread in his fingertips. He released the clenched fist. "There're consequences to your actions, Rosca. No matter the root. You put Jack in danger. He's twelve, and you had him hauling your bags and dealing with smugglers. You made him an accomplice and put him in harm's way."

Fire darted in the fox-like face. "I didn't tell him mescucha! He found out and inserted himself into my plan. It's who he is. For someone who talks a lot about family, you don't even know how those closest to you work or think. You could sooner hide a bloody bird from a bloodhound than keep Jack from a secret."

Towering over his sister, he lowered his voice. "You're being selfish, Rosca. Selfish and prideful."

Stubbornness gripped her features. "So are you. We all must grow up sometime. I just wanted to be active in deciding my fate. You know what the debna planned for me, and Deb Rez gave in years ago. If I hadn't fought for more freedom, I would've been locked down by some wealthy, stuck-up man at sixteen and never...never..." She faltered.

"Never what, Rosca?" He smirked as she stepped back, and her confidence faded to shame. He cackled like a crazed man. "You wanted to be *her*, didn't you?"

She flinched at the long-avoided reference.

"Of course you did." He looked at her as though seeing her for the first time. "You always have."

A season best buried, yet somehow always resurfacing. She that pirate. "I'll bet you didn't even have a plan, did you? You just wanted to travel. To go on an adventure, is that it? Well, let me tell you, little sis, the world isn't like your books. You'd be dead within a month on your own."

"I had a plan." Her voice screeched in his ears like metal on metal. "Besides, so what if I fail? That's my business, not yours."

"Your dreams are bigger than you are, Rosca. One day they'll get you killed."

"Better that than never pursue them. To sit in false comfort all my life never knowing what I could have seen or who I could have been."

"Is that what we are? False comfort?" Too angry to continue, he spun his elbow into the bag, and she flinched. Disgust curled his lips into a snarl. He gestured towards their home. "They'll be waiting for us. Hurry up."

Chapter Fifteen
The Ball

The family portrait hung high in the ballroom, so it drew the gaze of each visitor as they entered. Stationed on the balcony, Deb Rez caught the squeals of admiration and gasps as the guests flooded in and caught sight of the fifteen-foot masterpiece. A boy, one of the many fighters he'd trained, waved and pumped a fist from below. Rez nodded in acknowledgement. Letting his thin grin grow, he waved. At his side, Debna Le echoed the motion.

For the first time in a while, he was happy. The dim thought grew with the lightness in his chest.

He released a pent-up breath, tension squeezing out of his traps, head, and neck. His mind cleared. It had taken the better part of a lifetime, but the Banli islanders accepted him as their own. He'd moved past "the Valsquelian that fought his way to the top" to a familiar face. A man of the community. A deb. A father. Twisting to look over his shoulder, he studied the painting.

In the back, he and his wife appeared perfect specimens of success and beauty, respectively. In front, primped and accessorized, stood their six children. Pride coursed through him as his attention fell on the oldest. The twenty-one-year-old Silohski, nicknamed Ski, placed a protective hand on his sister. His lean body held plenty of muscle, like all of the Ishels. One of the benefits of raising fighters. Rez smiled to himself and sipped the Nilealian ale. The spice and warmth pooled in his chest. He had raised a good family. It was one he would have given anything to be a part of in his younger years. One that he did give everything to create.

Yet it wasn't enough for Rosca. Drowning his drink, he turned and leaned against the rail overlooking the ballroom floor. Below the marble balcony where he and Le stood, young and old women twirled around, dressed in gowns bulging with froufrou. Rowdy men led them through the skips and jumps of a dance like frisky puppies. Even Jack, he saw, had found a silky-haired young girl to suffer through his jolting renditions of the fun.

He stopped when he found his daughter. She spun in the midst of it all, her maroon dress flowing out like a blooming rose. Her partner, a tall, energetic Banli Boxer, watched her with an eagerness that made Rez dig his nails into the wood railing. Her beauty and status made her an attractive conquest, but he didn't have to like it. Beauty and title would do her more harm than good in the rest of the world. Yet, according to Le, they were all that saved a woman here.

But she wasn't built for here. *Maschiach,* he prayed, *show me how to prepare her for what's out there.* They had their own world on the island, with dangers you could laugh at and people you could trust. She didn't know true evil. She couldn't imagine.

The scene blurred before him. Rosca's long braids, decorated with golden clasps and jewels, fluttered like those of another he had known. His daughter's visage shimmered and vanished. Another girl took the space in his thoughts. He took a deep breath, sucked into memories he had sworn to never think of again. "Renelia." The Valsquelian pet name rolled off his tongue like honey.

His wife started. Her knowing, sorrowful expression reeled him back to reality. She tried to reach for his hand, but he pretended not to notice. He would not be pitied. Not tonight when they should feast and rejoice. With a huff, she retreated down the stairs to the dance floor.

Undammed, the flood of the past rushed in, drowning the present. Panic crept upon him. The memory took flesh. He and his older brother scoured the earth for their young sister. Their cries for "Renelia" echoed fruitlessly among the Valsquelian woodlands for three days. Finally, they found her curled up and starving in a field of wilting dandelions. The harsh, icy days of Dascansi were coming. The freeze would've killed her.

Phantom arms encircled him in a bear hug as a young girl thanked him for saving her. He'd promised then, if anything happened, he would be there. He would rescue her. He would protect her.

How wrong he had been.

Two years later, a neighbor found her shoes and cloak near the Achelois Ocean. Renelia had vanished. They searched for months for a body or sign of foul play, but she'd either drowned or flown away. Lured, he imagined, by her love for adventure, she'd fallen prey to the unforgiving sea. The water had taken her without apology and without farewell. At least, that was what the city's officials told them. It was no wonder Rosca was dissatisfied. She had her aunt's blood in her.

He watched his spinning rose below, surrounded by admirers and lauders. She was a boar in a glass castle here. She wouldn't stop till she got herself killed. Or someone else.

He swallowed his pain, wishing his wife had stayed close by.

***

Rosca excused herself from her clingy partner, feigning an ache in her calf. The boy offered to accompany her anyway, and she quickly paired him with a passing debna girl for the next dance. Satisfied he wouldn't follow, she slipped out of the ballroom, and into the parlor. A smaller ring of dancers filled the room, but card and drink tables lined the walls.

Gawking up, Rosca lost herself between the gold-gilded arches mapping out the wide ceiling. Images of the sea at different seasons covered the spaces between the beams, sometimes curling strokes of frothy white, other times cutting lines of emerald, and, most enchanting, royal blue so blended with pearl that it sparkled and shone like an aquamarine galaxy. Painted nama branches spread out from the walls, slithering over the multicolored images like snakes. Twisted in their grasp were vines, vegetation, and flowers. Silver lesp trees contrasted the rich red of the nama branches, and the colors of the sea. Her head spun from staring up, but she took a step forward as though she could fly into the beautiful images. Her mother's voice cut into her reverie. "Debna Rosquevalarian!"

With a gasp, Rosca ducked behind a servant. Shel it. Tonight was not the night for debna games and gossip. She would not be dragged into a circle of gawking, chittering women during what may be her last ball for many years.

"Rosquevalarian!" Sizzling anger seeped into the call.

Rosca hunched lower.

Fading, the sound soon became masked by the music and stomping feet. Mercifully, the dancers circled in front of her, and she snuck into a lounge adjoining the ballroom. Several Banli soldiers sat around the fire, playing cards and joking. Raucous and egged on by drinks, the group taunted each other.

As she entered the room, she glanced back to make sure the debna did not see her and muttered to herself in Ikuela. "Mifu kique shelnigias."

A playful shove drew her attention to the present. "Only you could find something to complain about at a ball, Rosca. Don't you ever have fun?" The handsome boy slouched carelessly, but his eyes, slanted with hard-lined and nearly lash-less lids, avidly watched her reaction.

Her heart skipped like a child's. "Saniz!" Rosca hugged the boy, then stepped back. Just a year ago, they'd been studying their lessons and broadboarding together. Then he dropped out and became a soldier.

She examined him, blissfully aware of the way his clothes pulled tight over his chest and shoulders. He'd grown. A lot. Always on the scrawny side, he'd never painted an impressive picture before. But now... well, he certainly could hold his head higher. She hoped he'd attributed her heated cheeks to the stuffy room, but the way his mouth twitched said he hadn't missed her reaction. She rubbed her arms, chilled though no drafts cooled the room. "They kick you out of N.A.F. yet?"

Saniz led her closer to the fire, his matured face shimmering with silver mirth. "They were going to, but then they found out I was friends with Deb Rez's daughter. So they just put me on kitchen duty instead."

"Like I'd let you within ten yards of anything I eat." Another soldier, clearly one with higher rank, sipped at a flask and stood to let Rosca sit. "I'm Captain Reko. Nice to meet you." He paused and examined her. "Debna? You look as beautiful as your picture."

"Thank you." She glossed her smile with delight, the way her mother taught her. She took the offered armchair, its plush red surface pulling her into sudden comfort. "Just Rosca is fine. Nice to meet you. You know, I've seen Saniz cook. He can grill like nobody would expect." Rosca struggled to maintain a masked expression.

"Really?" The man cocked his head.

"Really?" Saniz furrowed his brow.

"Yeah, remember when you caught your hand on fire at your brother's wedding? No one expected that."

The older soldier howled with laughter and a drop of ale spilled from his flask onto Rosca's dress. "That's where you got those burns? I knew something was up with that saved a child from a fire mescucha. Err, lies. Pardon my tongue, Debna."

She giggled. "No matter."

Saniz cracked his knuckles. "We should show Rosca the game we invented."

Reko shook his head. "Have some class, Saniz. She's a debna."

Intent on drying the wet spot on her clothes with a handkerchief, Rosca jerked her head up and tried to guess at Saniz's intentions.

Amidst the protests from the other soldiers, Saniz spoke louder "She's a boxer. She's used to this sort of stuff."

That shut them up. Indignation clouded Rosca's brow. Boxer or no, she was still a woman. What exactly were they planning? The allure of the challenge stayed her impulse to march away.

"Well," Reko drew out his sword. "The game is to chug an ale, spin three times, and charge. First one to disarm the other wins." He grew stern. "You're just trying to disarm."

Rosca gaped at Saniz. He knew sword fighting and her went together like boars and bathwater. Even Jack and Mar could beat her now.

Reko prepared the weapons. "Don't worry. We got wooden tips to put on the end of the swords, so you don't kill each other."

She rolled her eyes. "Lovely." She only had a whole blade to stay wary of.

"You don't have to do it." Saniz spoke in a chivalrous tone, as though he hadn't trapped her out of spite for revealing his secret.

He may have had a new body, but the same old cockiness strutted in the shadow of his grin. All brawn, no brain. And no idea about how to treat a lady.

Her heart sank. If he saw her as a lady.

"Don't worry, Saniz. I'll try not to hurt you." She grabbed a sword from Reko, and the soldiers cleared a space for the two. The crowd quieted. She took a deep breath to steady her pounding pulse.

They faced each other. She wrapped her hand around the hilt. Its solidity comforted her. Gallant images flashed in her imagination, and she blocked them behind a mental wall. She had to focus.

Shaking hands, they took a few paces back. Eyes locked as their companions handed them each an ale. Downing them, they did their spins. To her chagrin, Saniz finished first. More had changed about him than his size. A year ago, she would have bested him out of sheer confidence, but now he sped through the movements, sure of his skill. He shot forward.

Her blade reacted of its own accord, and their swords clashed. Grinding metal rang in her ears. A shock of pain hit her bones at the force he applied. Her sword fell to the ground. She cursed under her breath in Ikuela.

"Again!" Her booming voice startled her. She burped. A few men laughed and heat coursed her neck and cheeks.

"Rosquevalarian!" Her mother's tone made her view of the soldiers melt away like ice. "Come here. Now."

Cheeks burning, Rosca returned the sword, unable to look Saniz in the eye. She followed her mother out of the room. "Why'd you have to embarrass me like that?"

"Me the embarrassment?" Her mother snorted in that dignified, perturbed way she had. Whiffing, the debna pulled up short. "Were you drinking?"

"No." Rosca ducked away, but her mother gripped her arm and pulled her back as though handling a young child.

"Debna Remalu was asking for you." Her mother dragged her through the crowd. "It's very important—"

"I know. Women are not like men." Rosca gestured in cheap imitation of her mother. "They watch your clothes, posture, tone, and you can't impress them with fighting. You have to use tact, diplomacy, grace… You give the same speech every time but fail to remember that it's been eighteen years, and I still don't have tact, diplomacy, or grace."

The debna released Rosca and gave some staring couples a sweeping curtsy. Rosca copied the motion, and the two hurried on across the ballroom. She all but loped to keep pace with the older woman.

Soon, the sheen of polished white and gray swirled above them in the chiseled lilt-stone. Impressed in the crown molding were images of women in gowns and capes of flowering splendor, their cupped hands holding suns, children, and stars. Beside almost every woman pranced a mare, a Nilealian sign of nobility. A thrill climbed Rosca's spine, and she wondered how the legends of the noble debnas could so contrast the women she knew to carry the title.

"You know, Rosca," her mother whispered in a reconciling tone, "Debna Remalu never stops raving about your beauty or charm. Even she admits you have quite a talent for diplomacy. When you choose to use it."

Rosca barely caught the repulsion from slithering onto her features. Diplomacy? Another word for people-pleasing.

Her mother swelled as she saw the women at the end of the parlor. They huddled around in silk tarped armchairs, rose pink and set on ivory legs.

Rosca puffed her breast to the sky and braced herself. "Debna Remalu will say anything to get on yours and Father's good side."

Her mother surprised her by stopping to study a wall tapestry they'd both seen a hundred times. "How is you judging her any better than her judging you?"

Rosca observed the image. It stretched from under a stair-cased crown mold to the mahogany floors. The weathered, wise gaze of a white-haired woman stared down at them from within the silver tasseled borders. She turned to her mother. "Because I don't ask her to impress me."

"No." Her mother's stare froze like the first chill on a virgin sapling. "You don't give them a chance."

"Karol cried because her mother wouldn't let her buy a dress last tempa. A dress! She's a grown girl crying over clothes."

"Karol is also extremely smart." Her mother pushed her flyaway hairs back into place. "She finished her studies two years early to help with her mother's embroidering. You know how much concentration that takes? Not to mention she helps take care of poor widow Lastije's children. You can't live your whole life avoiding people you don't like, Rosca. It's selfish and weak. You shouldn't let people make you bitter. Why do you think these women respect our family so much? Because they know they can trust us. We stay ourselves, and we don't sit there grumbling and whining about other people."

Rosca guffawed. Ourselves? "And here I thought they liked us cause Father's a powerful deb."

Storm clouds brewed in the debna's expression. "There are many debs, Rosca."

Rosca tilted her head, willing her mother to see the obvious. "But not many chief debs."

Her mother's grip on her arm turned vicelike. "This isn't about debs. This is about debnas."

"I'm not sure I want a part of that."

Hurt tightened her mother's features. "They're waiting."

They maneuvered around a circular mahogany table so fast Rosca bumped into its side and sent a swan shaped ivory statue tumbling. She caught it and gave the watching debnas a practiced smile. After replacing it, she curtsied and greeted the women. "Evening debnas."

"Evening, Debna Le. Debna Rosca."

Rosca felt her smile become genuine when she saw Janel, a debna her own age and of some similar mindset. They exchanged the knowing glance of shared sufferers.

There were three other debnas besides Rosca, Janel, and Le. A handsome grandmother named Debna Remalu and her granddaughter Karol. Both had full, cinched figures with masses of glossy chestnut hair as wavy as the sea and thin, elegant eyes which men swooned for.

The third debna, an unattractive woman named Thelrose, lived a demure, quiet life in her old age. The only times Rosca had seen her look alive were in in the middle of heated political conversations. A flush in the woman's cheeks told her that this was the topic now.

"They raided West Salme last tempa." Thelrose practically skipped on her aged legs.

Discomfort slithered down Rosca's spine. She shifted.

"Well, then let's hope they do not come here." Debna Remalu dabbed a tissue to her nose and sniffled.

"Who?" Rosca leaned forward, expectant.

"Pirates." Janel stiffened. "They killed ten people and stole months' of supplies from the seaports on West Salme."

Rosca's heart leaped to her throat, and she masked her reaction under one of those diplomatic expressions Debna Remalu admired. Pirates hadn't attacked the Speckled Region since her father order the N.A.F. to kill them on sight. Ray alone had dared to cross that line. But she was far away in Kenst. Her letter had said as much. As few as she sent, there would be no reason to lie now, right? She would have just not written. Like she had the first year after her disappearance. Rosca feigned a yawn. "Well, we don't have any reason to suspect trouble, right? They wouldn't dare attack. There's enough men at this ball alone to fend them off."

Debna Thelrose opened her mouth to answer, but Debna Remalu cut in, cooing, "Rosca, I was searching everywhere for you. It's been so long since I've seen you. Where have you been hiding all night?"

"With Saniz and the soldiers." She sprinkled mischief into her laughter. Let the woman think her a flirt. It'd probably be a relief to have something they could relate on.

"Oh. I see you haven't changed." The woman did not hide her disapproval. Not that Banli women ever did. "You better let her free, Le. We all know Rosca would rather be with the men than us boring, chittering women."

Rosca chewed a scab on her bottom lip. Guess the debna understood more than she realized.

"Nonsense." Le directed a sharp look at the old lady. "Rosca knows her place like all the young debnas."

"Certainly." Debna Remalu raised a hand to fiddle with her necklace, and the bangles on her arm clattered like a dinner bell.

"Rosca doesn't have a place." Karol pulled a strand of rich, smooth hair between her fingers, twisting it. "Before you know it, she'll be off again. Rubbing elbows with sailors and taking hits like a caned dog."

Rosca glared at the smug-faced beauty. They were just words, but they stung.

Debna Remalu clucked in agreement. "Well, we will not judge you too harshly, Rosca. You're young. It is the way of the young to be free and not heed the wisdom of their elders."

"I strive to heed all that is called wisdom." Hands shaking, Rosca resisted the urge to get in the woman's face. "But perhaps not all tradition is wisdom."

"And perhaps restless children should not be given their way so often." This time the woman looked pointedly at Le. "They may spend their time trying to fix what is not broken."

Anger boiled in Rosca's chest. She grinded her back teeth and released a saccharine smile. It was bait. A trap. A test. *Don't react. Don't react.* "My mother raised me impeccably. She allowed me to have a mind and will of my own." Rosca tried to bite her tongue, but the words spilled out. "To be something more than just a pawn in life."

The woman did nothing to alter her taunting features or acknowledge her offensive words to Debna Le.

Fresh fury clenched every muscle in Rosca's body. "I wouldn't trade my mother's teachings for thousands of the counsel you've filled Karol's brain with." Debna Le was going to kill her. Great.

"Rosquevalarian, that is enough!" Her mother's dark expression crackled, like a full storm cloud, ready to pound the earth and all that lay within. Trembling, she steadied her voice. "Debna Remalu is a wise woman and perhaps I was a little too easy on you at times. You certainly would benefit from learning to hold your tongue like Karol."

A wild ache filled Rosca's heart, as though one of the suction pads of a giant sea beast stuck to her breast. Tears that had leaked all day threatened to flood. She lifted her chin, stiff as a nama tree. She would not cry in front of these vultures. "Karol has no tongue to hold. That requires wit and a mind of her own."

"Those are two things any criminal may have." Le glared at her daughter, face drained and pale with shock. "Not so with servitude and patience."

Recklessness convulsed Rosca's mind. She ran a hand down her face, squeezing her temples. A cross between a cry and a cackle escaped her. The pause allowed a moment for her thoughts to settle, and she viewed the women earnestly, wishing she had the words to explain. "It is not virtue if you have never had the urge for selfishness or impatience. I will not praise a girl too scared to live life!"

Silence enveloped the group. Rosca counted down. When no one offered a response, she gawked. For all their pretentiousness, they wouldn't address a direct attack. For all their show of power, they shifted, weak and unsure.

Finally, Debna Remalu managed a weak smile that went no farther than a curve of her plump lips. "We do not doubt you are full of urges, Rosque. Some just are."

Rosca seethed, but Karol's pink cheeks caught her attention. She hadn't meant to put the girl in between herself and the grandmother's crossfire. Even if the girl was a snippy minsk-head. Guilt muddied her vexation, and she gave a curt curtsy. "Good night, Debna Remalu. Debnas."

The women didn't protest, but Rosca found satisfaction in the tight lipped, aghast faces as she left. She held her head as high as she might, every ounce of her pride chiseled into the erect neck. Digging into the hope she'd felt hours earlier, Rosca put an image of the SOE in her head. She would be gone soon.

Dancers thronged around her as she marched away. Debna Remalu's implications burned holes in her spirit. Selfish. Untraditional. She shook her head in silent protest. But hadn't Di and Mother said the same? Consensus won elections. Maybe. Or maybe her dreams were too big for others' eyes.

Frustration shortened her pace, each step hammering the floor. She turned too sharp and bumped into Adnesi. Taking one look at her, he raised his brows. "What's wrong?"

She hesitated. A surge of emotions crushed her throat. "Debna drama. It's not important."

Forced to the side of the ballroom by a bustling server and a line of frolicking dancers, he waited for her to join him. "Rosc, you'd tell me if it was, right?"

His gentle tone surprised her. Dium or Jack must have told him what happened. Why wasn't he mad?

She peered about for a chair to sink into, but excited, cheerful crowds covered every inch of free space. "How would I know if it is? Just about everything pisses me off these days. Doesn't have to be important." She bit her lip. "I'm sorry. I shouldn't complain so much."

The muscles around his mouth tightened as though in annoyance, but Rosca knew him well enough to read confusion, not irritation.

She rubbed her hands together vigorously. "I just mean," she stopped short. She hardly knew what she meant. Her emotions spiked erratically. Every thought seemed to suspend in midair, waiting for her to command a cease-fire before they dared return to ground. An urge to be done with everything and everyone arrested her. The night couldn't get any worse. May as well slay all her dragons at once. "You know where the rest of our family is?"

"You mean Mother and Father?"

"No. Di, Ski, and the boys."

"No."

"Well, find them. I need to tell you all something. In the kitchen."

"What is it?"

"You'll find out in the kitchen."

"Okay." He froze for a moment, examining her one last time then disappeared into the crowd.

She wished her brothers would stop looking at her like that. Like she was some new sea creature to be examined and not the sister they'd helped raise.

It took a while to collect all five of them, but finally they crowded into the hot, stone-walled kitchen storeroom. Glass lanterns, hanging on hooks from the ceiling, lit each face with an eerie glow. They might have stayed in the kitchen if the cooks hadn't shooed them out with wooden paddles and iron cooking rods.

The storeroom's tall, long walls held racks of bagged flour, crumbling vines with vegetables still attached, and spices that made Dium sneeze in Rosca's face. She wiped the spittle off in disgust. "It won't take long." She turned to close the door.

As they gathered around, she took a deep breath. It wasn't too late to bow out. Give up the SOE and stay with them forever. But she'd go mad.

Jack and Mar, the babies of the family, worked together to shift around several flour bags. One fell to the floor, and a white cloud burst in the room.

"What are you two doing?" Ski blinked comically in the white dust, and his flour covered brows drew together like two wrestling garden grubs.

"Sorry." Atop Jack's shoulders, Mar reached to the back of a shelf and produced a full platter of du-ca cakes. The crispy, golden rectangles puffed, gooey dough filling the fried crust. A sprinkling of powdered sugar and thick lines of melted chocolate decorated each one. The siblings ignored Rosca's cry for attention as all hands grasped at the platter.

"Calm down," Jack yelled as Adnesi's long arm swiped two cakes while Dium pulled at Jack's elbow. "There's enough for all you bottomless pits. We hid two more platters."

A celebratory cry went up. As a favorite treat of almost all Nilealians, the cooks tripled the required party amount. Yet, somehow, they were always the first to disappear from the dessert table. As the group munched, Rosca addressed them. "I'm leaving to study at the Valsquel SOE."

Except for the steady munching of the two youngest, the room hushed.

"You're leaving us?" Mar's boyish pout ballooned his stuffed cheeks.

Beside him, Jack paused licking his fingers to stare in disbelief.

Rosca tried to gulp, her throat dry as a crisped fish. They would be grown by the time she graduated. She'd miss all those years… A whimper escaped. Why did becoming independent have to mean leaving the ones you love? "I'll be back every sunstruck for the 4 month break." Praying they'd forgive her, she sunk onto a sideways barrel of ale, exhausted. "It's only a few days by ship. You can come visit."

Adnesi broke the spell by spreading his arms. "I'm proud of you, Rosc." She rose, and he enveloped her in a hug that threatened to introduce her ribs to her spine. "You're finally getting your dream to travel."

Gratitude soared through her, slicing off the weight on her shoulders. "Thanks, Adnesi." She dropped out of his embrace.

"I always said you were the smart one."

Tensing, she spun to scan her only blood brother in the dim lighting. Ski, with his broad, lean shoulders and bushy hair, relied on her. Counted on her steadiness when life had given them none. Since entering the Deb's care, they'd been a team. Always there for the other. And now, she would leave him.

He pulled her into a hug. She grabbed his arm, hanging on a little longer so she could master the tears threatening to spill. "I'm sorry," she whispered.

"Don't be." He kissed the top of her head. The tears won out, drizzling down and off her chin. When he pulled back, sorrow tainted his look. Regret? As though her leaving was somehow his fault? No. She couldn't comprehend the look.

"Mother and Father are going to kill us if we don't get out there." Dium's stoic features did not lessen, but he nodded when she looked his way.

She smiled through her tears. He would come around. They still loved her. They cared.

"Shut up, Di. This is more important." Jack asserted his youthful authority with a puff of his small chest.

Rosca laughed. "We're already on Father's bad side, Jack. Do we really want to dig that hole deeper?"

"Fair 'nuff."

They filed out, Rosca and Dium last in line. A hand gripped her arm and yanked her back.

"Come on." Dium gestured for her to follow him. "I want to show you something."

Rosca glanced to the ballroom, torn between curiosity and fear. "What about Father? Isn't he pissed enough at me?"

"He won't even notice we're gone. After all, he's got enough kids to watch."

"Fine. Let's go. It's not like I wanted to live to old age anyway."

"Not like you were going to with all the dumb mescucha you pull."

"Fair 'nuff."

Chapter Sixteen
Anchored

Fuerzalin "Lin" drew a breath deep enough to suck some freshness out of the fish-laden air, but not enough to cure his curdled stomach or throbbing lip. With a yawn, he slapped his bare feet onto the worn boards and forced himself off the cot. Scattered maps, journals, and books made walking nearly impossible, and, for the hundredth time, he cursed himself for losing his desk to an ill-fated hand of cards. As if saving for a new home wasn't bad enough. How was he supposed to furnish it for three people? A molten ache filled the crevices of his heart.

Shaking off the self-pity, he ran his hand over his head, and the short hair scraped his calloused palm. "As it is." Shrugging, he yawned. He would figure it out. He always did. "At least they couldn't take the shelves." He plucked his shirt from the almost-square niche of a log he had hollowed out and bolted to the wall. Two more "bookcases", a wash basin, and his untidy cot completed the furnishings of the room. A tiny amount of money, earned from winning his morning fight, sat on the shelf, mocking him. Months of training for as much as he could swipe in ten minutes. He gritted his teeth. The straight and narrow was set on crushing him, wasn't it?

The more he won, the prize money would grow. If it didn't, he'd have to sell the ship. He'd rather sell his foot. You could still sail on one foot.

But his family couldn't wait forever. Assuming they were still alive, he would need a place to put them once he brought them back.

After pulling on his shirt, he splashed stale water from a metal bucket on his face and ate some besemini leaves picked earlier that day. Icy hot spikes swelled in his mouth, and he spit it out. "Blegh. Good for the breath, bad for the buds." He marched out onto the open deck.

As he double-checked his ship's anchoring, he rubbed his tongue with his finger, trying to rid it of the strange sensation. Everything proved satisfactory, but he hesitated and looked about. The small rikkey ship proved a comfortable home for a single man. For over a year, he had lived anchored at Nileal's back door. Yet his stomach twisted every time he had to leave her unattended. Especially at night.

"I'll be back, girl," he promised the mass of wood, rope, and sails, dimly lit by moonlight.

An impatient whinny sounded from below. Falia, his sesaquill, must have caught his voice. "Women." He rolled his eyes. "Always jealous. Won't even let me say goodbye without a protest."

Lithe as a squirrel, he slipped over the side of the ship and plunged into the teeth-chattering water. Falia, the half-horse, half-fish beast of beauty, neighed in greeting and pulled at the rope fastening her to the ship.

"Falia," he patted the beast's velvet neck. "You're gonna have to learn to sit still. If I'm gonna be a good boy, you can be a good girl."

In the moonlight, her amethyst pupils dilated, and she threw back her ears as though she didn't like that idea at all.

"I know, I know!" He threw up his hands, treading water with his legs. "You're a Pagne girl. Maschiach knows you lot can't be tamed, but work with me, please? If we win this race, I'll buy you sweet cod. I know you love the tentacles." He wiggled his brows as if she could understand his human gibberish or even see him in the dark.

She snorted, sending ripples in the waves. Maybe she did get part. He cocked a brow at himself. He needed to find some human friends to talk to, before he truly went insane. But he preferred solitude. Only in moments like these did it feel strange.

"You know, for a Pagne girl you ain't very appreciative of bribery." He untied Falia and climbed onto her back. "I won my fight this mornin' and winnin' a race right after would make a shel good day, okay? So work with me." With a click and pressing of the knees, he nudged her to swim parallel to the coast.

Slouched backwards, he could see the millions of white lights decorating the sky, with Fat Man Moon thrusting his belly into the midst of the scene. Shel. Hadn't he told Dium he'd be there before sunset? At this pace, he'd be another half hour. But any faster and Falia would have to race tired.

He grimaced. "I just had to take a nap, didn't I?"

Not that Di would mind if he was late when he'd done his part of the set-up already. Still, he'd given his word, so he ought to keep it. Squeezing his legs, he leaned over Falia's neck. A beautiful face floated in his imagination. Di's sister seemed the type to appreciate a man who kept his word.

Her plump lips curved around his mind. The abundance of soft, black hair that framed her fox-like profile shoved out every other thought, as did the confidence with which she entered a room. It didn't matter what room, she walked like she belonged.

Dipping and rising, Falia's steady rhythm soothed the ache in his chest. The waves blurred past, spraying him with icy-cold drops.

An ethereal beauty soaked the night air, and he drank it in. Fresh wind washed over his face. Above, stars danced and laughed. Silver moonbeams highlighted the froth tipped waves as they curled and crashed into the inky sea. It was a perfect night to see a beautiful girl. To go from admirer to friend.

Her presence could convince Alarog himself to fight for beauty. When she spoke, she did so with conviction. Eager with hope and excitement for life, her earnest voice reminded him of the older legends of the hebl-jirdens, who believed singing to flowers made them grow faster. She inspired people to fight and love. She embodied the noble ideals she ranted on. Virtues like tenacity, honesty, and compassion. Not the most practical or pragmatic view for dealing with the outside world. He certainly could never make use of 'em, but she made a pretty show of each.

Slowing the sesaquill, he shook his head. "Fredge was right. Women are my weakness. I got one goal, and nothin' to give anyone before that. Least of all a debna like her."

Falia whinnied, and he decided to keep these thoughts to himself. Maschiach knew how'd she'd pitch and roll if she caught wind of even more competition.

But he risked one more sound, just to practice forcing its odd shape around his unaccustomed, foreign tongue. "Roskavaleen. Rosqu... Rose. I see why people say Rosca."

Chapter Seventeen
The Party

"If Father finds out about this…" Rosca dismounted her horse and slipped off his bridle so he could graze. Torches lined the inside of the parallel city walls, illuminating the manicured trees, flowers, and vines. Planted between the two borders of gray brick, a garden encircled Nileal.

The pure black gelding dropped his head, plucking at the grass as though she starved him. She rubbed her pet's neck with affection. "We'll be back soon. Enjoy getting fat. Well, fatter."

Dium tugged at Rosca's arm. "You act like you'll never see them again."

"You never know." She shrugged. "Life can change in an instant." Not that it ever did.

Dium stopped at Nileal's entrance to talk to the guards. Their father had forbidden leaving horses in the garden, but the guards would see to it the creatures did no damage. Dium slipped a few coins in their hands and hurried off.

Rosca ran to catch up with him. He didn't slow, and they jogged on without a word. From their path, Rosca guessed they headed for Slipknot's beach. A quiet stretch where Ieculians youths often met for parties or sesaquill races. A tradition started by Hela and the Ishels.

With each stride, a rock formed in Rosca's stomach. "Look, I saw that stupid gleam in your eye you always get when you have some horrid scheme up your sleeve, and I'm already in enough hot water with Father so I'm not taking any of the blame if we get caug—"

"Do you ever stop talking?" The moonlight made his silhouette just visible in front as he pushed on. Rocks and overgrowth as well as steep hills cluttered their way.

"Oh, come on, Dium. You should know me better. 'Course I don't. Why did this have to happen the night of Father's party?"

He pulled up short and ran a hand through his curls. "You're not going to shut up, are you?"

She crossed her arms.

"Okay. What we're doing isn't exactly... legal, and I needed the cover of Father's party to distract everyone."

Definitely sesaquill race. "Why didn't you tell me...?"

"We all have our secrets." He threw up his hands defensively. "I didn't want to distract you. You seemed busy. 'Course, I didn't realize you were planning on running away." An edge crept into his voice.

Since she couldn't think of anything to say that didn't involve sarcasm, she opted for silence.

They made their way through tropical trees and brush. Grass and sticks morphed to soft sand, still warm from the day's hot sun.

"We're here." Dium grinned and made a sweeping gesture.

"'Bout time." Rosca growled. In her hand hung her heels, her braids fell heavy and hot, and sweat stained her new dress. "Woah." Looking out on the scene, she took in a gulp of night air, letting the breeze wash over her.

Wooden chairs covered the beach, and a sequence of five roasting bonfires lined the twinkling waves. A plethora of stars and nebula clustered in the sky like a cloudy spill of interstellar dust and gas interrupted by pinpricks of light. A wave of recklessness and thrill filled the air alongside the smoke blown about by the sea breeze. The beat of a skilled drummer, the chant-like rumble of singers bursting with energy and sounds of other musicians grew in volume as they approached the middle of the party. Not far from the small band and spectators, a cluster of youths surrounded two arguing men.

Dium approached the throng. "What's going on?"

As though rehearsed, the kids fell silent. The two apparent instigators laid the problem before him.

"We messed up, Dium." A man stuck out his chest, clearly pleased with the attention.

Rosca tried to keep from rolling her eyes. She'd accepted the strange, worship-like reverence the islanders rendered her father, but Dium? He was a loudmouth. And stubborn enough to call the sea orange.

"I don't look into minds, Rollins. Especially not yours." Dium crossed his arms and tightened his lips into a straight line, surprising Rosca. Not his bluntness, but the authoritative gaze he gave the man. He appeared, someone other than her might say, like a leader.

"We agreed on tonight for the sesaquill races—"

The crowd murmured and Dium turned about, giving each a glower. They quieted.

Rollins voice took on a faux command that squeaked at the end. "But it's too dangerous. Coquerielle's Current is here. We must tell someone, or we'll starve. Sunstruck's ending, and supplies are scarce."

Rosca chewed the inside of her cheek to keep from a snarky comment. It was the middle of the Sunstruck season, and supplies were not scarce. Rollins' constant attempts to use drama to claim second in command to Dium sickened her as much as Debna Remalu's sweet talking her parents.

Her disgust melted as the man's claim hit her. Coquerielle's Current? Last time that appeared, Dium had accused Ray of inviting it. Like she was a witch. Rosca curled her lips. He was wrong, of course, and time had proven it. All sign of the water shadow, as the fishermen called it, had vanished soon after Ray. But, when the damning, dark suction pad returned, Ray had long been gone. It had swallowed their best barques just before the season of Dascansi, leaving the island low on food and supplies. It'd been helski and chaos, but Ray had been nowhere near.

The man formerly arguing with Rollins jumped in, voicing her own skepticism. "Rollins, if you didn't make a career of lookin' for problems, we might believe you. But sunstruck just started and supplies ain't low."

Rosca glanced at him, then jerked her gaze back when he smirked. She recognized him as Lin. Though she didn't know him well enough to truly dislike him, he'd made a reputation for himself as a fast-tempered know-it-all. Continuing to stare at her, he seemed intent on grabbing her attention, even mid-argument.

Cheeks burning, she scowled. Men.

"I'm telling you!" Rollins short-lived bravo shrunk into a whine that even Mar had outgrown. "This is what happened last time. History is repeating itself."

Rosca rolled her eyes, but fear wound her heart in nets and her chest ached. If he was right, no one would laugh. Too many of them still remembered the hopeless hunger and bone chilling cold that had gripped the island that Dascansi. The unparalleled strength of the current had sucked down their biggest ships, yet, like an indecisive woman, it would leave some entirely free to pass by. It had a mind of its own. Maybe that was why Dium believed it witchcraft. That and the giant black shadow which filled the water wherever it took up station.

Lin shook his head. "Give us proof, not theories, Rollins. Why do you say the current's here?" Apparently enjoying the small squabble, his wolf-like face held a ready, wide grin that looked as sturdy as the rest of him. His whiskey-colored eyes flickered under full lashes. The blazing bonfire lightened his bare shoulders to bronze, highlighting pale scars and the defined abdomen of his athletic body. As though recently shaved, his black hair grew close to the scalp. When he looked up, her stomach clenched.

She was staring. She tried to focus on anything else. It was his fault. He'd noticed her first.

Rollins spun around as though to convince the crowd. "Three of Iecula's top trade ships are missing. All three were on different trade routes, coming in at different times and different ports. None of them have returned. There's no practical explanation for all three to miss their deadline."

"Trade ships are late a lot." Rosca huffed, thinking of her time at the Sailor's Solace. Among weather patterns, star mapping, trade routes, and other nautical topics, the sailors spent their days crying over extended voyages, complaining about the unpredictability of the sea.

"Two of these ships were Mmelarium and Raspit. They're our top trade ships, you know why? Because of their punctuality! Besides, I investigated and I... I saw it."

Rosca scratched the back of her hand, unease tickling the corners of her mind.

"What do you mean you 'saw it'?" Dium broke in, his brows furrowing.

"And why haven't you told anyone else?" Rosca spread her hands in an exasperated motion.

At a look from Dium, she lowered them.

"I needed to stop you all first. From getting in that water." He seemed sincere and full of urgency. "I climbed Mount Peskill just before sunset to see the current. They say wherever it is, there's a large dark shadow in the water. And it was there. Right on this beach. I'm sure I saw it. Well, I think I saw it."

"You think?" Anger poked holes in Dium's steady tone. "This is bigger than you think, Rollins. Anything could have made those ships late and, no offense, but you have some of the worst eyesight known."

Rosca raised a brow. Ironic but true. Rollins did have a tendency for running into things right in front of him. He'd even complained of a reading problem.

"I got a simple way to solve this." Lin crossed his burly arms. "Let's just go."

His mischievous tone reminded Rosca of Jack, but his voice held a deep richness which twisted her stomach into a burdensome bundle of nerves.

Frowning, she tried to remember the exact gossip concerning him. *Other than being a bit rough around the edges,* Ski had informed her, *he's one of the best fighters talent-wise. But he hasn't trained long enough to beat anyone of significance.*

He's a strange man. He won't last in fighting, Deb Sergio had argued. *You can spit in his face, and he'll just wipe it off, but other days, you look at him wrong, and he'll use sparring as an excuse to beat you like a mad man. He's got too much fire, and any experienced fighter can see it. He quits thinking and gets caught. Too much temper, not enough tempering.*

And yet he wins so much. Ski had retorted.

Rosca shifted her weight. "You can't beat a current like a man. This isn't sparring."

He'd been rocking on his heels, waiting acknowledgement from Dium. He looked at her in surprise. "Well, Rosquevalarien…"

She winced at the use of her full name as though it would summon her mother's presence. No one other than Debna Le called her that.

"...we'll never know anything until we try. I'll race." His golden irises crackled in the moonlight. "Who's with me?"

"Please, no." Rollins paled.

"No." Dium looked at Lin. "Racing sesaquilles was my idea. I'll go."

Lin cocked a brow, protest in the expression.

Dium's features hardened with resolve.

Nodding, Lin backed down. "This one's all yours."

Dium started for the water, clasping Lin's hand in a quick motion as though to thank him.

Rosca stepped in front of her brother. "Helski no! You could die."

He smiled at her but avoided returning the look. "Calm down, sis. It won't take long."

Did he have a death-wish? "Dium, I can't live with you getting killed. Really! Father will kill me."

"Sounds like a problem I won't be facing." His light-hearted tone grated her nerves.

She opened her mouth to protest but stopped suddenly when she caught the determined line scratched in his brow. Nothing she could do or say would change his mind. With grinding teeth, she stormed off. "I won't be a part of this." Looking back at her brother, she saw him already stripped down to shorts. "Minsk-head!" This was Lin's fault.

Chapter Eighteen
Waves

"Oof." Dium shivered as he lowered himself from the wooden pier onto the sesaquill's back. Above the water, the creature seemed like a normal horse. She snorted and tossed her mane at the familiar weight of the man.

"Good girl." He patted the paint's blotched neck. Leaning down, he hissed in her ear. "I'm sorry, Sash. I made a mistake." He straightened. Now he was the minsk-head talking to horses. But she deserved as much. If Ray really had returned... If the Current was here... Trembles shot through his body, and he blamed it on the frigid water. Shel. Why hadn't he reported that ship? Pirates brought on these things with their witchcraft and dark dealings, but he'd ignored the threat. And for what? A party? An adrenaline rush? "Minsk-head," he muttered to himself. If anyone died tonight, it'd be blood on his hands. The realization sucked on his conscience.

Without the flickering firelight nearby, the night grew and wrapped him in her clammy hands. Misgiving creeped up his tailbone. "I could drown tonight." He thought putting it into words might diminish the dread. Instead, he had to grip Sash's mane as he all but retched over her side. What did he have to fear? Death was just another adventure. Shel it. Maybe so, but he wanted to finish this one first.

It didn't matter. If he didn't ride, Lin would, the boar-brained minsk-head. Dium was a deb. A nobleman. He had a responsibility to protect the people of this island. A duty Maschiach had given him a second chance to uphold, and, this time, he would.

His lips pressed tight, and he gripped his reins with a balled fist. Some bodiless rat gnawed at his stomach. Did he have time to relieve himself?

No. No turning back. Forcing his spine into a straight line, he jutted his chin into the night air. The familiar feeling of the sesaquill beneath his legs helped bring his nerves in check.

The small group standing on the pier looked empty without his sister. He sighed. Rarely did she run from a challenge, no matter the danger. Bitterness tinged his taste buds. He'd stood at her side for her countless suicidal adventures, where was she for him?

Sash sensed his worry, and it echoed in her own swimming. Skittish, she threw back her head from everything from the waves to the small globs of iridescent, glowing jellyfish that floated past.

"It's okay, Sash." He patted the sesaquill's neck.

Below the water, four fins flipped in rubbery congruency, carrying them farther and farther from the pier. A fish jumped to their left and Sash spooked forward with a jolt, causing Dium to tighten his grip and to pat her assuredly on the back.

"All right, no reason to drag it out. Let's go, girl. One lap around the course and back. If Coquerielle's Current is here, it's going to have to be faster than us. Right?"

She snorted a disapproval or an insult, either way it wasn't polite. Ignoring her, he leaned forward and hoisted his rear into the air. Tension ran like a bolt through his body. Automatically, his toes pressed down to keep the stirrups from slipping. Smiling, he clicked her on, urging her into a steady swim-gallop.

A piece of driftwood, long as his arm and treated in a seed oil to make it more water resistant, made up the first marker. A metal hook at the bottom of the ocean anchored it. Two more of these homemade signals connected to the other by a rope, glowing with orange dye, formed a half circle of track.

They swished past the first point. The world faded until only Sash and he stayed, surging beneath the stars. Outrunning his worries, he leaned even closer until he touched the horse's neck. The seconds stretched into hours as he tasted life at its fullest. Not a bad way to die.

With a drawn-out whinny, Sash slowed. They'd passed the last marker, and she knew her stopping points. "Not about to let me overrun you on a Soonmae, eh?" He laughed. His muscles loosened, the stress slipping. She'd never run it that fast before. Ever. Had anyone thought to count his time? If only she could do that twice. He'd make his money plus some tonight. He patted her neck, smiling wide enough to hurt.

She nickered.

Not even two hundred feet away, the crowd cheered him on from the old pier. Waving and smiling, he searched for the gold and maroon of Rosca's dress, but with no result. It didn't matter. She had been wrong. He did it. The constriction in his chest loosened. He should have put money on it.

Then his world was water. The sea clutched him to her depths. Darkness drenched him. His throat developed its own heartbeat. His head and neck jolted, sparking with of pain. Desperate, he reached. Nothing. Sash had disappeared. Anytime he began to get a sense of an upward direction, he somersaulted again. Before he could finish one flip, the water spun him in a second direction, jerking like the strings on a puppet. Searching for the starlight offered seconds before, he opened his eyes. Met with salty water, his pupils stung as though a thousand tiny swords had been thrust within them. The pain exceeded any he'd ever felt in the ocean. He had to get out. This couldn't end here. He wanted to finish this adventure. His adventure. He cried out. Water forced itself down his open mouth, filling his lungs and burning his throat.

A white glare greeted him from above, as though the sun had returned to usher him on. He swung fiercer. Harder. A voice filled his head. *Birth takes pain.*

Chest burning, he elbowed the sea spasmodically. Pressure gathered at the top of his nose until it spread to his body. Numb, he blacked out.

Chapter Nineteen
Paralyzed

Ice-cold water needled into Rosca's brain. Her thoughts muddled. The thick, nautical rope tied around her waist squeezed and slacked sporadically as the kids dragged her back to solid ground. She'd done the knot in a hurry, determined to dive in before anyone could stop her. *Maschiach, please let it hold.*

The yelling grew in volume. Her arms, locked about her brother's chest, shook and threatened to go slack. Terror made bile rise in her mouth.

"Pull!" Lin's barking, flat voice cut through the waves filling her ears. "I thought you were all strong and brave fighters. Come on you shelled minsk-heads. Use your muscles." He urged them as though this was just another training drill, but his commands held no room for debate.

A violent last effort hoisted Rosca and her brother's sopping frames onto the deck. For a moment, it seemed the rueful sea would jump up and wrap around their ankles to pull them back. Nothing happened. The onlookers stared, dumb with shock. Her icicled fingers itched and burned. Then, slowly, she turned to look at her brother. In her arms, the limp Dium looked, even in the dim lighting, more dead than alive.

"Move." People scurried. Seconds later, Lin crouched beside them. She studied him through half-closed lids. He hooked his arms under hers and dragged her off Dium.

He pounded Dium's chest. Was he dead?

She fought to move. Exhaustion and cold turtled her actions.

After a few terrifying seconds, Lin revived her brother. Coughing and sputtering, Dium groaned and looked up in a daze. Numb, she barely registered the relief creeping through her.

"You're alive." Lin heaved a sigh.

"Not if I have anything to say about it." Another voice boomed from the crowd. "You really thought I wouldn't notice a sesaquill race the night of my party? I just didn't expect *my children* to be leading it." Deb Rez's voice thundered so loudly Rosca expected to see lightning strike in the background. The other kids cowered around her.

"Sash." Dium suddenly struggled to get to his feet and then collapsed once again, coughing.

Laying her head against the deck, Rosca twisted her neck to stare at the starlit night. Deb Rez shook her shoulder. Perhaps if she stayed put, he'd leave.

"Get up." He shouted at his children.

Rosca turned her gaze towards Dium. He lay still. Long as he didn't stir, she wasn't going to get up and take all the blame. A few scuffling noises tempted her to move, and a sigh indicated her father's impatience.

"Lin, carry Dium." Her father scooped her up as he spoke. His familiar smell and gait contrasted the chaos like the feeling of home stilled terror. He turned to the crowd of people. "Go home before I send praetis to storm this beach." Just like that, they disbursed.

Each step jolted her as her father marched up the hill in front of the city entrance. His beefy arms swung her like a baby. She wiggled in discomfort. "Put me down," she barked in a rougher tone than she meant to use. Especially given the deep, deep mescucha she was in. Clearing her throat, she tried again. "Please. I'm okay now." Coughs racked her body as he set her down.

"Here." Her father handed her brother's clothes to her, which he must have retrieved from the sand.

The typical sunstruck night breeze ruffled her torn and soaked dress. Chills tingled up her arms. "Thank you." She slid on the breeches and slipped on the coat.

"Now, what the helski happened back there?" Arms crossed, he tilted his head up till the moonlight caught the long scar splitting his cheek.

They were doing this now? He couldn't wait until the castle? A different fear, unlike the heart-pounding exhilaration danger induced, piled rocks in her stomach. Dread tarred her tongue. She may as well have been a statue.

She forced herself to respond. "Coquerielle's Current. It grabbed ahold of him and wouldn't let go."

"Coquerielle's Current?" A dangerous edge cut into his tone. "That's impossible."

"A kid said they saw the shadow in the water. The current…" she swallowed, "well, we don't know. But something took him under. Dium's a good…" she cut herself off. He didn't need to know Dium'd been riding sesaquilles. At least, not from her.

Sash! She frowned, sorrow draping her in a heavy blanket. Had the sesaquill drowned? Heart lodged in her throat, she couldn't find the will to continue the conversation.

"If you lot suspected the current, you should have come and found me. Someone could have died, Dium almost did." His even voice vibrated with tension, as though any second would send him into an explosion. But the deb knew how to remain calm. He had to.

"I'm sorry." Her whisper held less weight than an empty clamshell. Surviving death and saving her brother had taken all one night could take from her. She would sooner shout in gratitude for their spared lives than mope in regret.

His silence unnerved her more than his yelling. She wished her brother would wake up and share the blame.

He cleared his throat, the darkness masking his features. "We'll finish this at home. Did you ride?

"Our horses are…"

At the hesitation, he glanced over. "Yes?"

Zoning in on the moon above, she blanked her mind to force the confession. "In the garden by the entrance."

A disapproving guttural sound emanated from his throat. "You left the horses in the city garden? The world is not your backyard, Rosca. I may have spoiled you, but I thought I taught you about respect, too. That garden is a symbol of beauty and survival, planted by our founders to remind us of the gallantry of those warriors. And you… you drop off your horse to leave mescucha and eat the plants like it's a stable? Have you so little pride in your city? Your history?"

Rosca's ears burned. How much did he truly care about the garden and how much did he care about what people would say if they knew? As Mother often pointed out, part of his job included exercising an overconscientious awareness of their family's public image. She searched her heart for a mite of penance she could offer up. Nothing came. It was just… convenient. And the guards hadn't minded, why did he?

"You're immature, Rosca. And spoiled. Open your eyes. There're others in this world, too."

He hadn't yelled once, but somehow that made it worse. She lowered her gaze as they walked. The adrenaline from before, his cutting words, and the drama of the past few hours all crashed in on her. Her tears dripped in silence. Tonight… No, today had to be the worst day of her life. Why had she let Dium talk her into this?

Then again, if she hadn't gone, fish would currently be feeding on her brother's corpse. If only her father knew how hard it had been to jump in that cold water. If only he cared how scared she had been.

"Let me tell you something," he continued as though he couldn't keep the words in, "You may think you've got all life's answers in that little bookworm head of yours, but you don't know anything. How could you? I've protected you from most of it. I did what I thought best as a parent, and what did it get me? Ungrateful, know-it-alls. Shel kids, I told the debna not to have 'em, but she just had to argue." He made his voice falsetto, mocking his wife. "'Being a father is the most fulfilling thing you'll ever do. You scared of a few mini yous?'"

"I'm sorry." Rosca hissed, unsure of what to say.

"Not sorry enough, but you will be. When you have kids."

They had now reached the Nileal entrance, and Lion-Lok glared at them from above, shining against the dark night. A carriage waited for them just inside. "You and Lin get the horses. I will see you at home." He took Dium from Lin's arms and ascended into the carriage.

Lin laughed. "Well, that was entertainin'."

"Shut up." Snapping back, Rosca whistled for the horses, grateful the darkness covered her teary face.

Whinnying joyously, they appeared, then stopped. *What about Dium?* their perked ears seemed to ask.

She jutted her thumb towards Lin. "You'll have to take him home instead, Buco. I'm sorry."

Lin tilted his head. "You really don't like me, do you?"

"Have you given me a reason to?"

"Girls always like me." He said it so matter of fact. Almost without a trace of humor.

Yup, he was as self-satisfied as any fighter. No wonder Dium got along with him so well. She mounted her horse.

He refused to let it lie. "Well, I ain't given you a reason to dislike me, have I?" The same neutral directness dressed his tone.

She reined in the horse as he pranced. "Weren't you the one that suggested racing?"

He shrugged. "And I can admit when I'm wrong. But how was I supposed to know that ratface kid knew what he was talkin' about? You could hold a dog up to him, and he'd call it a horse."

Rolling her eyes, she urged Spirit into a trot. Clopping hooves echoed her own as Lin followed.

They crested the top of the hill. Between the brush and trees which curtained them, the view of their home swallowed her. Nearly one hundred yards away and nestled beneath their vantage point, it spiraled up with towers and mason work. Lantern lights flickered on the balconies and patios, dressed in green ivory and bright full flowers. She waited for the release of tension. The relief of being home. They were alive. This wretched day had finally ended. She slumped in the saddle. Who cared if today had ended? Tomorrow she'd have to pick up the pieces.

Rustling in the woods harnessed her attention. The tree line cupped her home on the left. Ant-like silhouettes crept out from it into moonlight. She squinted. Giant black shadow-monsters, like arms on stilts rolled out from the mosaic of branches. Flashes glinted in the sea of darkness. Were those swords?

The first explosion hit like a nightmare. Crashing sounds of stone on stone razed the stillness. A fist sized rock slammed into Lin's chest, and he fell to the ground. With a string of curses, he moaned and rolled about. Pounding filled her chest. Screams wombed her in.

Those shadow-monsters were catapults, and the silhouettes men and horses. Nileal was under-attack. Oh shel. Oh Maschiach. Nileal was under attack.

Numb, she watched her mangled home as a tree-sized catapult let off more boulders, some on fire as though by magic. At the head of the charge, a tall figure raised a sword and pointed it straight forward. Dressed all in black, the attackers hid any sign of allegiance to anyone. They had materialized from the dark forest like cats upon unsuspecting prey.

Her father pulled her down from Spirit and said something she did not hear. Spooked by the chaos and sudden movement, the horses pranced back towards the beach.

Through the black dust, orange and yellow torch lights flickered like giant, angry fireflies. Attackers slaughtered the ball attendees as they ran out from the rubble. Women and children fell alongside the men. Somewhere in Rosca's shock, horror paced and reared. The walls of the castle crumbled as easily as a sandcastle. The smooth, lilt bricks were no match for the massive boulders.

The thicket surrounding them did not stop the flying bits of stone from crashing down. Their carriage horse fell to the ground, dead from a stray chunk of rock which had split his skull. The horse's brother lay on top.

Rosca leaned over, mouth open. Patiently she waited for the churning party food to come up. It refused. Boiling and bubbling, her stomach ached. Never, never did she imagine such a day as this. She wrapped her arms about her and fell to her knees. Sick curiosity, more than courage, drove her chin up. She watched.

Below, a defense line had formed at the entrance of the Ishel's home. Banli Boxers, soldiers, guards, and even retired fighters, cooks, and servants took up swords and frying pans together. With hardened, war-like yells they held their ground. They slashed and bashed in protection of the home and community center. The fighters roared louder. Hope rang out with each clash of metal.

A blur beside Rosca made her nearly jump up, but exhaustion stayed her compulsion. Lin had run past the carriage and headed towards the battle when her father gripped his collar and yanked him back. The deb yelled at him above the sounds of falling men.

"Watch them. Protect them. From themselves if you must. No one else goes to battle." He gestured to his daughter and son before running down the hill.

Moonlight beamed on Lin. The muscles around his mouth drew too tight, and he refused to look away. His fingers jerked at his side, searching for something. Rosca waited for him to leave. To ignore her father's orders.

He started forward, then glanced back and froze.

Between shivers, Rosca saw the proud neck stiffen with decision. Hands clenched, he walked to her and her brother.

She looked at Dium. He had slipped back into unconsciousness. A whimper escaped her. Her head ached with panic. What if he didn't make it? The freezing water must have put his body in shock. She had to help him. *Move*, she told herself. *Move!* Another boulder hit the castle wall.

Each breath pounded in her ears. Sharp and harried, it held all the questions she neither had the time nor strength to ask. Discernment came in slow motion. Father had run into battle. He might not survive, but he had gone. For Mother and the boys. For her. For her mother. Her family. She could hear screeching. Her raw throat ached.

Lin clamped a hand over her mouth, incredulous in his sharp glare.

She had been yelling. She bit him, and he jerked it back.

He didn't understand. She didn't have the strength to play heroine. Not again. Not tonight. It had taken all of her to go after her brother.

Before now, she believed only selfish people would not rush in after their loved ones. She had decided that in such a moment as this, certain death could not stop her from fighting. Didn't most say the same? She thought she'd one-upped the "most" in doing it for Dium. But here she sat. Paralyzed. And not because she was selfish, but because she was terrified.

Chapter Twenty
Revenge

Deb Rez rushed through the clamoring crowds, calling Le's name. A hundred sweaty bodies pressed in as they scrambled around him.

"Rez!" a shout met his own, and he caught a glimpse of his wife.

Her expression reminded him of his boxing opponents when he hit them with a shot they didn't expect. The remaining children ran with her. Their wide eyes fixed on him, mute horror written in the concentrated stares.

Frantic, Le's gaze darted about, and her lips shook. "Do you have Dium and Rosca? I've looked everywhere... I—"

"They're safe."

"Thank Maschiach." She put a fist to her mouth.

Rez took her hand and led them through the chaos.

Attackers swarmed the castle, but the Banli warriors sliced them down as they got lost in the numerous rooms and halls. Rez took a moment to thank Maschiach he hadn't asked guests for their weapons at the door. He believed in staying prepared, and, tonight, that rule proved their saving grace.

The castle's crooks and crannies created a map of twisting halls which played to the islanders' advantage. The last king of Iecula, King Dahl, had ordered add-ons and remodels with the indecision of a fat man at a feast. In addition to the maze, Rez's enthusiastic collection of nymphs, lions, sesaquilles, and other life-size stone statues crowded these halls, rooms, and spaces. The Banli warriors used all to dodge, confuse, and attack the straight-on advance of the fighters.

A mix of Banli, Limurian, Valsquelian, and Kenstian blood spilled on the floor. Rage filled the air. The surprise and horror which locked the defenders in confusion and panic at first, now melted with the hot burn of animal-like anger. The attackers retreated beneath the war-like yells filling the castle and the blood-hungry blades which dashed and thrust like hummingbirds.

The catapults, which had risen like beasts of helski from the surrounding woods, had long since stopped their thundering. Rez prayed they were crushed and splintered in the muck of the debna's front garden. His chest swelled with pride.

Automatic, he flowed through the motions of battle. Parry. Stab. Roll. Adnesi and Ski fought alongside him, forming a protective half circle around his wife and two youngest sons. With slow, steady progress, they advanced to the servant entrance. If he could just get Le and the youngest out, he and his oldest could help the rest. He just had to get them out. They were going to be all right, Deb Rez continued to tell himself without conviction. Misgivings pitted in his stomach.

They charged into the empty kitchen. Rez did a sweep of the room, including all exits and openings. Two doors and one hallway. The hallway had been their entrance. One door led down to the wine cellar, while the other led out to the servant's quarters. He stepped towards it, but it burst open and six burly men entered. Behind them, a single authority followed, wearing a mask. Black and red dressed the slim figure, and it raised a circular wooden shield in defense. The other hand held a shining, straight Valsquelian blade. In surprise, Rez noted the womanly shape.

She removed her mask. "Good to see you again, brother."

His heart failed him. Renelia.

Prepossessing, cruel eyes complimented her crooked nose and small, stern features. The years had written hard lines on her brow and around her mouth. Even so, a youthful spirit enveloped her, accentuating the beauty she still possessed.

A boulder lodged in his throat. "It's impossible."

"What? That I managed to escape the helski you sold me into?" She gnashed her teeth, spit flying.

"Renelia." His sister had returned. All these years, but she had survived. Blank, his mind searched for a meaning to the madness. How had she found her way here? He stepped towards her as though in a trance.

One of her guards met his advance.

"You lost the right to call me that." Nostrils thinned and knuckles paled, she raised her sword. "Take a step closer." Her challenge hung in the air.

Rez went rigid. His jaw slacked. Everything outside of him faded to black. He'd never found her. Never saved her, and, now, she would make him pay. All those years dreaming for a reunion, ended. And in the worst possible reality.

A huff drew him back to the moment.

"Hela." Her name tasted like poisoned memories. Dropping his hands, he drove forward on compulsion. Her suspended blade poked his throat. "I'm sorry. I loved you. I love you. I spent every day praying that what happened... I..." He began to speak in words only she understood. The Valsquelian of childhood poured out as he tugged at the last connection they had. "Renelia, haj lo. Mie repegave!"

With fire in her gaze, Hela pulled back her sword for his execution. "You. Sold. Me!"

Chapter Twenty-One
A Look Back

FOUR YEARS AGO
Captain Hela

The rocking of the lifeboat could have lulled Hela to sleep under different circumstances. Her pulse pounded in her ears. As she drew near the shadowy shore, she examined the tree line.

"Movement, Cap'n?" One of her accompanying crewmates repeatedly dipped the paddles into the silky sea.

Hela squirmed. "We're still too far to see." Sharp with anticipation, her tone vibrated across the still water. Locking her jaw, she forced herself to look away. Everything rested on this. Everything.

A bitter taste filled her mouth. She spit over the boatside as sunken memories floated to the surface of her mind. The tempa she had turned thirteen, she fell asleep and woke to find herself on a pirate ship. For years, she tried to figure out what happened between those two events.

Aboard the ship, the captain dubbed her "Little Warrior" for kicking a crewman. The name had garnered more heartache than respect. Bullying and bossing her became a past-time aboard the ship, like knife throwing or wrestling. She'd carried piss pots over hot coals, sewn coats with armpit hair, and skinned cats only to throw them overboard. Still she had not seen the truth.

Mule-brained to the end, she promised her captors that her brothers would come. No matter how the pirates beat or abused her, she swore to hold onto hope. Each crisp morning, she searched the horizon for her brothers' sails. Her innocent heart could not resign so easily.

Why should she have? The boys had never failed her before. When Jingli made fun of her buck teeth, when she had been lost in the woods, even when fever had overtaken and racked her thin body, her brothers had stood by her side. She told herself that a kidnapping wouldn't be any different.

She tapped her fingers on the side of the boat. An ache filled her chest, but bitterness washed it away. "Foolish child," she hissed to herself.

"Cap'n? Cap'n?"

Hela shook herself and growled at the man. "What?"

"You seemed... lost."

"Then leave me bloody well lost." She rubbed her finger against her sword, and the man quieted.

Thirteen years. Thirteen years since she had first... She closed her eyes and recited her captors' conversation, overheard by chance. A few lines that solved every mystery and brought anything but peace.

I paid that Rez boy in gold for the girl. She's my own property.
The girl's brother?
That's the one. Said he needed the money to get out. To escape.

The second man had laughed. A short mocking bark which rang in her ears every day since. Three years she'd trusted her salvation to her brothers' cunning. Three years of deceiving herself. But no more. Her beloved brother was a beast. He had sold her. She looked out to the dark waves of that early morning, just as she did every day. When no sails of rescue crested the horizon, the last of her foolish innocence fled. She vowed herself to the black sea. Vowed to never hope again. Vowed to have revenge.

Their lifeboat bumped into the shore. The time to fulfill that vow had come.

She stepped onto the foul-smelling beach, her crew following. A sudden gust rose from the blackened, diseased trees like an incoming storm. The power of the wind startled Hela, pushing and bending her frame back towards the shore. It stopped without warning. As it died down and the ashy sand settled, three figures approached them. First, a skinny, tall man with graying hair and pale flaking skin led. Behind him, a short, buff woman covered in boils and blisters hobbled as though each step shot pain through her being. Following these two a beautiful man sauntered with eyebrows mere slivers of silver and hair like the waving black sea at night. His tall, thin body rippled with muscle, and he held himself with lofty grace.

"King Alarog!" Hela dropped quickly to one knee, and her men copied the stance.

The man chuckled humorlessly. "King Alarog does not leave his fortress. Certainly not for you."

Hela jumped to her feet. "But we paid the price!"

"The price?" Impatience twisted the thin lips. "The lives of you and your whole crew would not be enough to merit a meeting with the Dark King of the Sea. Still…" His gaze ran over her body like a wild cat assessing prey. "Your family has a history which would be disgraceful to ignore."

Hela winced. Her mother Gina had been persecuted for years for dark art practices. These cursed arts had drawn Gina and Hela's father, Role, together in the first place. *Mi Pita Lofu*, he used to call her mother. My little witch.

Hela's blood ran cold as she imagined her mother's bruised and bloodied face, crying out for mercy. Even at eight-years-old, she had grown accustomed to such things. She had believed every home acted the same in the shadows.

Her father had less control over the voices inside than he pretended, and his desire had warped to match the darkness he called into his home. Cruelty and viciousness reigned. Hela had spent waking and sleeping hours in terror. Out of control. Helpless.

She would never outgrow that terrified little girl, but neither would she show it. Lifting her chin, she met the handsome man's stare.

"If you aren't King Alarog, who are you?" With practiced precision, she scanned the coastline for the threat of more men.

"No need to be so aggressive." With eyes cold as stone, the man laughed. "I am Chief Bukii of the Zelxes."

Tremors traveled through her veins. "A Zelxe? That's…" The creature went rigid before her. Did she really want to call his existence impossible? She felt for the hilt of her sword. Why couldn't creatures stay dead in their legends? Life had enough worries without adding supernatural beasts.

"Would you like me to prove it?" His pupils rolled back into his head, and he shimmered, shifting into different faces as though masks flew around his head.

"I believe. Oh god, I believe. Stop." She took a step back, shuddering. "I'm only here to ask about my brother."

His face resumed its first form. "Ah, yes. Little Rez. Now all famous and loved. Quite the switch. I remember when he was a boy. My whisperers used to have fun with him."

Hela felt a chill run down her back. Was that what they called the puppets from helski? The damned ones? What an apt name. In her memory, a screaming, kicking Rez, no more than ten years old, cried out for the voices to leave him alone. She dug her heels into the ground and focused on Bukii's face. She would not swoon. Not in front of these bloodsuckers.

"I still remember the first time they made Rez lose control. Wasn't he seven?"

"Four." Hela's hoarse throat tightened. Her parents had crowed over the experience, as though the sucking of their son's life testified to enlightenment and a sort of divinity.

"He had so much potential. He was the brother who sold you, no?"

Hela's blood boiled at Bukii's knowing smirk.

"Yes," she barked. He had not bothered to hide his gloats, and she would not mask the disgust in her voice.

"So, you want revenge?" The man chuckled again. "But don't you wonder?" His face didn't change shape, but it may as well have. The slight eyes glinted with profuse hunger. Leaning in, he circled her like a vulture, dismissive of the way she gripped her blade. "Was it Rez? Or was it the whisperers which guided him? He'd blacked out many times before. How do you know this time was not the same?" Full circle, he stopped in front of her. Humor drained from the expression, and a blankness hooded his features as though he had died. "You don't know. You don't know anything."

"He wasn't a Zelxe! He had free will," she sputtered. This helski monster would not deter her now. "He stopped himself before! When they tried to get him to jump off the cliff, he had enough strength to save himself. To quiet them."

"But not enough to save you?" Tossing the angular head back, the beast exposed its papery thin throat. "And that's why you're hurt? My, my, how petty humans are."

"Just tell me what to do." Sick of his games, she had no patience for the Zelxe's speeches.

"Well," he clasped his hands, rubbing one through the other with a gleeful look. "Manipulation is the purest form of revenge. Forget swords and killing the body. They only pass onto the next life. Create so much confusion they can't help but tear each other apart. And, because I'm feeling generous, I'll give a few simple tricks to help you."

Hela shook her head. "I'm only here for advice. My brother lives in a fortress. Soldiers, warriors, and servants attend him night and day. Pirates are hated on his island. I just need to know how to reach him." She sneered. "Keep your dark arts in the shadow. I want no part."

With a smile, he raised a brow. "You became a part the day you made your vow."

Hela's heart pounded. "How'd you—"

"Know? I am here to hold you to it. It is my business to keep the dishonorable honorable."

Her dry tongue swelled, thick with words she didn't have the rishop to say. She cursed silently, unable to meet his slivering gaze.

"You've worked hard, Hela. You've become the woman you wanted. Why not reward yourself? After so many years? There's no reason to make things harder than they already are. Let me make this easy for you."

The words licked at her pride like a dog at his sores. It had been a long, hard road to garner enough respect to build a crew willing to be led by a woman. A bloody, merciless road, but respect was currency she couldn't afford to lose. If she went after Rez, her crew would suffer. They'd be lucky to escape with their lives, much less a reward for their endeavor. Assuming her crew stayed loyal after, she'd be watching her back for a knife. Pirates didn't forget quickly.

Why destroy everything for revenge? Why not get something more than a slit throat from the experience? "What are you offerin'?"

"A level of control over Coquerielle's Current, to pass through it unharmed, and strength equal to that of two men."

Her fingers curled into her palm, glory and triumph buzzing before her. *That of two men.* If she had accomplished this much as a woman, how much more could she do by surrendering her feminine weakness? And if she could control Coquerielle's Current, the beast of every sea traveler's nightmares, pirates from every corner would be forced to honor her. No one could deny power. It would be a weapon to use against Iecula. When she attacked, escape would be easy. She could mark Rez. Only he would be able to follow her. To chase her. And chase, he would. Her heart thumped as the possibilities multiplied.

She had clawed her way into becoming Captain Hela, but this simple gift would elevate her into Captain Hela, the first female pirate and powerful master of the seas. And who else deserved it? She'd sacrificed everything for this. She'd earned it with her own blood and tears.

"What do you expect in return?"

"But you already paid," he mocked her claim with a condescending false innocence.

She needed to learn to hold her tongue. She gritted her teeth. "For the advice, yes. But not for this… this gift." She shifted her weight and crossed her arms. It did nothing to ease the discomfort gnawing at the back of her mind. She would not be indebted to this helski beast.

"A woman of business." His smugness iced her soul. Then, his mirth vanished, replaced with hunger. "Carry my whisperers back on your ship and release them in Kenst."

Her guts slithered in sickening hoops within, but she hid her disgust. "You serve a water king, but you can't get yourself to the closest nation around?"

A muscle twitched in his jaw. "Breathing underwater is a bit of a health hazard. Most Zelxes can do it, but for some reason, the whisperers don't last any longer than you powerless humans."

Her lips curled. "Fine."

They shook hands, and she turned to leave.

His voice stopped her. "If you really want your niece and nephew to listen, I'd enlist a whisperer. They're helpful. If you can control them." He arched a brow.

A young Rez's writhing, helpless form filled her mind. "I wouldn't join up with a whisperer if it would save my life." She spat and marched away. She couldn't stand this place a second longer. The beach stank and her body itched. Business had finished, and she had nothing more to say.

Onboard, the whisperers seemed as determined to stay out of the pirates' way as the pirates were to stay out of theirs. Most took human forms. But some transformed into animals, forcing her to keep from shooing birds from the deck as they sailed to sea. She had no desire for King Alarog or his followers to develop a vendetta against her. She had more important things than fighting with a dark sea king. She had her plan, and power to back it.

Chapter Twenty-Two
Attack

CURRENT TIME

Raising her sword high above her head, Hela howled.

Deb Rez slipped safely away, and she crashed it into the hard floor with a *thud*.

She plucked it out as though it were a twig. "You will watch them die just as you left me to do!"

He pressed his back against his family, retreating step by step. He would not hurt his sister. His renelia. But neither could he leave his family to her bloodlust.

A wild, ferocious thirst dried Hela's expression, deadening it with stone-cold malice. Her blade thrust forward. "Prepare for suffering. Prepare for retribution. Prepare for me."

Instinct marshaled his muscles. He leapt forward, parrying her strokes.

Hela's blade whipped in and out like a bat's flight path. "It almost isn't worth killing 'em."

Kill them? Rez doubled his slashes. She's ludicrous. He did not have the luxury to lose. Hela's easy defense made him flush in shame. When had he grown old? Why had he let himself grow complacent?

Abrupt, she switched her gaze to his family.

His two eldest walled away Le and the young boys, ready for defense.

"What is loss to a stone? To a man consumed by ambition and selfishness?" Pure ferocity shown through Hela's bared teeth. "Can such a man love? Ach!" She sliced at Rez, pushing his sword back with the power of her blow before spitting at his feet. "You do not love. You are a dog, just as I had to become. Just as our parents were."

Rez parried left, then right before a nimble thrust cut her wrist. Revenge. That's why she was here. That's why she had found him. She wanted to destroy them. Destroy him. Hope ebbed from his soul. This woman's bitterness had consumed the little girl he once knew.

He charged, but Hela stood firm. She blocked his every attack. As each of his strokes fell on her metal, she twisted so that his own power would drag him forward. Each time he caught himself, his ragged gasps became more and more like their retired hound dog.

From the corner of his eye, he saw his wife and younger sons. "Run!" He urged. Another thrust of Hela's blade shattered his focus.

Jumping back, he returned her blow with one of his own. She stumbled. Excitement filled him. He had disrupted her rhythm. Thrust. Thrust. Swipe. She fell back. He swung again. This time, she did not block. Rolling under his sword, she dug her blade into his side, then retracted it.

Panic pierced his concentration. Swearing, he dropped his weapon. Years of training kicked him into action. He threw an overhand right at her temple. She crumpled.

Her men flinched, ready to jump forward. He hovered above her with heaving breaths, the wound in his side forgotten.

Life fluttered into Hela's limbs as she pushed herself up with the help of the wall.

"I have beaten you. Let me and my family go." Rez fell to the ground, pain spasming in his ribs.

Still swaying, she foamed at the mouth. "Get 'em!" Her screech summoned chaos. Her men joined the fight.

Adnesi and Ski sprang forward like leopards to meet them.

Pride fizzed in Rez's chest at the sight. Eardrum-shattering clangs of swords and cries of men in their last moments filled the four walls of their family kitchen. The fight did not end until his boys had left a pile of bodies spread about the room. But there had never been a hope for victory. The numbers were too great.

From the corner of his eye, Rez saw a mallet racing toward his skull. Then, all went black.

***

The stench of death clogged Ski's nostrils. A point at his back kept him moving through the castle. Any sudden move, even throwing up, could work as an excuse for the guard to stab him.

The floor glistened underneath the dismembered bodies of Nilealians and foreigners alike. Young, old, boy, girl, it did not matter. Each had fallen dead to the surprise. Each stained the stone with their bloody remains.

Pride kept him from crumpling to the ground. Nothing could keep the tears in. They dripped from his chin onto the motionless corpses. The Ishel's captors led them down the hall and into a tunnel.

All this just for the deb? This was Rosca and Dium's fault. They let Ray in. They let her tour the castle. They did this. They did this. Not him. It wasn't his fault. He didn't start this. Ragged gasps harried his breath. Shudders latched into his spine, vibrating down his back. Ray... no, Hela. That was her name. She'd planned this for three years. Waited three years, who knew if it was longer? Was the revenge worth it?

She could have killed them, but she waited. She calculated. It would have been low-hanging fruit to kill them as children. She waited till she could get all of them. Till she could make sure the deb was remembered as the first deb under which Nileal suffered an attack. She waited to make him look weak.

Under the numb sorrow, respect budded. Deb Rez had fallen to her. She may have lost the battle, but she'd taken everything from him. His reputation. His family. His *children*.

He nibbled a piece of dead skin on his lip. And now what? It wouldn't end here. She'd left Deb Rez alive. What madness was she planning?

Lifting his chin, he studied her through lowered lids. She led the run through the secret tunnel as though she had traversed it a hundred times. Of course she had. With him. With Rosca. With Dium. His stomach cramped and coiled, sending pangs up to his chest.

Their exit led out to a large courtyard, abandoned by guests or guards, but swarming with praetis. Straightening at the sight, Adnesi tensed. He nodded at Ski as though to say, *get ready. With them, we can win.*

Ski shook his head. His brother could be so gullible. So innocent of the world. "How do you think she snuck up on us?" he mouthed.

Adnesi stared, uncomprehending.

Hela walked up to the commander. Whispering something in his ear, she handed him a few coins. The man smiled and laughed.

Ski's heart faltered. With one swipe of her wealthy fist, Hela had tarnished and divided his home. Not that he expected any less. Money broke the strongest loyalties.

"Hela, let's go!" A brawny, gap-toothed man shouted, clearly her second-in-command. He pointed to a large black cart. A team of four horses pulled the jail on wheels.

With a pinched, formal sneer, the commanding praeti addressed Hela. "Change of plans. Too many soldiers out looking for you all. Go on Iculous road." The praeti gestured off to the right. "It's a little longer, but no one ever thinks of it. Take the first left. It'll lead you straight to the beach. Your ship is moored on Filmore's Beach still? And you're sure no one has seen it?"

"Yes, I've done this a few times, you know." Hela snapped, throwing her black cloak and mask to the side.

Ski couldn't deny the family resemblance. She had Rosca's face shape and hair with Deb Rez's ebony skin.

The praeti crossed his arms, clearly fed up with the woman.

"I don't care." The praeti's spoke drily. "Take Iculous or you may as well surrender now."

She nodded and turned to the muscular man beside her. "The mother and two boys?"

"Done."

Ski's insides lurched. What had they done to Jack and Mar? He'd seen them loaded on a different cart, but…oh Maschiach. He heaved.

"And Rez?"

"He'll live."

She smiled. "Well, fun part is over. Time to do what we do best. Sail away."

Ski didn't meet the pirates' eyes as they shoved him and his brother into the cart. The solid, wood box reminded him of a stable.

Why had she spared Rez? She certainly didn't do it for sisterly love. His head spun. She was playing a game. Shel. First successful attack on Nileal in fifty years and the very people meant for catching her were aiding her disappearance. And this was just setting the board. Death wasn't enough for her. She was playing Deb Rez, and she'd keep on till it killed one of them.

This was more than hate, this was obsession. He leaned on the back of the cart. Now what?

Chapter Twenty-Three
Parting

"LE!" Deb Rez pushed himself off the cold tile. His vision cracked and fuzzed.

Stumbling his way to the ballroom, he scoured the room. "LE!" He concentrated his energy into taking the next breath and step. Wetness coated his side from the wound. Several debs rushed to attend him. He pushed them away and yelled, "LE!"

"Rez." A chill ran down his spine, and he spun about at the croak.

His wife lay on the ground coughing, blood pooling outward from a stab wound in her stomach and a second in her leg. "Rez, you shel minsk... They... they took...." Her eyes were gray. Already, her hand had begun to grow cold. Rez gripped it tighter, tears falling like volleying arrows. "...my boys." With this, she leaned back. "I love you," she whispered and delivered her last breath.

He held her hand to his lips and closed his eyes, rocking back and forth.

"They will pay, Le. I promise. She will pay." His yell pierced the clamor of the ballroom.

***

"Where are they goin'?" Lin studied the coordinated retreat. From their position on the hill, they observed Hela's escape by carriage.

"Does it matter?" Rosca stood erect, locked in by the sight before them. "We beat 'em."

"It will matter a whole lot if they decide to come our way."

She harrumphed in response.

"They're takin' Iculous road." Squinting, he chewed his lip, noting the rolling black prison with unease. No one ever went on Iculous road. But how could they know that unless they were natives? They had to be natives. Or have native help. "They have prisoners. I'm gonna follow 'em."

"Are you crazy?" Rosca's tone pitched high.

He placed the back of his hand against an unconscious Dium's forehead. Burning. "Mescucha." Wistful, he searched the night. Why hadn't he grabbed the horse before they ran off? Why did he have to freeze?

"Lin, you're one man. There's no reason to take that risk. No one is asking you to take that risk."

He ignored her and examined the remaining carriage horse. The poor, overweight beast seemed the worse for having fallen, but other than that, uninjured.

Shudders ran through Lin at the sight of the dead one's glassy eyes and shattered chest from the killing stone. Drawing a knife from his britches, he worked at cutting and loosening the live horse. The beast shot to its feet, and he formed reins by tying leather strips to the halter. No bit. No saddle. This should be fun. He tightened his shoulders, tension springing up his neck.

"If you're going, I'm going." Rosca had crept up behind him while he worked.

He chortled, then met her eyes. Wide with fear, their soft shape framed a reflection of the flickering flames below. With the snap of reflex, her trembling lips pressed into a hard line while her throat muscles constricted into a bulging V. She lifted her chin, glistening with teardrops, higher and higher.

Pity and admiration fought for control in his breast. She was serious. A debna ridin' into danger with him? What a story that would make. He curbed the laughter rising in his throat. It was a noble gesture on her part.

He pointed to her brother, the one person he knew she'd never leave. "I've seen this happen with sailors before. The sea takes 'em and seems to give 'em back, but it leaves a sickness. A weary chill in the bones. He'll need a fire. He'll need to wake up soon. Else he'll die."

"Die?" Slumping back, she rolled the word out like it was foreign. Her small hands tightened into fists at her side.

"You're goin' to make sure that doesn't happen. Can you do that?"

"I'm not an invalid."

Her bite tugged a bittersweet smile from him. Good. She needed her fight.

She cradled her stomach. "But what do I do? I can't start a fire. We'll be seen."

"The attackers are already leavin'. Wait half an hour more, then go get help. But be aware. There's always a possibility of stragglers, although I doubt any of these helken men have the rishop to stick around at this point."

His strong oaths seemed to spur her into action. She traipsed to Dium's side and bundled him farther with the jacket her father had given her. At the sight of her torn dress and small figure, he debated the wisdom of leaving. They were going the opposite way, no one would touch her. No one would come near here. He followed them, not the other way around. Time stretched, but he could not force himself to action.

"Lin, tell me when you return."

Her question broke his spell. "If. Yes."

At his correction, she slunk back. Her hands folded together. "I want to know where they go. I want to know who they are. They won't get away with this."

Violent memories sprang to mind at the bitter underlining in her tone, and he stiffened. "Revenge is a slow death."

"Then it is the price to be paid. For many have died below."

"Two deaths do not make life. Never have and never will. If you can't control your anger, then there's no reason for me to tell you anything." His sharp words betrayed his own lost temper. Hypocrite. He mounted the horse. "Do you know Filmer's Beach?"

Her chin jerked up. Something flitted in her expression. Recognition? Guilt? She avoided his eyes. "Where we raced sesaquilles last time?"

"Yeah." He studied her, but a mask slipped over her features. "What's the fastest way there?"

"The mansion roads. Why?"

"I'd bet my good arm they anchored their ship there."

"How do you know they even have a ship?"

"It's how these people work." He gripped the leather strips he'd slashed to make reins, his pulse roaring within him.

"Do you know 'these people'?" Her tone cut with suspicion.

He growled. Did she think he was a part of this? He didn't have the time, or desire, to dignify that with a response. "That beach is the perfect place to lay anchor without much notice. What's more, the only road givin' access to it crosses Iculous. Besides," he tapped his sword, "it's what I would do." Probably didn't help his innocence to tell her, but it was true.

After a pause, she spoke. "If you use the mansion roads, you'll go towards the fishermen's districts. You know the way. There are parts reasonable enough to ride a horse."

He scooted back, the horse's high withers making a sharp seat. "A sure-footed horse, yes, but this hag is barely breathin'."

She raised her voice. "Once down there—"

"In the fishermen's district?" He clarified, still shifting in discomfort.

"No, the road leading to it. Before you enter the district, there'll be woods on your left. Ditch the horse and hike into them, up a hill. At the top you'll be able to see Filmore's. The island curve and trees block the beach from everyone else."

The torchlight of the retreaters dimmed in the distance. It was time. He kicked the horse into motion, forcing his fat rear down the hill and into the mayhem.

Dirt and rocks flew up as his hooves pounded on the crowded streets. People wailed, clutching their limp loved ones in their arms. He pressured the horse to avoid collision with wandering children and vacant-eyed adults. Finally, they broke free of the crowds and reached a narrow trail, winding through lok trees. An archway, holed into the city wall, covered the path. The entrance to the fishermen's district. The wooden gates were unmanned, every praeti drawn away by the chaos. They lay open.

When he reached the bottom of his descent, a group of about ten people, still in clothes from the party, crowded him, calling his name. Shocked by their insistence, he spun about. What did they think he could give them?

"Lin!"

In surprise, he jerked the reins. His horse jumped about. Too many people and too many voices. He called out for them to wait, but their shouts roared over his own. Their grabby hands reached out to clasp at him as if he could answer their prayers.

"Lin!" A single cry screeched above the others. That of a debna whose husband had helped train him for his fight. His win. She clutched his pants leg. "Please. Help us!"

Lin jolted as the horse tripped backwards. Spooked, the animal took off, bolting away from the crowd. The voices became indistinguishable from the wind. He bowed over the steed's neck. He couldn't help them. His heart pounded. Couldn't stop. The bloodied, injured citizens floated in his imagination. Their cries clung about him. Could he have saved one? His chest thumped with beats as quick as the horse's gallops. It didn't matter now.

A forest rising up the broad back of a hill came into view. If Rosca was right, the top would give him a clear view of Filmore's Beach.

Lin tugged at the horse's makeshift reins. The beast ran on, froth thick on his neck. He pulled again, jerking in aggravation. The animal sped up.

With the quick realization that they would soon pass the hill, he made his decision. Leaning forward, he grabbed the horse's mane. In one rushed motion, he swung both legs over and pushed off. Dirt and grass sprayed his nostrils as he rolled several feet. Unmoving, he groaned. Every bone felt bruised. His neck ached with whiplash. "Shel horse." Muttering and wincing, he rose and continued through the woods on foot.

Signs of early dawn shone through the towering namas and loks. The trees broke off, revealing a beach and a masterfully crafted ship anchored just offshore.

An acrid taste teased his tongue. He'd guessed as much, but seeing it brought home the reality. Pirates had come to Nileal. His hand shook and every ounce of strength drained from his muscles. "Shel it." He slammed his fist into a tree. He'd left that life. Why must it follow him? Swallowing, he lassoed his courage.

The ship glowed in the red sun, whose peak glimmered just above the water. How had they got past Coquerielle's Current? He scanned for a flag or name. On the side of the long, two-masted gilla read *Lady Scarlet*. Horror scraped his reason raw. Of all the shel pirates, her? Vomitous bile pooled in his mouth. He spat.

With a shake of his head, he shoved all his questions far away. It didn't matter that it was her. It only mattered that she had attacked his friends.

He waited in the foliage until the black carriage appeared. A good thirty yards of hillside stretched between his hiding spot and where the carriage had rolled to a stop beside the water.

"My father will have that snarl for dinner!"

A smack followed the speech. No pirate took kindly to back talk.

Lin growled. He knew that voice from Asium. Jack. The last of the puzzle pieces fell into place. The disguises. The small numbers. The retreat. This wasn't an invasion. This was a kidnapping. The realization hit him like a spray of icy water. He flinched, then froze, as if that would lessen the shock.

They were after the Ishels, and he'd left Rosca alone. Metal hit his taste buds. He'd bitten through the inside of his cheek. Half-rising, he froze.

Amidst the gang exiting the back of the carriage, a bound Jack kicked and bucked furiously while a scared young Mar shuffled along slowly. A pit as deep as the sea lodged in his gut. As if guided by a sixth sense, a man looked in Lin's direction.

Lin's mind raced. A helpless feeling dripped down his veins. If the pirates chased him, he couldn't go to Rosca. Assuming they hadn't already found her. Soon, the man turned back.

Lin released a pent-up breath. He was hidden. For now.

A second black cart rolled up. Waiting, he watched for them to open the back. Would it be Rosca and Dium this time? He should have followed Deb Rez's orders. Who was he to think he knew better than the chief deb? He never took orders well and if Rosca and Dium had suffered for it—! He dug his nails into his palm, the pressure anchoring his spinning head.

Before unloading the second round of prisoners, the men washed themselves in the sea, scrubbing the red stains and other signs of the fight from their bodies. Then they abandoned their military costumes, tying them down with stones and casting them into the sea. From beneath the shrubbery and rocks, they dug out bundles of ragged trousers, shirts, and overclothes then dressed.

Lifeboat after lifeboat left the sand till roughly sixty men had boarded, not including the prisoners. Maybe fifteen remained. He seethed with impatience. "Just unload the cart!" Maybe he should go back. He'd know the truth when he found them. Or didn't find them.

A branch cracked behind him. He flew to his feet and hid behind a lok tree. Crunching leaves announced each footstep. The newcomer didn't care who heard them. Must be another pirate, set to meet the rest.

He drew his sword.

***

Rosca watched Lin leave, Dium's moaning keeping her from following.

Lin had held something back, but questions would have to wait. He may have grated on her last nerve, but he spoke with authority. If he said he knew something, she believed him. Even if how he knew was questionable at best.

Dium stirred.

She lifted her hand from his cheek and waited, breathless. Seconds lingered into minutes.

"Rosc?" Throwing his head side to side, he woke himself little by little. Shaking, he pushed himself up to his elbows. "What happened?"

A jumbled description spilled out. He deciphered it with nods, questions, and grunts. By the time she finished, he had stood on his own, refusing her help. For a long second, he stared down into the valley at their crumbled home. The distant gaze held the same sorrow, shock, and desperation swirling within her. "God. Oh, God." His shoulders shook.

Her heart melted.

A long shrill note sliced her eardrums as he called for their horses, tottering about in desperate search. "I'm following Lin."

She resisted reprimanding him. It hadn't worked when he took Sash into possessed waters, it wouldn't work now. A lifetime living with stubborn males had taught her as much. "Lin said you might die. To stay and watch you."

Dium snorted, but the moonlight revealed his pale, sweaty face. "He must have forgot I'm an Ishel. Or he didn't want you tagging along."

Indignation lit in her breast at the idea. "That lying..." she stopped. Maybe he had, but that didn't change the slow, labored breaths Dium took or the stiffness shown in every movement.

He caught her studying him. "I'm going," he said in a tone that killed all debate.

She nodded. "And so am I. 'Live fast, die young', right?" she cited in a grim tone. Trite, the simple phrase still settled her courage into place.

Dium shook his head. Coughs racked his body. He wheezed, "You and your words."

Aiding her brother in his search, she retracked their route, calling and whistling in turns. They found the two horses wandering in the woods, skittish but obedient to their call.

In seconds, they'd mounted and loped off towards Filmore's Beach. Their horsemanship saved them more than once as they maneuvered the crowds and foliage. Hiding the animals in the woodlands, they crept up through the namas and loks towards Filmore's.

Only Rosca's boxing training saved her from a gory beheading. She ducked, and a metal blade flew over her. "Lin!" She yelped.

"Rosca!" Lin's voice reached dangerously low tones, and his sword still poised for a fight.

"Shut up!" Dium put a finger to his lips. He peered through the draping leaves at the pirates some thirty yards away.

"Lin, you minsk-head! You almost killed me!" All the stress, anger, and devastation of the past hour crashed into her. Torn between clawing at him or crying, she shook head to toe.

Dium reached out instinctively and deflected her attempt to punch Lin.

Still as death, Lin glared. "You followed me?"

"*We* followed you."

His brows clouded over. "You were supposed to take care of him! He can't be walkin' 'round like this... He'll end up sicker than a fish on land!"

"I'm already sick." Dium swam back and forth on his legs, his eyes glazed. "Can't get worse."

She placed her hand against his forehead. "You're burning up."

"I'm fine." Dium asserted as he hit her hand away.

Motion attracted her gaze to the shore. A series of prisoners exited a giant jail-like carriage. Bound and chained, Adnesi and Ski towered above the rest.

"Dium." Rosca struggled to steady her voice. She pointed at the men.

A figure like the one Rosca and Lin had seen heading the attack led the group onto the last lifeboat, and they set out for the ship. A driver took away the cart.

"That's ain't the worst of it." Lin watched them till Rosca's skin crawled with worry. "I saw 'em put your brothers Jack and Mar on the boat, too." Full of sympathy, his gaze cut through her.

She reeled. "No." She couldn't believe it. If she did, she would crumble. She held in a sob. It bubbled in her throat. "Anyone, *anyone* but them. They're just children—" Her words screeched with mounting panic.

Lin jumped forward, clasping a hand over her mouth. His fiery eyes pierced her own. "We'll do our best to get 'em back. I promise. But we gotta stay calm. Can you do that?"

His intense expression anchored her. They would find them. He would find them. Somehow, he knew about these things. Somehow, this would all work out. If only she could stay calm. She nodded.

"It was all for us." Dium stared at the hulking ship. His arms crossed over his stocky chest. Resolution flared his nostrils and chased away the usual mirth found in the half-cocked grin.

Gratitude filled Rosca. She had one brother left. She grabbed his hand. Together, they would get their family back or die trying.

Clear with repressed anger, his voice summoned her courage. "The attack, the deaths. All of it. They targeted us. Our family. We should have been on that boat, too."

"But why?" Releasing his hand, Rosca backed away from the tree line. Lin followed.

"Rosc, did you see Mother and Father get loaded up?"

"No."

"Then let's pray this is all for a ransom. They'd leave them alive for that."

"Ransom?" The trees spun around her.

"Rosca." Dium spat. "We have to get on that ship."

Lin started, his black brows shooting up. "They'll kill you."

"They'll kill our family." Dium pulled up his shoulders. "They'll be setting sail soon. This is our only option."

Rosca nodded. She chewed the inside of her cheek till she tasted metal.

Lin scoffed. "I got one better than turnin' yourself over to blood-suckin' pirates who have a vendetta against your family."

They turned to him.

"I've got a ship."

"*You* have a ship?" Rosca winced at the surprise in her voice.

"Yes." Lin crossed his arms, giving her a condescending glare.

"That's generous," Dium interjected, "but some little rig isn't going to keep up."

"It's a two-sail rikkey that travels near four knots a day." Lin beamed with obvious pride. "And she's outrun many a pirate brig with me captainin' nothin' more than a four-man crew."

"I find it hard to believe a rikkey can outrun a gilla like that!" Rosca gestured to the pirate ship emphatically. "That's a double-mast gilla with—"

"I know." Lin cut her off with a dark scowl.

"But we don't have a choice." Dium stood stiff as marble. "Lin?"

Lin nodded at him as though answering a question.

In bewilderment, Rosca watched the unspoken conversation pass between the men.

Catching her expression, Lin spoke in an even tone. "I'm comin' with you. I ain't about to leave my ship. We leave now, and we leave alone."

"Alone?" The siblings chorused their confusion.

Exhaustion in the drawn cheeks, Dium leaned against a tree. He winced with the small effort. "But we could have a whole party ready in the hour. We can't save them ourselves. We can't even sail a ship."

Lin slowly moved his broad head side to side. "This comin' from the minsk-heads that were just ready to hop in bed with the enemy with no plan?"

Rosca took a deep breath. Fair enough.

"We need pirates to chase pirates." He looked from one to the other. "We'll find a crew at Pagne. I know who we can trust. They're simple folk. As long as you hold the gold, you're safe." His skin drew taut over his cheekbones, tightening around his pressed lips.

Rosca threw up her hands. "Until they cut your throat for it." How could he be so minsk-headed? Pirates? He wanted to treaty with pirates? Did he not just live through what she lived through? She would die before sailing with those dogs.

Dium's brows scrunched over his deep-set eyes like a hood. "You're saying you trust Pagne's trash over Nileal's top warriors?"

Lin chortled. "Why did the praetis not step in sooner? How did the pirates know to take Iculous road? The castle layout? Your people aren't as loyal as you think. These pirates know the island and your people. Whoever you tell, whoever you run to, that's who they'll have set up to deter you."

The muscles in Dium's cheeks twitched like lightning. "Don't talk about my father's men like that."

Lin gestured in the direction of their home. "This wasn't an attack. This was a kidnappin', meanin' they expect a chase. But they're not expectin' people who think like 'em. Sail like 'em. Fight like 'em. I know you think Banli warriors are undefeatable, but pirates can fight like helski and sail like birds fly. If we're gonna keep up, we gotta have a crew that can do the same. One that ain't compromised. By the time you figure out who you can or can't trust here, the ship will be long gone."

Rosca rolled her eyes. Right, because pirates weren't compromised.

Something else he'd said fluttered at the back of her mind. *How did they know about Iculous road?* It couldn't be what she'd feared when she first heard Lin say Filmore. It'd been years since she'd given those secrets away. Ray wouldn't....

Rosca twisted to examine the pirate ship. Her breath caught. The letters etched into the side of the gilla branded her mind. *Lady Scarlet.*

In one second, the truth she'd always clung to changed.

Numb, she read the words again. Ray had returned. She'd tried to kidnap her. The raschuka.

Ski had been right. Dium had been right. The beautiful, adventurous woman was bent on treasure. On taking her family. She'd never admired Rosca. Never thought she fought well or would make a good pirate. She'd only been after her family. A ransom maybe. Just like everyone had warned. The world rocked.

Darkness blocked her vision. She popped open her eyes. When had she closed them? Did Lin notice? She glanced at him, but he seemed lost in his own musings. He couldn't know. No one could know. Deb Sergio, Debna Remalu... Never. She was the cause of her family's fall, just like her mother had always threatened she would be if she didn't become less selfish. Selfish and spoiled.

Why couldn't she have been made like Karol? Content.

Shel it. She'd taken her freedom too far. She was a selfish, arrogant, spoiled Nilealian brat. Even Dium had warned her about inviting evil in. Her mischievous, stubborn brother had figured it out. Now, they had to run to pirates for aid. They couldn't go crawling back home, begging for assistance from the ones they'd betrayed. They would make it right first. This was their burden.

Hoarse, she spat her next words. "Dium, Lin's right. We need a pirate crew."

Dium's curt nod told her he already knew. How long had it taken him to realize? How long would it take him to forgive her?

A heaviness fell over the group.

Dium faced Lin, his brooding features screwed tight. "We leave for Pagne. Are you sure you want to come? It's a suicide mission, and you know it."

A stab of resignation sliced the night air. The hairs on Rosca's arms prickled. No one dared give voice to hope or doubt, but their gloom-filled expressions each reflected the same thought. If Lin went, he'd probably die on their fool's errand. But if he stayed, they had no chance for victory.

"Lin," Rosca forced herself to meet his whiskey-colored eyes. Forced herself to think of someone else for once. "You can't come with us. You may die, and for what? You've built something here. At Asium. I know how good of a boxer you are. Word gets around. We'll buy the ship from you and pick up a crew, but don't come. It means nothing for you except death."

Surprise flitted across his open face before he settled it. A stern expression wrapped his features, but admiration glowed in his bright eyes. "Assumin' I don't die, I'll be back to make my career. Nileal ain't a bad place to settle down. After all, that's the dream." Despite the light-heartedness, his tone carried the sharp iron of a final decision. Nothing they said would dissuade him.

Warmth erupted in her belly. Unable to speak, she nodded. Her heart heaved with gratitude.

Gaze locked onto the sea, Lin drew himself up. In the black pupils, Rosca saw a flicker, like a distant star hidden by fog. "It ain't fair your family got taken." He turned his attention back to them. Deep wrinkles creased his forehead. "But life isn't supposed to be fair. We're supposed to be strong."

Dium shifted his weight from the tree. "You're a true friend, Lin."

"I think that's the first time anyone's used 'true' or 'friend' to describe me." Lin broke the stillness with a grin as wide as the ocean.

Rosca narrowed her gaze at him. What did he mean? Who had he been in his past? *It's what I would do,* he had told her on the hill about the pirates anchoring on Filmore's Beach. And he'd been right. She clutched her throat. Was he working with them?

The grief, fury, and suspicion spiraled together until all she could do was stand still and wait for orders. Wait for someone to pull her along to the next thing. Just like she'd been doing all night.

Dium tensed. "How are we supposed to get past Coquerielle's Current?"

Lin shrugged. "Same way they do."

"Which is?"

"How would I know? They ain't done it yet."

Rosca drew a breath. Was this how all his planning would go? If so, a long voyage awaited.

Chapter Twenty-Four
The Pass

She was gone. Lin eyed the horizon. No sign of the husky, billowing sails of the *Lady Scarlet*. He puffed his cheeks in frustration. Oh god. He hoped they weren't going in the wrong direction.

Above his head, the underside of the stern castle floor caved him in. Full view of the wide-open deck filled his vision as he manned the helm. The rikkey looked big without a crew.

The *Lady Scarlet* couldn't have sailed straight to sea. What about the current? Maybe she used Shadow's Pass. Maybe she waited among the deadly rocks and unpredictable currents to meet in a battle where they were down twenty to one. He rolled his shoulders in discomfort. As if maneuvering a cavern in the dark wasn't bad enough. Not to mention the rumors surrounding the pass. His gut twisted, and he tightened his abs.

These rumors kept him from mentioning his whole plan to the Ishel siblings. As Nilealians, they would have heard the wild tales. He could only hope their common sense would prevail over island superstition.

As they rounded the coast and the trees fell back, a jagged mass interrupted his reverie. It rose from the ocean like the world's ugliest and most uncreative sea monster.

"Lin!" Dium barked and jumped from the barrel he rested on. "We can't. Surely you know the stories!" With his face drained of color, Dium's eyes seemed to bulge beyond their usual shape till he looked like a bug.

Lin grimaced. So much for common sense.

Dium took a step towards him, and Lin gripped the handle of the whipstaff even tighter. "Lin, listen! We'd have to be mad to attempt Shadow's Pass, and if we aren't now, we will be after."

"Di..." Rosca soothed.

He nudged his sister gently to the side. "I said no, Lin. You can't risk it. Not with mine or my sister's life."

"What about my life?" Lin muttered and brushed past him. He had to lower the sails. They'd be torn up in the furious cavern winds. He despised superstitions, but numbers didn't lie. The unexpected pattern of Shadow's howling breeze had dashed many sailors to their deaths. Who knew if this meant mystical spirits played in the darkness? Who cared? They just had to survive.

"Lin, you're insane. Coquerielle's Current is better than this."

Rosca snorted. "Yeah, 'cause that worked so well last time."

Lin's lips twitched with a smirk.

Color rejuvenated her cheeks. The apples and cheese, the only food on board, had brought life to the weary, wet eyes. She'd had a good, long cry once they set sail, but the nourishment calmed her down. Thank Maschiach. He couldn't take the whimpering.

"Lin." Dium barked as though he expected obedience.

Fury washed through Lin. He spun. "Dium, I am the cap'n. If you don't like it, you're free to jump out and swim through Coquerielle's Current again. But seein' how you're on my ship, and the responsibility of gettin' us through safely is on my shoulders, I'll do as I shel well see fit."

Rosca jumped in with a pleading tone. "Dium, we don't have a choice. Lin knows the sea better— Listen!"

"The debna knows what she's about." The cavern entrance loomed ahead. Lin returned to lowering sails and shouted commands at them to do the same. The hairs on the back of his neck prickled.

They only had a few more moments before they would enter the pass. Dium would waste his breath and possibly kill their chances for survival if he didn't start lending a hand. Stubborn Ishels. Never taken a shel order in their lives.

Dium stood stiff as a board. "Lin, I will turn this ship around myself if I have to, but we are not going through those rocks."

Lin ground his teeth. Not a chance in helski would he let another man touch his ship. His rikkey.

Tying off another rope, he marched to Dium. Using his few inches of height to his advantage, he leaned over him and snarled. "Am I the cap'n or not?"

Dium's brow furrowed. "Of course, but—"

"There are no buts, maybies, or sortas! I'm either the cap'n or you can forget about trackin' down your family. I have the experience, the knowledge, and the resources. If you don't like the way things are, fine! We'll go back right now, and you can go to bed knowin' you turned 'round at the first test of trouble. I'll go home, sleep tight, win the tournament, and bring my own family to Nileal. I won't risk death or disaster. Best of all, I won't have to deal with a crazy, ungrateful, fish-eyed, spoiled deb's son anymore! Now, get to the oars if you want to survive. Oh, and if you do decide to prove the old wives' tales correct and go crazy, know that I will leave your minsk-head-self ravin' your lunacies on the rocks."

Dium glared and spit on the planks. Without another word, he stormed down the steps to the deck below.

Rosca stared, a smile on her smooth lips.

He glared at her, and she rushed to finish tying off the last sail.

Was this somehow funny to her?

"They're not just stories, you know."

He could barely catch her yells as he walked back to the helm. "That's the least of my worries right now."

Jumping a pile of extra ropes, she bounded over to him. "Yeah well, right now is when you need to know. Janel's father went insane going through Shadow."

"Okay." These people put new meaning into talking someone to death.

Rosca rolled her eyes. He was growing accustomed to seeing her eyeballs up in her head rather than straight forward.

"Janel's a debna. She works sesaquilles with Dium."

"Aye, I know who she is." He sighed. Couldn't anyone in this family sense the urgency? They weren't lying when they said they couldn't sail.

"They went through Shadow eight years ago when they came to Iecula. Their father has never been the same since. He goes on random black outs, beating 'em and screaming. Says he can see poison coming outta their ears or some mescucha. He wasn't like that before. The pass cursed him. Haunts him."

Anger flared in his chest. He could remember the man clearly now. The only deb on the council he knew besides Rez, and nothing to savor. Sloppy and prideful beyond reason. A drunk who didn't deserve his title. In a steely tone he hoped would shut down further conversation, he reassured her as best he could. "That won't be us."

"How can you be so sure?" She searched his face as if she truly believed he had answers.

Duty settled on his shoulders like boulders. "Sanity means keepin' your courage. That's something all three of us have, or we wouldn't be here."

"I think you may be oversimplifying it." Rosca's lips quirked. He held in a grin.

The rikkey shifted left and groaned. A lurching gut reminded him that courage did not make one immune to fear. "Go grab an oar."

"And do what?"

"If you see a rock, push us away from it. Try keepin' us in the middle."

Rosca nodded and left. A moment later, he could hear her voice ring out with more questions. He had kept the directions simple for a reason. How did she always manage to make everything so complicated? "Figure it out!"

She must have heard his answer because she disappeared below deck.

The jaws of Shadow's Pass towered above the rikkey. Her cavernous walls greeted them like the greedy fist of a child grabbing up a toy. The lazy current picked up speed until it pushed the ship into the gathering dark like a leaf in a river.

A few jolts and turns let him know Rosca and Dium did their job. The ship dipped and shuddered. A screeching sound made Lin groan. Something had scratched his rikkey. He dug his nails into his palm. If he could breathe through it, he could get through it.

Water sprayed and splashed over his ship. The reaching rocks closed in and around until only a small crack of light remained above to guide them through. It didn't matter that they could now barely see, for the water pushed and pulled too violently to steer. Dread settled in Lin's soul. The darkness before him bent and twisted with streaks of gray shadows and flashes of monster-like visages. Paranoia creeped up his spine, as though, amidst the chaos, something sinister planned an attack.

A resounding thwack from below made Lin search about. The shadows shifted before him, deeper layers of black pulling him in. An eerie feeling haunted his fingers as they gripped the helm staff in an effort to steer. But where to? Except for the thin crack above, nothing guided them in this wasteland.

A musty presence, like the smell of death, weighed him down. He considered prayer, but the words stopped in his throat. This was his job. Sweat poured from his brow and throw-up filled his mouth. Tightening his abs, he willed the sickness to still.

***

A thwack filled the air as Dium's oar caught on a rock and snapped. He held the broken stick for a moment, immobile. What was happening? This wasn't a monster you could fight. More like a storm from helski.

Rosca yelped and fell with the turbulence.

Dium evaluated the scene while he helped her up. Waves sloshed and sprayed through the oar openings until the water pooled up to their calves. Beneath his feet, the floor angled as though the whole rikkey threatened to topple sideways. Misgiving flooded the pores of his heart. He'd kept the pirate ship a secret, assuming it'd all just work out. Careless. Thoughtless. As always. Now, judgement had come. With bounding steps, he took to the deck above.

When he reached the top, nausea washed over him. Something sickly filled the atmosphere. Stench like that of months old, wet rice bags filled his nose and ears. He breathed through his mouth, but the taste reminded him of rotten flesh. Up, down, up, down. His intestines flipped like a fish on land. A massive fin, slate gray and tall as two men, curved out of the water before disappearing into the depths. What. The. Helski.

The ship rose then dropped as though something pushed it from below. It teetered and rocked, threatening to capsize. He scrambled up from where he'd fallen on the deck. Memories of his earlier drowning crowded his courage, the water closing his airways until his life all but flickered out. He clenched his fists. Alarog was doing everything to make this his tempa to die, but if he could survive that, he'd survive this.

Rosca's small hand wrapped into his own, and she clung to his arm as though the sea meant to whip them apart. "Light!" Her voice sounded thin and scratchy, as though it could break at any second.

He squinted at the glimmer of growing yellow ahead. Was that the end?

The ship lurched, whipping him to the floor and yanking him from Rosca. A warm glow encircled them, and he blinked repeatedly.

"We made it." Rosca's hushed hope sounded fragile, like a naked flame in the wind.

The burst of light vanished, and the ship stood still as death. Only the crack above their heads still shone.

Dread saturated Dium's senses. They weren't alone. That gray fin thing was playing with them. Scrambling to his feet, he drew a rusty broadsword Lin had gifted him from his own personal arsenal. "Weapons!"

A scuffling about told him Lin and Rosca obeyed his command. The anxious tension cast an air too thick to breathe through. If it killed them, it'd be no less than he deserved. But Rosca? Lin? They had to make it.

He took measured breaths to still his beating heart. He could feel it coming in his bones.

Something broke free of the water. It rose. And rose. The monster towered like a castle; its extremities spread out from a black wall of shifting gray shadow. Eel-like, they whipped and swung about.

Numbness spread through him, the sight turning him to stone. He clutched his sword as if it made a difference. As if they weren't all dead.

Rosca screamed. A barnacle encrusted tentacle encircled her waist.

Every vein throbbing with adrenaline, he reacted in blind defense, and severed the slimy appendage.

With a shriek of pure venom, the creature disappeared over the side of the ship. Dropping her blade with a sob, Rosca turned and sprinted below deck.

"Guess she wants to die alone." Lin growled, his eyes trained on the water like a cat for prey.

Dium ignored him. Never once had he seen Rosca with the sense to run. He doubted he was so lucky now.

Thick, deep shadows collected on the deck like black mist. They brushed Dium's leg. Deathlike cold and fur prickled his senses. His blood shriveled in his veins as though polluted. A rubbery tube slithered between the rikkey's railing and over the ship floor. Slobber pooled out from its path. Lin stabbed it, and its motion dragged him forward as he gripped his sword.

Spellbound, Dium watched. One constricting squeeze from the tubelike form and their venture would end. Their family lost. Suddenly, Coquerielle's Current didn't seem so bad.

Smaller snake-like shapes curled out from the dark fog, ripping ropes and burrowing holes in the rikkey. It would sink them.

Dium roared, a guttural thing which demanded action. With a single intent, he and Lin charged. Kill.

The sound of their blades sticking sizzling, rubbery flesh echoed off the walls of the cave. Only the screeches of their opponent told them they'd hit their mark. With each successful hit, the counterattack came with renewed vigor and desperation.

Desperation meant it feared him. Dium swung back his blade. He'd give it something to fear. "Agh!" A tentacle whipped out to his right, and then retreated. It shot out again, reaching and stretching for his head. He whirled the sword in an upward plunge, gutting the limb, then pulling so it sliced in two.

Hisses, thunder, and whispers swarmed in the cave like bats circling for a hunt. Dium shut the noise out, just as he'd done with the screaming crowds at his tournaments. One attack followed another, as if the beast craved the sting of metal to send it back to helski.

"What is this thing!" Charging, he caught something by surprise, and one of those ghastly howls filled his ears. No response came. Was Lin already dead? Was he alone?

Rosca burst onto the deck. Carrying a torch in each hand, she flung them at the dark fog like a blind man swatting at a fly.

Tortured squeals like pigs getting castrated filled the cave. Dium's head ached and burned. Shaking slightly, Rosca inched forward. She handed him a torch. Lin stood at her arm, sword in hand.

Dium met his eyes and nodded. They weren't beaten yet. He lit the way while Lin thrust and hit with his sword. The creature retreated, crying with noises that sanded his bones.

The water below flowed again, pushing them out of the tunnel. Sunlight streamed onto the deck. Like waking from a nightmare, it passed.

The sea stretched before them, blue and wide. Lin ran to the helm barking commands. Obedient, Dium and Rosca raced to raise the sails.

Shel. Dium bounced on the balls of his feet, amazed he still stood. Locking his focus forward, he tried to still the shudders rocking his body. Bile piled in his throat. Shooting out, his hand gripped the railing while he leaned over and puked over the side of the ship. Sweat coated his back.

So this was true adventure. Why in the helski would Rosca want her life to be like this?

Every now and then, he glanced back to reassure himself nothing followed them from the pass. If they survived this, he'd never ask for more than a fast sesaquille and a sturdy island hut. Everything else in life was decoration.

Bit by bit, Shadow's Pass sank from view, and he did his best to sink it, in the same way, from his mind.

***

Lin hadn't moved from the helm since exiting Shadow. Not that he had a choice. Rosca and Dium knew even less about sailing than they'd claimed, and that was nothing.

They passed a small trader vessel, burning to ash and devoid of life. He clutched the whipstaff as though he wanted to crush it to powder in his grip. The horrid sight twisted his stomach, but his hope strengthened. They were on her trail. He'd been right. More than likely the pirates were headed for Kenst, if they didn't stop at Pagne themselves. A sigh of relief escaped him. He cracked his neck, tension dropping from his shoulders.

Rosca froze starboard, soaking in the sight without a word.

He watched, waiting for the inevitable questions. For the reaction of seeing the outside world for the first time.

She turned and moved towards him. "Who—?"

"The Lady Scarlet." He flexed his neck. "She attacked 'em."

Pale, she cradled her stomach with her small arms. "Why?"

"'Cause she can. Good news is she don't realize we're after her. If she did, she wouldn't stop." And she couldn't know. If she did, they'd be seeing bodies floating past in warning. Gah, she better be set on a ransom or slavery.

"But I thought you said she expected a chase?"

"Maybe it's a warnin'."

Rosca nodded and lowered her arms to her side. A hard defiance etched its way over the despair in her look.

He curled his fingers, flexing the tendons. "I need you to keep watch up front."

"What for?"

He stared ahead. He didn't have the rishop to say corpses. Her family's corpses.

Taking his silence as final, she left.

Helski. Fredge had better be in Pagne, or— *Quit*. He shook himself of the piling anxieties. "One worry at a time."

The *Lady Scarlet* had everything needed to rule the seas: speed, able-bodies, and a strategic leader. He rolled back his shoulders. If the attack on Nileal hadn't happened, her growth would have gone unchecked. Within a year, she'd be master of the seas. Now they had a chance to stop her and restore some order.

Snorting, he shook his head. Order? These seas and all her vulturous port-cities gave up on order long ago. Nileal alone stood apart, and now she burned. Soon the sea would force each of them to the same chaos that commanded Kenst. The same chaos that drove him from his home.

Kenst may have had a king, but the thousands of residents stretched beyond the joker's ineffective reach. Every citizen knew the pirates, gangs, and crooked counselors truly held the power. The city reached over the entire south shore of North Resave with its open markets, three-story stone buildings, and slave auctions so large you could hear the whipcrack and chain rattle miles away. It drew all sorts of people, some by choice and some by force.

Slave buyers came from as far as the Molatineez Mountains, and sellers swore blood oaths to protect confidentiality.

If the *Lady Scarlet* sailed for Kenst, as Lin suspected it would, the infamous slave market would swallow and split the captive Ishels till they'd be impossible to track. Lin massaged the bridge of his nose. "If we fall too far behind, we'll lose 'em. But if we get too close, they'll see us, and we'll die. Great." Maybe Tholley was still in Kenst. Maybe he hadn't forgotten him. If he could just make it to the city, and he could get out a message. They could fight back.

"Lin."

He jumped then glared at Dium. "Yes?"

His friend grimaced, but not at him. A lost look clouded his features, as though some other world haunted his thoughts. "What do you think their plan is? Ransom? Slavery?"

"One of those." Keeping a grip on the whipstaff, Lin inclined against the wall to his back, that of the captain's cabin.

"And?"

"And?" He challenged. Dium's earlier comment about taking over the steering still irked. "We're goin' to Pagne. That's all we know."

Dium crossed his arms. "Lin, I've watched you fight. You don't throw a punch that you don't think will either land or distract. Young as you are, and much as it hurts me to admit it, I've only seen Champions compare to your level of strategy. You expect me to believe you haven't considered where they might be headed? Their route? Their goal? Please. This is my family."

Lin softened, shame pricking him. He could be kind of a minsk-head, at times. Dium had just lost everything, and he was splitting hairs over what? Some brash words?

He smiled wryly at his foolishness. "They're headed for Kenst. I'd bet my whole ship on it. There's nothing else north unless they take a sharp left for Valsquel, but they'll only find execution on that route."

"What do you mean?"

He raised a brow. How did a deb's son know so little about the world? "Valsquel's got little patience for pirates. They're a no mercy kind of kingdom. Their King, a royal ol' has-been, is pretty strict about keepin' things, well, how yah say, aristocratic. Point is, we know their destination which means we can take our time gettin' there. Not too much, but enough to keep 'em from realizin' they're followed."

Dium stiffened, squaring back his shoulders and narrowing his gaze. "Kenst is the city with the underground slave trade."

Lin shrugged. "Not that underground, but yeah."

"It's been a hundred years since a successful raid on Nileal." A grim light entered Dium's eyes. "You know what this means?" He seemed to have already decided, so Lin let him finish. "Every pirate will know Iecula isn't invincible. Those savages will smell blood in the water and set sail. Nileal's reputation of impenetrability has always been her biggest protection."

"Maybe not." Lin flexed his hand, studying the veins rippling over the back. "She's got castle walls and hordes of fighters to deter invaders too. A few more attacks and people will see she ain't to be messed with."

Dium huffed, wrinkles thickening his brow. The hooded eyes, high cheekbones, and thick black hair may have been of the debna Le, but the thick, sturdy way he carried his shoulders, the honesty with which he let care ride his forehead, and the thoughtful grimace all were reminiscent of Deb Rez.

Pushing the resemblance from his mind, Lin thought back to the fighters he had trained with. The militia men and boxers. Young, old, it did not matter, he hadn't met an untrained man in the city. How could Dium think they would fall so easy? That, at least, distinguished father and son. Rez would have had more faith.

"It isn't attack I fear." Dium's chin rose, and he glared as though facing an invisible opponent. "Pirates eat a place like Nileal from the inside out. They stop and blend in till it's time to strike. Because we welcome newcomers. Because we take pride in being a haven. The city of refuge will turn to desolation within a year. The strays she picks up..." He stopped.

In the pause, Lin took a deep breath. Strays like himself. He masked his features, careful to not let the man see the anger pooling beneath his skin.

"It will be another Kenst." Dium finished with a look that told Lin he had caught his reaction. "But perhaps there are worse things."

Lin turned back towards his ship. He heard Dium leave. "Perhaps there are."

***

Dium leaned against the rail beside Rosca. Her focus drilled onto the water, she didn't spare him a glance.

A vast expanse of shifting blue met the steady sky in a hazed horizon line. The lull of rhythmic waves rocked the ship like a giant cradle. A cool wind blew at their backs, propelling them forward while the sun wrapped them in a warm blanket. Salty and wild, the breeze sang past them. Lapping at the ship side, the sea drowned the anxious thunderstorm in Dium's thoughts.

"It's beautiful." She tugged at her hair, winding it slowly with her finger.

"Guess you're getting your adventure, after all." The bitterness in his voice took him by surprise.

Pulling away from the railing, she chewed her cheek like it would physically keep in the retort he could see aching to break forth.

It was cruel, but it wasn't like he was saying something new. She was too smart to not see the irony. Days ago, she was running away from the family. Now, after.

Relaxing, she sighed. "I don't understand how the Lady Scarlet got so far ahead. She attacked a trade ship, burned it, and still has knots on us. I know it took us a while to set to sea, but not that long. Certainly, she had to go through Shadow like us, to avoid the current."

So she wouldn't talk about it. Probably best for them both. "Why?"

"What do you mean why? Coquerielle's Cur—"

"Is a beast of evil, like that of Shadow." The sordid memory split his head with aching. He gripped the railing, a sad smile curving his lips. "We have the disadvantage in this world, Rose. We do not know how to feed such a beast, and those who do will always lap us. We didn't realize how good we had it at home." And, thanks to his silence, they may never see it again. Why hadn't he told the deb he saw pirates? Why had he been so minsk-headed? Slicing pains tore his heart, as though a butcher cut away the future he'd dreamed for himself. Tensing, he flexed his chest.

"So you think the pirates somehow… made a pact? With… with the current? Like magic? Oh, we're shelled." Her hopeless pout accentuated her baby face, and instinct told him to wrap her up and send her back with the next ship they passed. If only she wouldn't commandeer the ship to come right back. No. Better to keep her in sight and face the danger together.

"How are we going to win this, Di?" Expectant, golden orbs locked him in her gaze.

His heart sank. They couldn't. But neither could they walk away. Ignoring it would not make it disappear. He'd learned that the hard way.

He sucked in a breath through his nose, and counted to still his nerves, just like in sparring. "Do you remember what I told you when you kept losing your sparring matches?"

She rolled her eyes. "A lot more is at stake here than a busted nose."

He clenched his hand till his fingers ached. Eighteen-years and knows it all. "You got beaten up over and over again, till you wanted to quit. You cried about it like a little tiweekah."

Her jaw dropped. "I did not! And even if I did, I was nine."

"The point is you sucked, and you kept overthinking it and melting down believing Father wouldn't train you anymore. That he'd give up on trying to teach a girl. To be fair, I would have."

She gave him a look fit to scare the darkness out of night. "Thanks."

"I hated seeing you like that." He tapped the rail with his fist, wishing he had his hair to pull at. "You got beat up so much, people stopped staring when you came to your lessons with black eyes and busted lips."

"Is there a point to all this?"

"Do you remember what I told you? When you were crying and wanted to quit?"

The hardness dropped from her eyes, "You asked if I would rather be mediocre at something I love or great at something I hate. And it made me realize I couldn't live without fighting. Without adventure. That it was what I loved." She smiled, but sadness rimmed it.

"Out here isn't so different. We were blessed enough to be raised to do the right thing, but we forget it isn't always easy or rewarded. So the question now is, what if we don't win? Is it enough to know we acted like champions? Maybe success isn't based on the outcome at all. Maybe it's based on the person we choose to be."

"I want both. I want to do what's right and to win. I don't care what it takes. I want everyone home and safe." Ferocity spiked her voice.

Maybe that determination would pull her through, but it had to be balanced with reality. With the strength to face her problems. Face defeat. "Not everyone gets both." A humorless chuckle broke loose. "Almost dying twice in two days can really open your eyes to that."

She buttoned her lips. Tears brimming, she looked to the sea. As though sharing a secret with the waves, she whispered her oath, "I'll get both. Everything's going to be okay."

He took a deep breath. He could hope. For her sake, he would.

Chapter Twenty-Five
Honor

Deb Rez watched his trembling hand. It fascinated him. The way the pain made him physically grow sick and shake. Like a boxing opponent might make him double over and retch with a good body shot series. Except this enemy lived inside of him, and no matter how he screamed and tore at the ground and punched the walls, it did not leave.

Breathe. His children needed him. Breathe. Focus. The praeti was talking. Rez forced himself back into reality where a haggard man stood in the front threshold of the castle and spoke.

"Deb, it's been hours. They could be anywhere, including on a ship and gone from Iecula."

In silent refusal, Rez glared at the man daring him to continue protesting. The praeti could see Le's blood still staining Rez's chest from where he had lifted her, one last time, for a caress. He had told him of the kidnapping of his children, and the chief himself had reported that Dium and Rosca could not be found. So how did he have no compassion?

Rez resisted the urge to slam a rock-solid right into the old chief praeti's pooching stomach. How many years had he persevered persecution, pressure, and punches in service of his homeland? How many praetis had he trained into true soldiers and warriors? And now, in the face of the greatest injustice, they willingly said they couldn't do anything more?

Rez advanced until the man had to strain up to meet his eyes. "I sweat for this land every day of my life. I've poured my own blood into building a civil community, separate from the barbaric clans festering on every island around us. They train their children to fight because they do not know how to better themselves, but I taught ours to do it for love, justice, and peace. Where is that justice now? Where is your thirst for peace? Do you not know every pirate within sailing distance will descend on our shores at this… this weakness—? And we are weak. Only weak men do not protect what they love and fight for justice."

"Deb." Hopelessness caked the man's tone. "We did all we could."

"Then why do we not go now? Tell me Chief Praeti, did you surrender your honor when they gave you your title? Forget the very spirit of fight which made you become what you are? How can you say there will be no reparation?"

A thousand years settled on the man's brows as he lowered them and shoved his finger under Rez's nose. "Do not question my honor. I may not have achieved your title, but I certainly gave just as much, if not more, for my home. It is because of the honor you slander that we still have peace. If I had given in, worse than pirates would have consumed this city we arbitrarily call a haven."

Rez rubbed a hand down his face. "Don't be so naïve, Franz. I appreciate your service as chief, but if you fell, another would replace you. I've trained a hundred men with your talent."

"But not my good will." Franz cast a glance behind Rez and stiffened. He took a step back and motioned for Rez to do the same. "I don't like the look of that servant. Follow me. There are ears everywhere."

Puzzled, Rez cast a glance back at the gardener and men clearing debris from the walkway. He strode alongside the praeti, who looked about as skittish as a cat on a railing, expecting a fall at any moment.

"Deb, this is bigger than just a simple outside attack."

Stepping over the ruins of Rez's home, they entered the once perfect complement to the towering walls. Now, chunks of broken stone interrupted the manicured garden as though giants had played marbles in her flowerbeds.

An overwhelming pang filled Rez to see the greenery his wife had loved. She never again would walk its rows beaming at every tree and flower as though she hadn't seen them all a thousand times. Grief, still fresh, overpowered his step and he faltered. Franz stepped aside, averting his attention while Rez recovered his senses.

"I have reason to suspect the attackers had the help of praetis." Franz spoke quick and low, making it hard to understand. Not less so because the words he said seemed ludicrous. "I am personally investigating the idea. There is no one I trust to send after these… these rats. No one I would put by your side. Deb, from what you've told me, we know this attack targeted you. Who knows how long your sister was here, plotting, spying, building connections—? As much as I would love to leave and help you on your journey, I can't. Not when I have a duty to help this city recover and, furthermore, clean out the minsk-heads that pass themselves off as honest, servant-minded men. What I'm trying to say is you will not receive any help from the praetis because they no longer exist to help."

Stillness locked Rez's movements, like lava hardening into rock. Everything that had ever mattered— his family, his reputation, and his pride— stripped by the sins of an imperfect past. Sins he'd spent a lifetime atoning for. Was there no forgiveness on earth? Not on Hela's earth. And yet, he had expected this. He deserved this. He ran his thumb on the pommel of his sword. The small tic grounded him.

He held out his hand. "Forgive me, Franz. I'm glad that there is still someone left to care. To rebuild."

Franz jerked his arm in a steady shake. Deep sorrow hooded the chief praeti's eyes. "You will pursue them?"

Rez smiled. "I am old, Franz. I hardly think chasing killers across the globe is an advisable idea. In fact, I believe retirement and a much-needed return to my home in Valsquel are in order. Of course, some may choose to accompany me as old friends will do. I have many comrades who have expressed their desire to travel with me."

"I assume this is the story I am to sell for yours and several other debs' disappearances?" Chief Franz tightened his jaw as though already seeing the disbelieving stares.

"As you said, we can trust no one. Neither ocean nor land will stop me from restoring my children's freedom."

Once Franz left, Rez sank into the grass to pull at a clump of weeds. "Le wouldn't like you here." Tears fell and mixed with the upturned earth. "I will find them. I have to." He dug his hand into the dirt, enjoying the cool sensation.

He had thought it would be Rosca who would get herself killed, not his own treacherous past. God! He'd almost convinced himself his own memories weren't true. He'd believed… he swallowed a strangled cry. He'd claimed Hela's adventure-lust had killed her, blockading his guilt with ivory walls of lies. Shel it. He'd said whatever was needed to move on… to be that family in the portrait. When had he become such a monster?

Rosca had gotten the worse of it. He'd convinced her she was a volcano, set to erupt. No wonder she'd run away. Hadn't he put it in her head that she had adventure in her blood? That she wasn't fit to be a part of this family? Maybe not in so many words, but he'd trained her. He'd pushed her. Still, he never let her know it was enough. That she was enough. His fear had mastered him. He'd believed confidence would send her chasing after the sea like Hela, when all along, it'd been him who sent his sister away.

He raised a clump of dirt and molded it in his grasp. His lies might destroy them all.

***

The sun bore down, but Deb Rez shouldered the cloak anyway to tramp the long dirt road winding down the cliff. Franz was right. Hela and her gang would have been here, integrating themselves into Nileal life. They knew the roads and passageways too well. Bile frothed in his mouth. Some sign, some clue must remain. Someone must have seen them.

As he walked, the image of his home's wreckage festered in his thoughts. It would be years before they could remedy the architectural devastation, and even then, the castle may never reach its former glory. The Ieculian casualties didn't compare with the slaughter they'd inflicted, but the suddenness of the attack and the smoke-like disappearance cut deep.

He could see it on the faces of the passers-byer. The trauma of seeing evil's touch scar their home. Disgust bristled the hair on the back of his neck. "Our own vanity has overthrown us." He hid his face in his cowl despite the warm sun and suppressed a scowl. He never should have relied so heavily on reputation. He should have prepared more. And they called themselves warriors. The Valsquelians were right to think them hotblooded fools. All fight and no calculation.

The Nilealians' accusatory glares and mournful whispers haunted each step he took. He had failed them. And now he must do so again.

The scenery of the cliffside melted into the crowded fishermen's district. He searched the marketplace for his target and finally caught sight of a round woman tottling off a boat. In her hands, a barrel overspilling with fish slipped and leaned precariously. Two of her sons worked alongside her, but the oldest stood motionless, gazing at the sea.

"Chuwui! You just goin' to sit there and watch your mother struggle or grow a pair and lend a hand?" She yelled.

Her son started, then finished tying the boat to the dock and went to help his mother.

"It's not even heavy." The boy lifted the barrel easily.

"So? You think your mother should be lift'n things, doin' men's work when you stand right there—? Useless minsk-head of a son." She smacked him upside the head.

"It isn't as though you're a debna." The boy's chuckle broke mid-note when he caught sight of Rez.

Suppressing a smile, Rez gave a polite nod. "Good evening, Chuwui."

"Sir." The boy bowed in respect. Although Rez often came by their market stalls for fish, Chuwui still scurried nervously around him, all his bravado and bantering shrinking away.

"Madam Isla, I see you had a good haul today."

"And it'll feed many if my son loads it 'fore it rots."

"But it's almost night. Aren't you going home?"

With a shrug, Isla exited the boat and tugged on the ropes to ensure they held. "Deb Zedrick commissioned me and my boys to catch as many as we could and give 'em out for free. Whoever needs it. Just a little someth'n to help after—" She stopped, watching him with small, calculating eyes.

"The attack." He forced the words out.

She dipped her head. "I'm sorry for your loss. Truly."

He nodded. It was all he could do without breaking.

Taking the cue, she forged ahead. "We're late today. Took longer than expected. As long as you're wast'n my time, why don't you help us give out some of these things?"

"I don't think my people really want to see me right now."

"Oh, the great Deb Rez fears a few snide comments? They need you."

Rez leaned forward, lowering his voice. "I must talk to you. Privately. I don't have much time."

"Good, because I don't have any. If you won't help, get off my dock." Waddling towards the wagon, the squat, fat woman pushed Rez to the side and nodded to her sons.

Chuwui and his younger brothers waited for their mother to take her place at the front of the cart. They climbed in after her.

"Isla, wait! They took my children." His voice pleading, Rez bartered with the woman's back. "Including Mar."

Whipping her neck to face him, she gestured to her wagon. "Chuwui, trade places with the deb."

Obediently, the boy hopped down from the cart, and Rez ascended.

Chuwui gave his mother a smug stare. "Is this because I'm the only one who speaks the Trader's Tongue?"

"And because you like to give unwanted opinions." Isla clucked at the mules, and they started off. Chuwui stood by watching them leave. "He'll take the village route," she explained quickly.

Rez glanced back at the two younger boys, awkwardly smushed between fish barrels. "They do not speak the Trader's Tongue?"

She shook her head. "They don't have time for lessons. Anyways, it's a waste. Honest work is plenty enough to be found."

Rez nodded. He had never seen the woman without her trailing trio. It shouldn't surprise him that they only spoke Ikuela. "I wasn't educated either."

She contemplated him, then yelled back after her son. "Hurry to meet us there. There's still a lot of work to do tonight." Her attention fixing on the road, she noted a walker unable to avoid her storming mules and pulled the beasts up short. "Get out of the street, minsk-head!"

People jumped out of her way. With another whip of the reins, she urged the animals to go faster through the city. "What do you think I know?"

"Chief Franz thinks the attackers may have come in on a ship."

"He figured that one out himself, did he?"

"No one knows the ports better than you. Not a ship lands on this island that you don't know about. So I figured if anyone might give me a clue, it would be you."

"You call'n me a gossip?"

"I'm calling you the only person who can help me. I'll pay you well. Please. All I need is information."

"Information has the highest price." She lowered her eyebrows, a cloud settling on her dark, acne scarred face. "But take this for free. For Mar. He brought me soup and vegetables when my boys were sick. Kept us from starving. It's the least I can do."

A mixture of pride and ache swelled in Rez's chest.

"The Chief is right. A mystery ship did land some days ago. No pirate flags or trouble, but people still talk. Some say it looks awful similar to a pirate ship called the Lady Scarlet."

"Is it true?"

"I never saw the ship. A few kids spotted it while playing in the woods. They said it docked on the north side of the island, near Filmore's Beach. I don't have time to go chas'n down gossip."

With a side-eye and raised brow, she harrumphed. "I'll listen to it, but I don't tie my ropes to it."

"Of course." Lost in thought, Rez waved her on.

"If they aren't pirates, I'd bet my boat they're slave traders. Either way, they'll be headed for Kenst. You can count on it. Where else would you take prisoners?"

Rez nodded in agreement. "One last question. Say Coquerielle's Current was sighted in the water. How would you get around that?"

"Coquerielle's Current has been sighted? And you haven't sounded the alarm. Are you mad? Or do our lives not mean as much to you?"

Her comment hit a mark. He gritted his teeth. She was right, but he'd forgotten. A deadly current, risking all their lives and trade routes, and he'd just forgot. Like it was a cloak or another scroll to sign.

She softened and placed a hand on his arm. "I'll tell Deb Zedrick and sound the alarm."

He nodded his thanks.

"And where will you be?"

"I am taking a very much-needed voyage home. As I have given my children up for dead and my wife..." he swallowed, "...nothing else remains for me."

"That's why you want to know about the ship that took them."

His stomach clenched. "No one else knows that."

She puckered her lips. "Your story won't sell."

He rubbed his sword's pommel. "It doesn't matter. The people need an answer for my departure, and I can't tell them the truth. If the attackers do have connections here, then they'll send word soon as I set sail. A little misdirection, however flimsy, won't hurt."

An abrupt stop and crowding of hungry, complaining mouths told Rez they had arrived.

Isla gave one last yank on the reins and leaned in to whisper. "Shadow's Pass is the only way around the current and noth'n bigger than a rikkey will fit through. A small rikkey at that."

Rez nodded. "I happen to own five of those."

Chapter Twenty-Six
Good Judgement

"Rosca!"

"I'm coming, minsk-head." She opened the door of her small cabin, abruptly ending Lin's ferocious knocking. "Yes?"

"Put these on. We're almost there."

She took the outfit from him. "Almost where?"

"Put your hair in a bun and tie the bandana around it." Looking her over intently, he nodded. "I think the clothes are baggy enough. It'll have to work."

She scowled and squeezed the bundle closer to her chest. Sometimes she wished Maschiach hadn't answered her prayers for a womanly figure. Not often though. "Work for what?"

He plucked a tricorn hat from her arms and put it on her. It fell down to her eyebrows. "Why is your head so small?"

She opened her mouth, then shut it. "You do know the only reason you're captain is 'cause you have a ship and a bad habit of stickin' your nose in other people's business."

"And you're welcome for it."

"You could at least tell me where we're goin'."

With a look as pained as though she had asked him to swim the entire ocean in one breath, he nodded. "We're goin' to Pagne, so it's best if no one knows you're a pretty girl or a debna. In fact, imagine you're invisible. And mute. And deaf. And shy." His expression held little faith in her ability to act according to orders.

"This is the last place you want to get into a fight, with your fists or your mouth. Your families' lives depend on your silence."

"They always did say I would talk them to death." When he didn't laugh, Rosca quickly wiped the smile away and dipped her head. "I understand."

"You're sure?" His brow bunched into one anxious knot that had threatened to take up permanent residence since they set sail.

She swallowed. He hadn't bothered correcting her in calling it a pirate island. "I get it. Pagne isn't the place to go runnin' your mouth, and we're desperate for a crew. Di and I are hardly top-notch sailors."

He didn't hesitate. "You two aren't sailors at all."

"It's not my fault I didn't learn." She checked the whine in her voice. "My mother expected me to drink tea and socialize for a lifetime, not chase pirates."

"You chose what you chose."

She rolled her eyes. "Trust me, I didn't choose to be a debna. It was chosen for me. It was the last thing I looked for."

"We always choose our paths. Inaction is choice."

Inaction? Unsure of whether she wanted to keep in a tongue-lashing or a laugh, she bit the inside of her cheek. "So what? I should have abandoned my family?" She'd tried that. And why was he talking like he knew? Did Dium say something? She twisted a bit of the linen blouse in her hand. "I need them. More than the adventure." Now that she might lose them all, she could see that.

"No, you don't."

She stared.

He spoke with authority. "You should always fight for what's important. If something is strong 'nuff to pull you away from what you love, then it's for a reason. It's purpose."

Her chest tightened. That's almost what Ray had said. Except her "purpose" was killing and looting. "What about loyalty? Relationships? You don't think those are important enough to stay for?"

His cheeks dimpled with amusement. He crossed his arms. "I'm here, ain't I?"

Delicate twirls swirled in her stomach, and she clenched her gut. Priorities. Her shoulders pressed back. She barely knew this man. She would stay reasonable. "How are you so certain we'll find a crew in Pagne?"

"There's cutthroats by the hundreds, just waitin' for jobs."

Discomfort rippled across her skin. She squirmed. "And we're going to sail with 'em?"

A flash of annoyance crossed his eyes. He jerked his head in a nod.

Forcing out the apprehension electrifying her nerves, she swallowed. She'd have to get used to more pirates, but at least she didn't have to trust them.

He lifted his eyes to the ceiling. "Just get ready. We're only a few hours out. Unless you want to stay on the ship? You can sound the alarm if anyone attacks, and it'll be a lot safer." With a thoughtful cock of his head, he seemed to have already talked himself into the idea. "Yes, much safer. I think it'd be better—"

"No!" Rosca blushed. She hadn't meant to sound so adamant. What was wrong with her? They weren't here to adventure. What if the ship got stolen because she wanted to sightsee?

Lin's cool, calculating gaze ran her over. He nodded before she could change her answer. "Fine. We'll pay someone to watch the ship but stay behind me and Dium. And don't do anything stupid. Keep your head down and your mouth shut. No snooty comments or you may end up with a slit throat."

"Aye, Cap'n."

"This is serious, Rosca."

"I know. Won't Di be a problem though?"

"Why?"

"He's clearly part Banli. Banlis don't set foot on an island like Pagne. People will think it's strange."

Lin laughed and stared in disbelief. When she grimaced back, his eyes went round. "You're serious?" Doubling over, the laughter turned to hooting. "Who in the ocean told you that?"

"Banlis." Suddenly tired, she turned and placed the clothes on her bunk.

"And you believed 'em?"

"They didn't give me a reason not to." Careful to keep her tone from frustration, she pulled back her hair as he'd requested. She could follow orders. When she wanted.

He looked at the ground. When he faced her again, mirth shrouded his face. "Rosca, you can't be so trustin'. It's a death sentence in this world. People don't value honesty and honor like you. It ain't practical."

She scowled. "What kind of man doesn't value honor?"

His brows puckered.

Wrestling her thick braids into a bun, she hurried on before he could attempt an answer. "I'm not a little girl. One lapse in judgement doesn't make me a minsk-head. I have good judgement most the time."

"And how do you judge me?" Flirtatious, his grin betrayed both curiosity and doubt at her claim.

Rosca's cheeks burned. Shaking her head, she cleared her throat and examined a knot in a floor plank. "I'm not going to read you." Not that it would have been hard.

"Why not?"

With a single-minded effort, she forced her chin up. "Because you might not like what I have to say."

He dismissed her words with a wave. "I doubt you can call me anything worse than I've been called before."

Rolling her eyes, she shook her head. "I have no problem name-calling, I..." She froze, already saying too much. Her family told her she needed to learn when to quit talking, but his goading called to her ego.

"I'm not askin' for flattery, just honesty." He stared at her unabashed.

She chewed her lip, resolving cracking. What was the use of having an ability if she couldn't use it? "Promise you won't make me walk the plank?" She didn't wait for a response. "You want to prove yourself. Not to others, it's not insecurity. You're too confident in your abilities. It's like..." She rubbed her fingers together as if poising to pinch the word from thin air. It eluded her grasp, and she settled for the next best. "...weight." Weight? Disappointment clamped her jaw shut. That wasn't the right word.

Surprise coursed in his puffed cheeks and high brows. The muscles around his mouth drew too tight.

Something had struck. Her courage grew. "It's like you want to atone for something, not just prove yourself." As she spoke, the full revelation hit her. "You are. You're trying to atone for something." She stared at him, a knowing settling in her gut. His sarcasm, constant smile, and jokes all interlayered to build a brick wall around who he was. The blockage served one purpose, keeping others from watching too close. But was it really because of shame?

His wolfish expression tightened like raising hackles. She'd put him on the defense. That was proof enough. Well, he could keep his secrets. As long as they didn't interfere with the mission. "Whatever your goal is, you'll have to change to achieve it. That's not easy." Experience had taught her that.

Sternness cemented his features into their usual hardness.

Rosca's pulse pounded with warning. She had crossed a line. She always crossed a line. But what? What had she said?

What had he done?

"I'm not chasin' any goal except gettin' your family back." He shoved a finger at her accusingly. "I'm cautious, but I'm not haunted by some shame or whatever it is you think."

She rolled her eyes. "You asked for an honest—"

He cut her off. "Well, next time, don't oblige me."

She struggled to keep from rolling her eyes again. Having brothers had taught her better than to push a man about his private thoughts. Why did she break her own rules? Press too much, and even the most honest would turn liar enough to shame evil incarnate. "Fine." She shrugged. "Like I said, I haven't known you long." And his reaction proved she was right. An inkling of smugness slithered through her spine.

He found her gaze with a sudden softness in his own. "No, you haven't. But trust me. I'm gonna do whatever it takes to get your family back. And get you all home safe."

Trust me. The words rang in her ears as he left. The first request he'd given her. She lowered herself onto the bed. The floorboards swayed beneath her. "Trust is like respect. You gotta be worthy of it." And who was Lin, anyway? He didn't even seem to know. From one side of his mouth, he mocked integrity, but the other asked for trust? Jumped at the chance to prove himself loyal?

Her heart flipped. *Maschiach, help him. Please.* She grew cold. *Oh God, help me.* What business did she have praying for others when her last prayers for an adventure got her family taken?

Her mother had warned her. *Great people never lived for themselves.* Never lied and threatened and rubbed elbows with a pirate in the hopes of more. Her soul was black, and her family paid the price for it.

She had sworn to become someone, and now she was. Oh God, she was.

Maschiach, have mercy.

End of Ships and Silhouettes: Setting Sail

CALL TO ACTION!

Liked what you read? Leave a review with your email before July 2024 for the chance to win a zoom call with the author where you can ask about the writing process, the characters' secrets, and more!

This is just the beginning! *Open Waters,* book two of *Ships and Silhouette*, is written and under construction. Be the first to pre-order and get a bonus translation to learn the meaning of the Ishels and pirates' favorite cusses like shel and rishop!

By visiting **allysonfaith.com**, you can sign up for the exclusive newsletter and be the first to get the sample chapters of *Open Waters*. Stop in to see photos of your favorite characters, their world, and maps!

Follow the author on Instagram at Allysonfaith2023, Tik Tok at Allysonfaith, or Facebook at Allyson Faith for a series on how to write, updates, and book recommendations! Leave a review on Amazon to let the author know what you thought of their work. Allyson tries to respond to all reviews.

In addition, message Allyson on any social media platform or email at **allyson@allysonfaith.com.**

Thank you!

Full Dictionary:

Titles:

Deb: A nobleman of Iecula, meaning someone with status. Usually someone who has proved themselves in combat.

Debna: A noble woman, usually receives her status because she is a member of a deb's household.

Chief Deb: The head of the council of debs which handles all governmental issues of Nileal, and, by extension, the island since Iecula follows Nileal's lead.

Iecula Praeti (Pray-tee): The civil protectors organized and funded by the Deb Council.

Places:

Iecula (EE-coo-ay): The biggest island in the Speckled Region.

Nileal (Nih-lee-ool): The capital of Iecula and fight capital of the Eastern Realm.

Valsquel (Val-skwell): A nation which sprawls the plains across the sea. Known for their large universities and knowledge hungry culture.

Kenst: A port city located across the sea. The capital of the kingdom Kenst.

Pagne: An unaffiliated, ungoverned island where pirates go for business and pubs.

Asium (Ah-sea-um): The outdoor pavilion which houses rows upon rows of punching bags for training. It also holds practice rings, training equipment, and wooden boxes for storage. It is situated behind Deb Rez's castle and part of his grounds. Named "Asium" because this means red in Ikuela, and the wood which holds the boxing bags has red grains. When the sun shines, these grains cast red sunbeams on the ground.

Zafiere (Zaf-fee-air-uh): The monstrous, tiered outdoor stadium built some four hundred years previously for Banli Boxers. Its name means *Fire of the Sea* in Ikuela. It was named this because of the red blood spilt there in the middle of the sea, as, originally, all fights were to the death.

Cotto ali fimili: The main room in castles for the family to gather. Translates to *Family Room* in Trader's Tongue

Languages:

"Trader's Tongue": Slang for ewl, the language used by all port cities for trade, hence the name.

Ikuela(Ee-cuh-ay): The native language of Iecula.

Eastern Realm Tongue (Ewl): The language used by all port cities / nations in the Eastern Realm for communication across multiple cultures and dialects.

Legends:

Maschiach (Mass-chee-ack): The one true Creator, around since before time.

Alarog (Al-la-rog): The one who destroys. His kingdom is located in the sea. Nobody knows where. He is banished there by Maschiach until the world ends. He's also known as the evil sea king or witch king.

Whisperers: Invisible creatures who work for Alarog. They whisper lies in a host's ear until they begin to listen. When the host follows their counsel, the whisperers gain control until eventually possessing them. In a state of possession, the host may black out and do whatever the creatures bid. The host, if they can figure it out, which is rare, has the power to tell them to leave at any time.

Zelxes (Zelx-ziz): Beings who listen to the whisperers until they become fully possessed. They fall so in love with dark power and use it so often that they begin to physically rot and change shapes into grotesque things.

Flora and Fauna:
Sesaquilles (Ses-ah-kwills)): The half-horse, half-fish creatures which run wild in the Achelois ocean. They're caught and bred for racing. Islanders are wary of the beast because legends claim they have supernatural powers from Alarog.
Lok trees: White trunked, tall trees known for their hardness. Their leaves are large, three-pointed, and only grow on the branches at the top.
Silver lesp trees: Thin, spindly trees with silver moss which grows over the small brown leaves.
Nama trees: Giant, red-grained trees with diameters of up to forty-feet, but on average twenty-five.

People Groups and Influential Figures:
Banlis (Ban-lees): The people native to the island Iecula.
Valsquelian (Val-skwell-ee-an): Those who live in Valsquel. Generally have sharp bone structure and dark skin. Known for their intelligence.
Limurians: Bulky, pale skinned people who often dress in animal furs. They live in Limur.
Kenstians: Those who live in the port city Kenst, the capital of the kingdom Kenst.
King Dahl: The last king of Iecula before Banli Boxers overthrew him and created a council with a chief deb for governmental purposes.
Ieculians (Ee-cool-ay-ee-ans): Those who live in Iecula, whether they be immigrants or a Banli, the race native to the island.

People (The two ages represent the time jump in the book):
Ishel (Ish-el): Family last name.
Reznaldo (Rez-nal-do) Ishel and Le (Lay) Ishel: Father and
Mother of the four Ishel boys. Adopted parents of Ski and Rosca.
Silohski (Sih-low-ski) "Ski" Ishel, 19 then 22.
Adnesier (Add-neese-ee-er) "Adnesi" Ishel, 18 then 21.
Obedium (O-beh-dee-um) "Dium" Ishel, 16 then 19.
Rosquevalarian (Roska-val-ar-ee-an) "Rosca" Ishel, 15 then 18.
Jack Ishel, 9 then 12.
Mar-Iecula "Mar" Ishel, 6 then 9.
Hela (Hell-lah) Ishal: Rez and Adnesier's sister.
Adnesier Ishel: Rosca and Ski's father and Rez's brother.
Arienvalarian Ishel: Rosca and Ski's mother.
Fuerzalin "Lin": Dium's friend and newcomer to the island.

The debna's Four Pillars of Femininity:
Alson: Noble.
Sabini: Wise.
Vera: True.
Davit: Life-Giver.

Phrases and food:
As it is: There's nothing I can do about it, so I'm just going to
keep my chin up.
Spit rookah: Slang for telling lies or nonsense (used by pirates,
sailors, and all seafarers).
Spit mescucha: Nileal term for spit rookah.
Doesn't mean fish eggs: Banli saying for doesn't mean anything
or worth dirt.
Free days: The two and half days when most people don't have
to work at the end of a tempa.

Tempa: An eight-day cycle.

Dascansi – The 4 months of chilly weather and snowstorms which often forces people indoors.

Sunstruck – The 4-month period of unbearable heat where children are released from their studies to work.

Du-ca cakes: Fried, puffed dough covered in powdered sugar and chocolate drizzle.

Chalips: Dried fruit, often covered in a sweet and spicy sauce or honey and cinnamon. An island treat.

Mifu kique shelnigias: An elaborate Ikuela cuss.

Haj lo! Mie repagave: A dramatic Valsquelian supplication for forgiveness.

Renelia: Endearment for *little sister* in Valsquelian.

Ships:

Rikkey: The cheaper, more popular option of ship for small-time sailors, pirates, and fishermen. It has a sleeker and shorter body with a single mast. They are run by a whipstaff – a long stick—rather than a wheel. This is located in front of the captain's cabin in the stern. They have oars below deck. They have two rooms, one for crew and one for storage. The captain's cabin, if it has one, is above deck, situated underneath the stern castle.

Gilla: A large ship with a belly for rowers, cells, canons, and rooms. It has two masts, and occasionally a triangular third at the back. Built for fast getaway and wartime, it uses a wheel connected to the rudder for steering. Their giant sails, which can be up to hundreds of pounds, require constant repositioning. The able-bodied crew must switch off between sleeping and work, generally measured with an hourglass.

Barques (Barks): Built for trading. Fatter, slower ships made to carry lots of goods, especially barrels or big fish.

Coquerielle's Current (Coc-cur-ree-ell): A possessed current. It appears in the water as a giant shadow and swallows what it wants to.

Bow: The front of a ship.

Bunk: a bed on a ship.

Cabin: A room on a ship.

Deck: A level or floor of a ship.

Bridge: The navigational hub of the ship.

Captain: The person in command of the ship.

Helm: The device used to steer the ship.

Port: Left side of the ship.

Starboard: Right side of the ship.

Boxing terminology:

One, also called jab: A left straight forward punch.

Hook: Punch which digs into the opponent's side and requires the arm to be crooked at a 90-degree angle.

Three: Right hook.

Four: Left hook.

Uppercut: A punch which comes from punching up into the opponent's body from a lower angle.

Counter: A punch in response to the opponent's punch

Slip: A dodging motion created by moving your head off the center path by squatting to the side.

Pivot: Turning on one foot to the right or left.

Caught them: To hit someone, usually with power.

About Author:

Allyson Faith grew up in Springtown, Texas. When she wasn't stuffing her nose in a book, she spent her days doing archery, tree or rock climbing, writing, and sword fighting with sticks. Her college days were split between basketball, boxing, construction, and body building. At twenty-two, she now lives happily in Fort Worth near her family and friends. She's fluent in Spanish, writes literary analysis papers for fun, and loves to cook, fight, and camp. She graduated from the University of North Texas with a degree in Language Arts and a certificate in teaching. She now teaches English II at a public High School and splits her free time between her twelve (and counting) nieces and nephews, studying the bible, and working out.